# Atlantis
# in
# Peril

# T. A. BARRON

# Atlantis in Peril

Philomel Books • An Imprint of Penguin Group (USA)

## PHILOMEL BOOKS

Published by the Penguin Group
Penguin Group (USA) LLC
375 Hudson Street, New York, NY 10014

USA | Canada | UK | Ireland | Australia
New Zealand | India | South Africa | China
penguin.com
A Penguin Random House Company
Copyright © 2015 by Thomas A. Barron.
Map illustration copyright © 2013 by Thomas A. Barron.

Library of Congress Cataloging-in-Publication Data is available upon request.

Library of Congress Cataloging-in-Publication Data
Barron, T. A.
Atlantis in peril / T. A. Barron.   pages cm.—(Atlantis saga ; book 2)
Summary: Promi and Atlanta continue the fight against the evil spirits and their mortal
counterparts on the island of Atlantis.  [1. Fantasy. 2. Atlantis (Legendary place)—
Fiction.] I. Title.  PZ7.B27567Aq 2015   [Fic]—dc23
Printed in the United States of America.
ISBN 978-0-399-16804-8
1 3 5 7 9 10 8 6 4 2

*Edited by Jill Santopolo. Design by Amy Wu. Text set in ITC Galliard Std.*

------------------------------

*Dedicated to*

O Washowoe-myra

*and her fellow gods and goddesses*

------------------------------

# Contents

# Atlantis in Peril

# CHAPTER 1

# Revenge

Far, far away from the isle of Atlantis . . . something stirred in a place where no creature had ever stirred before.

That place, in the most remote reaches of the spirit realm, was a bottomless pit darker than the darkest void. Black clouds swirled around its center, roaring constantly, ready to suck in and tear apart whatever fell in. Any creature who came too close faced almost certain annihilation.

The Maelstrom.

• • •

Yet at this moment, something appeared in the Maelstrom's stormy center—the first sign of life ever to emerge from its depths. No other being had come out of that violent place before—because no other being possessed the same will for survival, hunger for power, or desire for revenge.

Of course, no one saw it happen. For to come anywhere near this place was to risk being swallowed forever by the black hole. And besides, what first appeared was very small, so small it would have gone unnoticed.

A hand.

The first bony fingers reached out of the swirling center, grasping at the shreds of clouds, climbing slowly higher. Then came a wrist and arm, wearing the shreds of a tattered robe. Next emerged the head of a man—narrow, as sharp as an ax blade.

Dark, jagged scars lined his face. A black earring, chipped and battered, dangled from one ear. And from both sides of his pointed jaw grew menacing, bloodred tusks.

But the most terrifying features of this face were the eyes. Dark gray, with fiery red centers, they seemed to swirl with their own vengeful storms. Any creatures who looked into those eyes would quail in fright—and know the truth.

Narkazan had returned.

For centuries, the immortal warlord had battled to seize control of the spirit realm, to dominate all its places and peoples. From there, he hungered to conquer all the mortal realms, as well—starting with the one called Earth that was the stepping stone to all the others. And in recent times, he had nearly succeeded, vanquishing almost all the spirits who opposed him. Only a ragtag group of rebels remained, led by Sammelvar and Escholia—spirits who believed that every creature, whether mortal or immortal, deserved to live freely.

Then, when he was just about to crush the resistance once and for all—by destroying them with the ultimate weapon, the corrupted Starstone—a most unlikely foe had appeared. A young man named Promi, a lowly mortal, challenged him and stole the Starstone! Aided by a wind lion, the young rebel managed to escape

Narkazan's entire army of warriors. And then, most surprising of all, he hurled the warlord into the bottomless pit from which no one had ever returned.

Until now.

Narkazan's eyes burned wrathfully. Clenching one fist, he vowed to the roaring clouds, "I shall find you, worthless rebel who bears the mark of the Prophecy. And I shall make you suffer as no one has ever suffered before!"

He continued to climb out of the swirling hole that had swallowed him. Using all his will, as well as his remaining dark powers, he pulled himself higher, clawing his way toward the rim.

Slowly . . . steadily . . . Narkazan advanced. What was left of his robe, shredded by the swirling winds, barely clung to his body. His skin had lost its normal silvery sheen from the constant battering; it now looked like dark gray metal. His narrow face was thinner than ever. And his legs and arms shook with strain.

The fire in his eyes, though, had not dimmed. If anything, the sheer rage in those eyes had only swelled.

Finally, after many more hours of climbing, he reached the rim. Hauling himself onto the edge, he stood there, arms crossed. Narkazan peered into the dark, spinning depths of the Maelstrom. Then he turned to face the rest of the spirit realm.

"I have returned," he snarled. "Soon that will be known throughout this world—and all the other worlds, as well."

The winds shrieked and howled even louder, as if the black hole itself felt his wrath.

Narkazan's eyes narrowed. To demolish all his enemies, including that rebel Promi—and to seize control of Earth and the rest of the mortal realms—he would need to raise a whole new army of spirit warriors. And that army must include a host of mistwraiths, the most terrible fighters anywhere.

"I will need something else, as well," he declared to the swirling black clouds. "A mortal—someone greedy and arrogant enough to do my bidding."

Closing his eyes, he turned his full awareness toward Earth, searching the minds of mortals for the ally he required. After a long moment, he opened his eyes. His search had been successful.

He had found a ship that had recently sailed from a land called Greece. Its mainsail bore the design of a blue dolphin. And the ship's captain, who was steering steadily out to sea, burned with desire for power.

Narkazan chortled to himself. "Yes, that one will do. Soon he will have a dream that will change his life—and his world."

He clenched his fists. "But first . . . it is time for revenge."

CHAPTER 2

# Worlds Within Worlds

F ar from the Maelstrom where Narkazan had just emerged, in a much more tranquil part of the spirit realm, three people sat on a dome-shaped cloud. Surrounding them, thousands of purple honeyscent flowers grew, filling the air with the unusually rich sweetness unique to that variety. So many of the flowers sprouted here that the entire cloud shimmered with purple.

One of those people, the wise elder Sammelvar, leaned forward to study a single flower. Gently, he slid his finger along the stem, even as his golden eyes observed every detail of the blossom. Yet he didn't touch the blossom itself—for each honeyscent flower was, in fact, an entire miniature world.

This one, Sammelvar noticed, held a dense forest of tiny purple trees. In those branches, he could see a family of orange-tailed chimpanzees swinging freely from tree to tree. And on the highest canopy fluttered hundreds of minuscule butterflies, each one no bigger than a mote of dust, whose radiant red wings flashed like prisms as they flew.

Like a microcosm of the spirit realm, this cloudfield of flowers held an endless variety of worlds. Some blossoms gleamed with buildings made from the tiniest blocks of vaporstone. Some cupped purple seas that held islands of immense magic. Some erupted from time to time with dazzling bursts of light. And some shrouded themselves with mysterious lavender cloaks that hid their worlds from view.

Those worlds and many more filled the cloudfield. As the elder spirit gazed around, he thought, *Worlds within worlds . . . ever changing, ever the same.*

"Your favorite poem," said the young woman sitting beside him.

"Reading my thoughts, are you, Jaladay?" said Sammelvar with a grin.

"Only when they're interesting enough," she teased. "Which isn't very often."

"On that I must agree."

Jaladay smirked. She could easily read her father's thoughts. As well as those of her mother, Escholia, who was seated farther away, near an especially sweet-smelling cluster of flowers—wondering, as Jaladay could tell, just how these small blossoms could create such potent aromas.

But Jaladay's sensory gifts didn't end there. Far from it! Although she wore a turquoise band across her eyes, she could still see this entire cloudfield and the vistas beyond. She could also sense the underlying meaning of things—and even sometimes glimpse the future. For she could, as her parents discovered when she was only an infant, *see the unseen.*

Which was how, at that instant, she knew to hold out her hand—just before a small furry creature dropped out of the sky. Catching him easily, she hugged him to her chest.

"Hello, Kermi. I'm always glad to see you."

"Even if you *don't* see like anyone else in the universe," the blue monkeylike creature said. "But I'll still take the compliment."

Kermi waved his long tail in front of her turquoise band, watching her with round blue eyes that seemed much too big for his face. "Tell me, now. How many tails am I holding up?"

"As many as you were born with," Jaladay answered with a chuckle. "Which is to say . . . one."

"Hmmmpff," he replied. "Next time I'll ask you something harder."

"Like how many bubbles are you just about to blow? That would be three."

Kermi's eyes opened even wider than usual. "Impressive," he muttered, even as he opened his mouth and released three blue-tinted bubbles that floated skyward. "Like any good, upstanding kermuncle, I enjoy blowing bubbles. But normally they come as a surprise to everyone but me."

Jaladay stroked his tail—which looked very much like the squiggly blue line that decorated her white robe. "Now Kermi, you must be tired after traveling all the way here."

"Right, so I am." He yawned, releasing another stream of bubbles. "Flying without wings isn't as easy as it used to be."

"Well then," she suggested, "how about taking a nap?"

"Oh no," he objected, shaking his little head so hard that his whiskers seemed to jump. "You're not getting rid of me that easily! I don't want to miss anything."

Ignoring him, she set him on her lap. "As you say, Kermi."

"Good," he replied. "I'll be the one who decides whether I need a nap." He yawned sleepily. "Not . . . you."

He closed his eyes, fast asleep.

Still stroking his tail, Jaladay grinned.

Beside her, Sammelvar sighed. "It's good to be here," he said, gazing at a pair of flowers whose tiny peoples had built a glittering bridge between their two worlds. Like a thin purple rainbow, the bridge stretched from one blossom to the other, binding the worlds for all time.

"And something else is also good," said Escholia, who had walked over to join the others.

Sammelvar raised a questioning eyebrow. Jaladay, meanwhile, nodded in agreement, since she already knew what her mother was about to say.

"That you're not worrying right now." Escholia bent to greet her husband, her white hair mixing with his. She gave his forehead a kiss. "Which you do entirely too much these days."

"Too true," he replied, turning from the flowers to look into her misty blue eyes. "But there is a lot to worry about."

She sat down beside him—with such lightness that she didn't disturb a single stem of any flower. That might have seemed surprising, given her age. Yet she'd long been called the spirit of grace, both because of her loving nature and her ease of movement.

Placing her wrinkled hand upon his back, she suggested, "Perhaps we should come here more often."

Sammelvar blew a long breath. "Alas, my worries spring from real problems. And those problems won't just solve themselves if I bury myself in flowers' sweet perfume."

"Nor will they solve themselves from your efforts alone," she replied.

"Of course, my love." He pushed a hand through his white

locks. "But I am the leader of this realm, and if I don't give any attention to the problems, who will?"

Escholia peered at him, unconvinced. At the same time, Jaladay sat quietly, taking in their conversation while showing no hint of her own feelings. Her only movement was to keep stroking Kermi's tail.

"Listen," Sammelvar explained, "life in the spirit realm is good these days. The whole realm is largely tranquil for the first time in centuries, now that Narkazan has been destroyed and the Star-stone returned to Earth. Yet that tranquility itself can prove dangerous if it lulls us into complacency—which makes people ignore future perils."

"What perils," asked his wife, "do you mean?"

Sammelvar's expression turned grim. "Narkazan may have been vanquished, but what about his old allies? Many of them still roam the spirit realm, bringing their violent ways with them, raiding peaceful settlements to take whatever they want. And let's not forget about the mistwraiths."

Just the mention of those shadowy beings, dark predators who devoured magic, was enough to make Jaladay shudder. She had met a mistwraith just once—and had only barely escaped.

"What will happen," Sammelvar continued, "if a new leader emerges who can unite them?"

Escholia nodded sadly. "You are right to worry about that."

Furrowing his brow, he lowered his voice to a whisper. "And what will happen if somehow Narkazan himself returns?"

This time, Escholia stared at him in surprise. "How could that possibly happen? No one ever escapes from the Maelstrom."

"No, my love. It's more accurate to say that no one has ever *yet* escaped."

Escholia turned to her daughter. "What do you think, Jaladay?"

The young woman pursed her lips thoughtfully. "Can't help, I'm afraid. Every time I've looked for Narkazan, which I've done several times, I've seen nothing but dark, swirling clouds."

Focusing again on her husband, Escholia asked, "What other perils are troubling you?"

"The veil," he replied solemnly. "It's growing weaker. And we all know what could happen if it is destroyed. Wicked spirits will surely attack the mortal world."

"Yes," agreed Escholia, shaking her head. "The great war was fought because of that—and so many suffered dearly."

"Despite my commands and even my new patrols, spirits keep traveling there," grumbled Sammelvar. "Each visit seems small—and individual spirits tell themselves it really won't matter. But every passage rips a new hole, endangering everything."

Bitterly, he added, "Even my own son . . ."

Escholia took his hand, her eyes full of compassion.

Jaladay leaned toward her father. "That's not your only worry about Promi, is it?"

The elder frowned. "No, it's not. He is angry—at me especially, but also, somehow, at his life. I can feel it . . . though I don't fully understand it."

"I feel it, too," agreed Escholia. "He feels that we forced him to leave us, lose his childhood memories, and spend those years disguised as a mortal. He had no say—no choice at all—in any of that."

"But," objected Sammelvar, "by doing that we saved him from certain destruction by Narkazan—who, as we know, specialized in tortures so painful that even the strongest spirits couldn't survive."

His face looked still more grim, as he recalled the loyal spirits who had perished in the war with Narkazan. Especially those who had chosen to end their own lives—to go out of existence for-ever—to end the warlord's tortures.

Escholia squeezed his hand. "Sending Promi to Earth saved him from that fate. And also enabled him to return when we most needed help—to do what no one else could have done."

"Yes," said Jaladay. "It's only thanks to him—plus the wind lion Theosor and little Kermi here—that the Starstone was saved and Narkazan destroyed."

"Now, now," her mother chimed in. "Let's not forget that you, too, played a role in all that."

Jaladay's silvery skin showed the slightest hint of a blush.

Sammelvar looked down at his robe, which bore a design almost identical to the mark on Promi's chest. Even the size of the soaring bird was the same. Only the color differed; Sammelvar's was gold instead of black.

"We shared this mark through all those years of terrible strife," he said quietly. "Yet now, I fear . . . we share little else."

He glanced up at the sky, then added, "Which is why I've asked him to join us here today."

# CHAPTER 3

# The Song

J oin us?" asked Escholia, surprised. "Are you sure that's a good idea?"

Sammelvar ran his fingers through his white mane. "Honestly, my love, I don't know. But he's already so upset with me, I doubt it will make things any worse."

Seated between her parents, Jaladay turned to each of them, viewing them with her second sight. But she didn't speak.

"I know," said Sammelvar ruefully, "Promi doesn't want to talk about anything. At least not with me. He's made that very clear. But we *do* need to talk about the veil. It grows weaker by the day . . . and he insists on continuing to travel through it."

"Haven't you already warned him?" Escholia questioned. "Made the dangers clear?"

The elder spirit nodded his head. "I've done

everything short of banning him from all travel outside the spirit realm."

"I doubt even that would work," commented Jaladay. She stroked the tail of her sleeping friend, Kermi. "He's just determined to keep going to Earth."

"Yes," replied Sammelvar. "To visit his friend."

"Her name," declared a new voice, "is Atlanta."

All of them turned to see Promi, striding toward them across the cloud. Though purple honeyscent flowers bloomed all around, filling the air with their sweet aroma, he didn't pause to enjoy them. Nor did he take the time to notice that each flower was actually a miniature world, complete with creatures, buildings, and flowering meadows of its own.

Promi's parents stood up to greet him. So did Jaladay, after gently setting Kermi down on the cloud so he could stay asleep. Yet the young man's expression remained grim. As he joined them, he looked at Sammelvar and demanded, "Am I in trouble again?"

Calmly, Sammelvar answered, "Just because I sent a wind lion to find you doesn't mean you're in trouble."

"It does if the wind lion is my old friend Theosor and he gives me a look that says *you'd better be careful*."

Before Sammelvar could reply, Escholia said, "It's good to see you, Promi."

Tossing his long black hair, he answered, "Is it really?"

Escholia moved to his side and gave him an awkward hug. Then, peering at him with her misty blue eyes, she declared, "No matter what you may think, Promi, we are always glad to see our son."

Jaladay raised her hand, trying to signal to her brother not to say the words she could tell he was thinking. But Promi ignored her warning.

"If you're always glad to see me," he grumbled, "then why did you send me away as a child?"

Taken aback, Escholia blinked the mist from her eyes. "We did what we needed to do to save you."

"Even if that meant erasing all my memories?" Promi shot back, his voice rising. "You stole them from me completely!"

Clenching his jaw, he shook his head. Then, in a whisper, he added, "The only shred of my childhood I have left, through all those years living on the streets, was that little scrap of a song you used to sing to me. Do you know how that feels?"

Escholia started to say something, then caught herself. Sammelvar took her hand, his face more careworn than ever. He heaved a sigh, then spoke to Promi.

"I didn't ask you to come here to rehash your grievances. But rest assured, we had ample reasons to do what we did. Including saving your life."

"Then why," snapped Promi, "did you send for me?"

"The veil." Sammelvar locked gazes with his son. "Right now it's barely strong enough to hold back any spirit warriors who might want to invade the mortal realms. And, Promi . . . every time you make one of your journeys—"

"I know, I know," said Promi with a casual wave of his hand. "It tears another hole in the veil. I've heard your theory before."

"It's not just a theory!" Sammelvar struggled to contain his temper. "If you really care about your friend Atlanta—and all the rest of Earth's creatures—you'll heed my warning before it's too late."

The sheen of Promi's skin darkened. "So I should simply *trust* you? Take your word for all this?"

"You can trust," his father replied, "that whatever I've done that affects you . . . I've done because I thought it was best."

"For who?"

"For the spirit realm. And the mortal realm, too."

Promi frowned. So did Jaladay, as she watched him with compassion. *I know how much that hurts you, Promi,* she told him telepathically. *But he really doesn't—*

Promi shot her a glance, cutting her off. Then he turned back to their father.

"You're always talking about what's best for the world," he declared. "What about what's best for *me,* your own son? Do you even care about that at all?"

Sammelvar winced, while Escholia held her breath.

"All I want," Promi continued, "is to go down to Earth whenever I like. You should support me in this! That's what a parent who really cared would do."

"I *do* care," Sammelvar said in a voice as quiet as a whisper. "More than you know. But our personal needs must come second to the needs of our world."

"Easy for you to say," snapped Promi. "You didn't lose your whole childhood! You didn't have everything in your life ripped away. And now you're telling me to trust you that you know what's best?"

Sammelvar reached for Promi's arm. "My son . . . I never meant to—"

"What?" Promi brushed aside his father's hand. "To hurt my feelings? To make me angry? Well, maybe you should have thought about those things before you sent me away."

"We're not talking about only you," said Sammelvar sternly. "We're talking about *everyone,* mortal and immortal. That's why saving the veil matters. It's more important than any one person."

Promi's eyes narrowed. "You don't even know for sure the veil is getting weaker! You're just guessing—it's totally invisible, after all. Do you have any real proof?"

Sammelvar muttered, "Well, I—"

"Just as I thought," said Promi with a smirk. "It's a guess. Nothing more."

"Promi," objected his mother. "You're going too far."

"Am I? Listen, I know what you're doing! Don't think you can fool me. You're trying to keep me from seeing Atlanta. Just because she's mortal. You don't want us to be together!"

"No, no," insisted Sammelvar.

"That's not true at all," said Escholia. "You must believe us."

"Why?" demanded Promi. "The only person I can believe is *myself*. That's what I learned in those years on the streets."

Jaladay shuddered, feeling more pain in her brother than she could bear. She drew a deep breath and sent him one simple thought: *I'm so very sad, Promi—for everything you've been through.*

He gazed at her somberly before sending her a thought in reply: *Glad someone understands . . . at least a little.*

*But you make it hard sometimes,* she added teasingly. *By being as stubborn as a herd of ox-wyverns.*

He almost grinned. *Just like you.*

*Got me there,* she admitted. Cocking her head thoughtfully, she asked, *Can I ask you question?*

*Do I have any choice?*

*No. Here it is: Since you want to be on Earth so much—to be with Atlanta, which I truly understand—why don't you just go down there to stay? Then you'd get what you most want . . . and also, if our father happens to be right, avoid any risk of tearing the veil.*

Promi shrugged. *Guess I just want to do whatever I want for a change! After all those years . . . I feel I'm owed that much.*

She nodded sympathetically.

*And also,* he added, *I like flying through the spirit realm. So many amazing places . . . and amazing desserts.*

He paused, eyeing her. *Besides . . . there's someone up here I'd miss. Even if she's much too stubborn sometimes.*

Jaladay smiled. *No idea who you mean.*

"Promi," said Sammelvar, interrupting them.

The young man stiffened and turned to him.

"We really do care about you, son. Even if you don't know that. But we are talking about something here that's bigger than any of us."

Promi gazed frostily at his father. "If you really cared about me, then why didn't you ever come down to Earth after you sent me away, just to look in on me? To see if I was even still alive?"

"Because," Sammelvar said through his scowl, "to do that would have thrown away all the protection we had won for you! That would have led Narkazan's warriors right to your hiding place—and all would have been lost."

He paused thoughtfully. "Even so, let me say, it was hard not to visit you. Very hard."

"Yes," agreed Escholia. "As hard on us as it was on you."

"I don't believe that." Promi shook his head, swishing his locks against his shoulders.

Escholia chewed her lip, then admitted, "In truth, Promi . . . I *did* visit you."

"You *what*?" exclaimed her husband, eyes wide with surprise.

"I visited Promi," she declared. "In his dreams! I just . . . forgot to mention it to you."

Sammelvar's scowl faded, replaced by a look of astonishment.

Turning to Promi, Escholia explained, "Through dreams, spirits can visit those on Earth. In the same way mortals can reach us with prayers, we can reach them with dreams. And so I came to you, my son, every single night you were gone."

She turned to Sammelvar. "I know it's strictly forbidden, for the same reason you barred any direct contact with the people on Earth—it's just too intrusive on their lives, their free will. But my dear . . . I just *had* to see him."

Her husband stood in silence, then slowly nodded. Meanwhile, Promi stared at her, his eyes full of doubt.

Moving with the grace of a floating tuft of mist, Escholia took both of Promi's hands. Softly, she said, "How else could you remember that song? And my voice? I sang to you every night."

A wave of emotion flowed through Promi. He wanted so much to believe her . . . yet he still couldn't be sure. Summoning his composure, he asked her a pointed question.

"If you came to me in my dreams, then why didn't I have any memory of what you look like?"

A shadow of sadness passed over her face. "It *is* possible for spirits to appear physically in someone's dream. But only if they truly love that someone with deep devotion."

Though his throat felt suddenly dry, Promi swallowed. "So that's not . . . how you love me?"

Escholia's eyes brightened. "No, that's *exactly* how I love you."

"Then why did you only sing to me? You sent me your voice—but not the rest of you."

"Oh, how I wanted to appear fully," Escholia lamented. "More than words can express! But if I had done that, the sight of me would have triggered all sorts of other memories. And the more you remembered, the more you'd have been in danger of realizing your identity and returning to the spirit realm. Which would have put you right into the hands of Narkazan."

Sammelvar nodded. "That's right. Your best protection was ignorance. The greater your knowledge, the greater your danger. So keeping you ignorant was best—both for you and for the Prophecy."

The young man's anger rekindled. "Keeping me ignorant—that's easy for you to say. But it's *me* we're talking about! My memories. My life."

"But," protested his father, "the Prophecy—"

"Face it," snarled Promi. "You cared more about the Prophecy than you did about me, your own son!"

"No, no. That's not—"

Sammelvar's unfinished sentence hung in the air. For Promi suddenly sprang into the sky, leaving behind his entire family. In seconds, he vanished into the swirling mists above the domelike cloud.

A cold wind passed over the cloud, making the purple flowers tremble. Promi's parents and sister also trembled . . . but not from the wind.

CHAPTER 4

# Feather Crystals

A realm away, on Atlantis, the
mortal world's most magical
island, a voice rang out. Deep
in the forest, the young woman's cry echoed among the trees.

"Hide me!"

Atlanta pleaded with the ancient blue
spruce tree, leaning her whole body against its
trunk. "Now! Before he finds me!"

The old tree seemed to shudder. Its upper
branches tossed as if caught by a breeze. Except
there was no breeze.

Atlanta rubbed her hands against the
rough, rutted bark, using her gift of natural
magic to awaken the tree—one of many in the
Great Forest who had known her since that day
she first came here, lost and alone, as a child.
The trees, back then, had protected her and

become her friends. But even now, as a fully grown young woman, she still turned to them when in need.

"Please, Master Spruce," she begged. "He's coming . . . and there's not much time!"

Again, the tree shuddered—this time so forcefully that hundreds of blue needles poured down from the branches, showering her. She shook them from her curly brown hair, not even noticing how their tangy-sweet scent filled the air. She only clasped the trunk harder than ever.

"Now, old friend. Only seconds left!"

With a sharp crackling sound, the trunk started to expand. A whole new layer of bark sprouted from the ruts and wrapped around the tree—as well as Atlanta.

Seconds later, no sign of her could be seen. She was completely covered—her head, her purple gown woven from lilac vines, and her bare feet. Only the spruce's unusually wide trunk gave any hint of her whereabouts.

Safe inside the blanket of newly grown bark, Atlanta sighed. She squeezed the tree thankfully.

Meanwhile, all around the spruce, the forest hushed, as if holding its breath. All the other trees in the grove fell utterly still. So did the animals in their branches, ranging from a normally chattering squirrel to a pair of cockatoos. Even a small butterfly with green-striped wings froze in place.

Then a slight movement entered the grove—so subtle it was almost invisible. A faint whirring of wings . . . a hint of blue . . . a blur of something passing through the air. Nothing more than that.

The faery landed on one of the old spruce's lowest branches. Now fully visible, his luminous blue wings opened above him, shimmering with light. Between his delicate antennae sat a white cotton hat; a translucent cloak rested on his tiny shoulders. Hollowed-out red berries served as shoes.

The faery's antennae quivered ever so slightly. Then, after a few seconds' pause, he placed his little hands on his hips, waiting impatiently. Once again, his antennae quivered.

Suddenly the new layer of bark around the trunk trembled, buckled—and split open. As quickly as it had grown, it receded into the old folds of bark. Atlanta, fully exposed, caught her breath.

Above her on the branch, the faery cocked his head.

She peered up at him. "All right, Quiggley. Stop your gloating!" Her eyes narrowed. "Just because you found me, you don't have to look so smug about it."

With a gentle flutter of wings, the faery glided down to her shoulder. Atlanta turned her head toward him and grumbled, "How did you do that so fast? It's no fun hiding from somebody like you!"

Quiggley shrugged modestly. But even on his tiny face, the grin of satisfaction couldn't be missed.

Because faery language is so densely packed with magical symbols, very few of Atlantis's mortal creatures could even attempt to understand it. Some elder unicorns, it was said, could banter freely with the faeries. And Falaru, the oldest of the great whales, often sang ballads with deepwater faeries that could last several weeks without pause. The only other known instance of someone conversing with a faery was when Promi, in Atlanta's presence, had tried it. That had required a great sacrifice on Promi's part—and he survived only because he was, in fact, immortal (though he didn't know it at the time).

And so . . . ever since Atlanta had first met this little fellow—and healed his wounds after he'd nearly died from an attack ordered by the wicked priest Grukarr—Quiggley had found other ways to communicate with her. Sometimes all it took was a grin like the one he was wearing now. More often, he sent her a wave of *feeling*, an emotion so clear it always touched her heart.

That's why Atlanta started to laugh. A wave of sheer amusement, so full of joy she couldn't resist, flowed through her. That joy wasn't just from playing their little game. Most of it came from simply appreciating their rather unusual friendship.

For an enduring friendship it had become. The attack that Quiggley had barely survived destroyed all the magic—and all the life—of his faery clan. He'd lost his young daughter, his wife, and both parents. Atlanta, meanwhile, had no relatives of her own. She possessed nothing more than a few memories of her parents, who had died in a terrible swamp near a place called the Passage of Death. So the two of them had bonded as tightly as bark and sap on a tree.

Since finding each other, the young woman and the faery had shared some perilous adventures—including a few with serious consequences for both the mortal and immortal worlds. And on days like this . . . they shared some lighthearted moments, as well.

As Atlanta's bell-like laughter quieted, she kneeled to smell a clump of lemongrass growing at her feet. She inhaled deeply, as did Quiggley while balancing on her shoulder. The scent made her feel peaceful, as always. And it also reminded her of the first day she had met Promi—over a freshly baked lemon pie he'd just stolen.

Suddenly she frowned. Standing again, she shot a glance at the faery. He nonchalantly twirled a loose lilac vine on the shoulder of her gown, looking carefree.

"You can't fool me," she grumbled. "You know *exactly* why I'm so upset at him."

Quiggley merely gazed at her, cocking his head innocently.

"Why does he have to go on acting this way?" she demanded. "When he knows it's just impossible?"

One corner of Quiggley's mouth lifted in a grin.

"Of course he likes me! That's obvious. Any buffoon can see that! But he doesn't have any right to assume I feel the same way about *him*."

Now the faery's whole mouth was grinning.

Atlanta slapped her hand against the old spruce's trunk. "But it's impossible! He should know that. We're from two different worlds, separated by the veil—and a stack of ancient laws, too!"

Her eyes narrowed. "And besides . . . he's, well—he's such a *problem*."

Biting her lip, she shook her head. "I know, I know . . ." Her voice grew quieter until, in a whisper, she said, "Maybe not the only problem."

The faery merely gazed at her.

She sighed. "Right. *I'm* the real problem."

Quiggley waved his antennae sympathetically.

For a long moment, she stared at her feet. Briefly, that game with Quiggley had lifted her spirits. But now here she was again, feeling the weight of all those thoughts that never took her anywhere, like a circular path in the forest that she couldn't escape.

Glumly, she sighed. She *was* the problem. If only Promi could understand how—

She caught her breath. Right before her eyes, a sparkling crystal appeared. It glistened and swelled rapidly, twirling as it floated through the air. A snowflake!

*But it's springtime,* she told herself in disbelief. *And it's much too warm today for snow.*

More surprisingly, the snowflake kept growing, stretching out delicate arms that continued to swell. Soon it looked more like a big white feather, glowing in the light. On top of that, it didn't fall to the ground. Instead, the crystalline feather just hung in the air, twirling slowly.

"You're not snow," said Atlanta, awestruck. "What are you, then?"

She reached out to touch it, but a subtle breeze made it float just beyond her reach. At the same time, more feather crystals appeared. They glistened as they grew, spinning lightly through the air in a luminous, magical dance.

Watching this radiant display, she held her breath. Never in her whole life had she seen anything like this!

"Quiggley," she whispered. "Have you ever—"

She glanced at the faery, then stopped. For his bright eyes, together with the slight trembling of his wings, explained it all.

"You!" she exclaimed. "*You* made this happen."

He shrugged modestly, making his cloak shimmer like the crystals.

Atlanta peered at him, full of gratitude. "Just to cheer me up. Even if that means making it snow on a warm spring day! Quiggley . . . you are, well, you are something! I don't know the right word to describe it."

Adjusting his cotton hat, he struck a casual pose.

"Yes, I do," she corrected herself. "The word for you is *friend*."

His expression didn't change . . . although his eyes might have gleamed just slightly.

"And, my friend," she added, invoking her favorite blessing that she saved for the most special occasions, "I bless your eternal qualities."

The feather crystals started to fall, at last. Gracefully, they settled down to the ground, decorating the roots of the old spruce and all the surrounding rocks, ferns, and grasses. Even an elderly bullfrog, seated on a mossy root, seemed to have sprouted crystalline wings.

For a brief instant, the forest floor glowed with sparkling radiance.

Then, with a quiver of the faery's antennae, the feather crystals melted away.

Feeling much better, Atlanta started walking. "Let's go, Quiggley. We're not far from Moss Island."

Indeed, only a few minutes later, they came to a clear stream. Following it deeper into the forest, they found a spot where the stream split into a pair of splashing waterways. In the center sat a small island covered in thick moss. And, to Atlanta's surprise, right in the middle of the island sat a young man.

Promi.

# CHAPTER 5

# The Starstone's Hiding Place

Startled to find him sitting there, Atlanta froze. "You!" she exclaimed.

Promi nodded, swishing the long black hair that contrasted starkly with the misty sheen of his skin. With the hint of a grin, he said, "Nice to see you, too."

Despite all the doubts she'd felt only moments before, her heart leaped. She dashed to the stream and jumped across to Moss Island, landing right on top of Promi. They rolled on the moss sparkling with spray, laughing together.

Quiggley, who had taken flight as she jumped, flew up to a willow branch. Amused, he watched the scene below. Then he turned his attention to the stream itself, listening to its constant splash as it swept around the island.

Closing his little eyes, he recalled the family he'd lost in Grukarr's attack—a whole clan of faeries who delighted in places just like this. Places where they could zip playfully through the vapors, turning cartwheels in the air, even as they made magical flowers sprout from streams or dined on the nectar of water lilies. Of all their communal activities, though, his most favorite had been telling stories to young children . . . including his daughter. How bright their eyes had glowed when he told tales and drew colorful pictures in the mist!

Ever so slightly, his antennae drooped. When his tales had ended, those pictures melted away, gone forever. And now . . . so had those children.

In the moss below, Atlanta and Promi weren't aware of the faery's musings (although, if they hadn't been so distracted, they might have noticed the temperature grow a little cooler). Having rolled to a stop, they sat beside each other, still laughing. Finally, Atlanta spoke.

"How did you know I'd be here?"

"Just a lucky guess."

She peered at him skeptically.

"You're more predictable than you think, Atlanta."

"And you're more ridiculous than you think."

"Besides," he added playfully, "what makes you so sure I came here to see *you*?" He ran his fingers through the thick green growth beneath them. "Maybe I just love moss."

"Right. So much that you came all the way from the spirit realm just to touch it."

"Well, maybe I came here to touch something else." Promi leaned closer and lightly stroked her cheek. "Like that."

She held his gaze. Then, feeling suddenly awkward, she wanted to change the subject. "How was the journey?"

He hesitated, tempted to tell her about the fight he'd just had with his parents. But the last thing he wanted to do right now was ruin the mood with Atlanta. Maybe he'd tell her later . . .

"The journey," she repeated. "How was it?"

"A bit bumpy," he replied. "I flew into some, er . . . unexpected winds."

Suddenly brightening, he added, "But I actually hit a snowstorm! With really huge flakes. It didn't last long, ending just before you arrived."

She almost grinned. "That's hard to believe."

He shrugged. "Most of my life is hard to believe."

"That's true, Promi. You've come a long way for somebody who started out as a pie thief, prisoner, and all-around vagabond."

"And don't forget," he added with a chuckle, "the Divine Monk's proclaimed Worst Criminal Ever in All History. Not because I broke all those laws to sneak into his private quarters on a high holy day, mind you. But because I . . ."

"Stole his favorite dessert!"

They laughed, the sound of their mirth mixing with the gleeful thrum of the stream. When at last they paused, she looked at him with an expression that was not quite serious.

"The worst thing you ever did back in those days—"

"You mean the days," he interrupted, eyes twinkling, "before I figured out the Prophecy, regained the Starstone, saved the world, ended the war in the spirit realm—and, oh yes, became immortal?"

"Right," she parried. "Back in the days before you became the humble fellow you are now."

"Right." He tapped her forearm. "So what was the worst thing I ever did?"

Atlanta opened her arms wide. "Right here on this island, that first night, when you told me—and all those forest creatures who had fed you so lavishly—that you absolutely wouldn't help us."

He winced. "Did I really?"

"You did. And nothing could change your mind! You didn't budge even when the centaur threatened to kick off your head, the birds tried to peck out your eyes, and the smelldrude wanted to make you stink like a field of rotten fish."

"And I suppose it's no excuse that I was still just a stupid, sweets-loving mortal?"

She raised an eyebrow. "As opposed to a stupid, sweets-loving immortal?"

"You got me there," he said with a sigh. "And there's nothing I can do to make that up to you?"

Thoughtfully, she stroked her chin. "Like what?"

"Well . . . like creating a whole new island in the middle of the sea?"

She shook her head. "That's been done. By somebody—can't remember his name."

"Hmmm. Then how about naming the island after you?"

Again she shook her head. "Also been done."

"Then how about this?"

Promi leaned over and gave her a kiss on the lips.

After the kiss ended, Atlanta sat back. Thoughtfully, she ran a hand through her curls. "Well . . . that's a start."

"Good. Maybe I should practice some more."

She smiled. "Good idea."

Reaching for each other's hands, they stood in unison. Seeing this, Quiggley fluttered down from his perch on the willow branch. He landed on Atlanta's shoulder, his radiant blue wings whirring softly.

"Welcome back, little friend." Atlanta tapped one of his red berry shoes. "Missed you."

"Quiggley!" exclaimed Promi. "How are you?"

The faery turned toward him. Suddenly Promi held up one hand.

"Wait! Don't answer that question! The last time you spoke to me, my head almost exploded."

Quiggley's grin returned. A wave of merriment flowed into both young people, making them chuckle.

Promi turned, scanning the moss-covered island and the forest beyond. "You know, a whole lot has happened since that night. Including the prediction by that gloomy centaur."

"Haldor," said Atlanta. "Not the most cheerful fellow around."

"I've met corpses more cheerful."

"You're right, though—he did predict this place would actually become an island. But don't forget what *else* he predicted."

"That one day," recalled Promi, "Atlantis will be lost forever, sinking deep into the sea, after a great disaster. What he called *a terrible day and night of destruction*."

Inexplicably, the temperature seemed to drop. Feeling the chill, Promi and Atlanta moved closer. Even the faery drew his cloak around himself.

"Brrr," said Promi. "Feels like it could snow again."

"Anything is possible around here," she replied. Then, recalling something, she added, "Why, on that same night we were also visited by a whole family of mist maidens. And by the river god himself! Remember?"

Touching the magical dagger at his side, Promi nodded. "You bet I do." He glanced at its gleaming, translucent hilt and the silver string that would wrap itself around his wrist whenever he threw the dagger. "That memory—like this blade—I'll never lose."

She gave his hand a squeeze. "And now, thanks to you, this little island has something else unforgettable. Something with infinite power."

Catching her meaning, he uttered a single word—and merely saying it made him feel somehow stronger. "Starstone."

"Yes, Promi. It's here."

He thought about the first time he'd held the Starstone. Resting in the palm of his hand, the magnificent crystal glowed with pure, pulsing light. At the same time, it filled him with its mysterious power, magnifying his own inner magic.

For that was the Starstone's gift. As the old priest Bonlo, whom Promi had met in the dungeon of Ekh Raku, first explained, this crystal did for magic what a magnifying glass did for images. It took simple magic and transformed that into something bigger—as well as far more rich and complex. So its very presence enhanced everything around it.

That quality made the Starstone, quite simply, the most powerful object on Earth. Its power could be used for good—as it was now, deepening the natural magic of the Great Forest. Or it could be used for evil, becoming a weapon of unlimited destruction—which had been the goal of Grukarr and his master, the spirit warlord Narkazan.

"But where is it?" Promi asked. "I don't see it anywhere."

Atlanta grinned. "Oh, it's here on the island, all right. Just hidden from view."

He continued to scan Moss Island. Yet he saw nothing unusual—just lots of moss beneath their feet, the old willow, and the surrounding stream. Maybe, he thought, if it can't be seen . . . it could still be *felt*.

Closing his eyes, he remembered what he used to do as a Listener—*to hear the unheard,* in his sister Jaladay's words. He felt grateful that, now that he'd become fully immortal, he no longer needed to make a sacrifice every time he tried to do it. In fact, Jaladay had told him that he still possessed all the ability to listen he'd had before, and that the power would never leave him.

Even so . . . he hesitated. He hadn't tried to use that power since Atlantis became an island. What if he'd forgotten how? What if he just couldn't do it?

*Might as well try,* he told himself. The worst that could happen was he'd embarrass himself in front of Atlanta. And he'd already done that more times than he could count.

Opening himself to the sounds all around, he listened. Not just with his ears, but with his bones. His blood. His innermost feelings.

At first, he heard only the rushing stream. Then his own breathing, as well as Atlanta's. Then their heartbeats. And then . . . the very gentle pulse of the faery's heart.

Meanwhile, Atlanta watched him intently. On her shoulder, Quiggley leaned forward.

High overhead, Promi heard the steady flap of a bird's wings. An egret, he felt sure. Seeking a fish to bring home to a nest of young ones.

Then . . . a sound unlike any of the others. Both very near and far away, it seemed to beat like a heart, but with a resonance that echoed in all the living beings on the island. This deep, steady pulse echoed in himself, in Atlanta, in the tree—and even in the tufts of moss. As well as in the stream and in the ancient rocks on its banks.

Slowly, keeping his eyes closed, Promi turned. The sound's origin, its source, was calling. He could almost hear it.

Almost.

Stretching his listening to the limit, he caught hold of the sound. *There,* he told himself at last. *Over there.*

He opened his eyes. With a certainty he couldn't explain, he stepped over to the willow tree. Kneeling by its roots, he lay his hand on one especially gnarled, moss-covered root.

"Here," he said quietly. "The Starstone is buried under here."

"Yes!" Atlanta rushed over and kneeled beside him. "I asked the tree to keep and protect it. To hide the crystal away—and never to release it unless Atlantis is in terrible, terrible danger. And that root lifted out of the ground, grasped the crystal, and carried it deep underground."

As they stood, she gave him a smirk. "Not bad for a pie thief."

## CHAPTER 6

# Strange Magic

"Come on," said Promi as he nudged her shoulder. "Let's take a walk. Can't think of how many weeks it's been since I saw you—but it's too many."

Atlanta nodded. "That's true! Shall I lead?"

"Of course. You know if I lead, we'll get completely lost in no time."

"Also true." Pointing at Promi's feet, she smirked. "Remember when you gave up your boots and walked the first time in bare feet?"

"Most painful thing I've ever done," he answered. "Except maybe . . . when I had to put up with that crazy blue demon riding on my back."

"Kermi? Oh . . . he was so *cute*."

Promi scowled. "Cute as the plague."

"Let's go," declared Atlanta.

With the faery perched on her shoulder, she

darted to the island's edge and leaped across the rushing waterway. Then, without breaking stride, she strode across a patch of lemongrass, between a pair of olive trees, and up a fern-covered slope. After glancing behind to make sure her companion was coming, she veered into a grove where passion fruits were just beginning to ripen.

Promi joined her—but as usual, without Atlanta's grace. Compared to her, he resembled a hippo trying to run with a gazelle. Yet he did try hard to stay by her side . . . except whenever they encountered a smelldrude.

When that happened today, fortunately, Promi was lagging behind. When Atlanta emerged from a stand of birches, the smelldrude saw her and waddled over. Looking like an oversized otter with enormous eyes, she placed one of her webbed feet in Atlanta's open hand. The smelldrude's powerful scent glands produced an aroma as sweet as wild roses. But the instant Promi appeared, that aroma took on a hint of something more like curdled milk mixed with dead fish.

Promi immediately turned around and retreated into the birches. Only after the smelldrude had waddled off—and Atlanta had waved to let him know all was clear—did he rejoin her.

Through the Great Forest they roamed, occasionally stopping to drink from a spring that bubbled up from the ground, eat some juicy pears, or split a sweet cakefruit. After a few hours, they climbed a massive fir tree (whose branches held a whole clan of chattering squirrels), just to enjoy the view from the top. Later, they came across a steep hill covered in fluffy blue moss—which they immediately rolled down. Throughout the day, the woods resounded with their conversation, laughter, and, whenever Atlanta felt inspired, song.

As late afternoon light touched the trees, painting branches with gold, they came to the western edge of the forest. Before them, at the bottom of a sloping meadow, sat three clear lakes. Like puzzle pieces, the lakes fit together perfectly, with narrow borders of rushes growing between them. Sunlight sparkled on the water.

"Shall we go for a swim?" Promi started to pull off his tunic. "Before the sun goes down."

"Not there," cautioned Atlanta. She put a hand on his arm. "Those are the Lakes of Dreams . . . and there is strange magic in that water."

"But they look so inviting."

"Look more closely."

Peering at the lakes, Promi noticed that there were no birds on the surface. Nor did any other animals wander the shores. Indeed, he saw no signs at all of animal life—not even a path to a favorite spot to drink.

"I see," he said. "There's something, well, *unfriendly* about those lakes."

Twirling one of her curls thoughtfully, Atlanta gazed at the scene. "The rumor I've heard—ever since childhood—is that anyone who stands on the shore and looks into that water will see their most frightful dream."

She glanced at him, then went on. "And anyone who stays too long by that water . . . will be condemned to *live* that dream."

On her shoulder, the faery shuddered.

Promi raised his eyebrows. "Well then, I guess we won't be going for a swim after all."

For a long moment, they sat in silence at the top of the slope. Then, in unison, they turned, reading each other's expressions.

"You're sure?" asked Promi.

"Yes," she replied. "Just a quick look. For the adventure. Let's do it together! That won't be so bad."

Quiggley flew in front of her face, wings whirring, waving his small arms in distress.

"It's all right, little friend. Just one look. How bad can that be?"
The faery waved even more frantically.

"Listen," she explained. "My whole life I've been hearing about
the Lakes of Dreams, and I've always heeded the warnings. But
now I'm old enough to handle whatever the water shows me."

"And I'm here, too." Promi slid his fingers into hers. "We'll
help each other."

Dejectedly, Quiggley shook his head, almost losing his cotton
hat. Then he flew over to the nearest tree, an elm, and perched on
its lowest branch. He tucked in his wings, as if to say, *I'll wait for
you here.*

Holding hands, Atlanta and Promi walked down to the nearest
of the lakes. As they stepped into the rushes, their bare feet made
the stalks snap and hiss. Finally, at the water's edge, they stopped.

They traded uncertain glances, then released hands. As one,
they kneeled—and looked into the still water.

Atlanta saw a sudden blur of images. Her own face as a child,
clouds of noxious fumes, menacing shadows, murky pools, twisted
trees. The Passage of Death was near! She ran into the swamp, dodg-
ing quicksand pits and slithering snakes whose fangs gleamed darkly.

*Mama! Papa!* she screamed, her small voice swallowed by the
night. *Don't leave me all alone!*

Images of hunched creatures flashed by, with more eerie shadows. Swamp specters! Feeding on human misery—following her.
Reaching for her hair, her neck, her arms . . .

Dark vapors swirled. The scene suddenly changed to a sunlit
meadow in the forest. Two people were lying together amidst the
sweetstalk fern. Atlanta and Promi! She relaxed, reaching for him,
even as he gently stroked her arm. Lovingly, they embraced, starting to kiss. Just an instant before their lips touched—

He burst into laughter! Not with joy, but with wrath—a harsh,
vengeful laugh. Roughly, he shoved her away.

*You!* He stood, looking at her with revulsion. *You are nobody. Nothing! I am leaving you forever.*

*Wait,* she cried. *Wait, Promi. Don't leave me all alone!*

• • •

Kneeling by the lake, Atlanta reeled so violently that she fell over backward. Looking down at her was someone with long black hair. Promi!

She shrieked and rolled away from him, still feeling her anger and pain at what he'd done. What he'd said.

*A dream,* she told herself. *It was just a dream.* But if that was true, why was the pain so raw? Why was her whole body shaking?

"Atlanta," he said, watching her worriedly. "Are you all right?"

Slowly, she sat up. "Sure," she said weakly. "Just . . . a bit shaken."

He sat down beside her. "Want to talk about it?"

"No."

Gently, he placed his hand on her knee. But she recoiled from his touch, moving away.

"No," she repeated. Lowering her head between her knees, she moaned, "That . . . was . . . a bad idea."

Promi frowned solemnly. "I know."

After a moment, she raised her head. "Was your vision just as horrible?"

He nodded.

"Want to tell me about it?"

"No."

She gazed at him, this young man who had saved the world, who had cast the wicked spirit Narkazan into a swirling maelstrom, who had created a whole new island—and who now looked so shaken and vulnerable. Drawing a deep breath, she slid over to his side. Their bodies leaned against each other. But they didn't speak.

In silence, they sat there. The sun dropped lower to the horizon, splashing pink and purple rays across the sky. Yet neither of them noticed.

Finally, Atlanta whispered a few words. "I'll tell you something about mine . . . if you'll do the same."

"Well . . . ," he said hesitantly.

She tapped his knee. "I think it might help. Both of us."

He sighed. "All right. Shall I go first?"

"No," she answered bravely. "I'll start."

Chewing her lip, she paused, deciding what to say. "Mine was about . . . losing my parents. Searching for them, all by myself, in that terrible swamp. Calling for them . . ."

She started to cry. As Promi wrapped his arm around her shoulder, she said through her sobs, "But they . . . never . . . came back."

As the sobs subsided, she wiped her eyes with her sleeve. "That's what I saw." Then she added, though it wasn't true, "Nothing more."

"That was enough."

Looking away, she murmured, "Yes, enough." Then she turned back to him. "And your vision?"

"A bit more scattered," he replied. "Funny thing is . . . most of it was feelings, not places or people."

"What sort of feelings?"

He cleared his throat. "Well, when I was a child and I found out my parents wanted to send me away—all the way to the world of mortals—I was angry. And confused. And very hurt."

"Of course."

"So what if they thought they were protecting me? They totally ignored what I wanted! They wiped away my memories, stole everything I knew—my whole past. Then they disguised me as a mortal, sent me to Earth, and forced me to fend for myself on the streets."

Atlanta shuddered. Until now, she hadn't really understood what Promi had survived.

"All because of *this*," he growled. He opened his tunic to show the strange black mark on his chest—right over his heart. Resembling a soaring bird, it was the sign of the Prophecy that had rocked both the mortal and spirit realms . . . and changed his life forever.

"The truth is," he lamented, "I've been used my whole life."

He paused, thinking about the fight he'd just had with his parents. Those childhood wounds were still so raw! Could he ever forgive Sammelvar and Escholia? Could he ever move beyond all that?

Reliving that pain, as he'd looked into the water, had been brutal. If that had been all he'd seen, it would have been bad enough. He blew a long breath and thought, *But that wasn't the worst of it. No—not nearly.*

Promi chewed his lip. Should he tell Atlanta the rest?

*No,* he decided. *I can't possibly do that. Can't possibly tell her how we were almost together—before we were ripped apart. Time after time after time!*

Feeling her stroke his back soothingly, he told himself, *And I certainly can't tell her that the person to blame, the one who tore us apart, wasn't some outsider. It was me!*

He shook his head. That was the most frightening part of the dream—the fear that he could never truly love anyone. Not his parents. Not his sister. Not even Atlanta.

She took his arm. "It's going to get dark soon. Should we find somewhere to spend the night?"

"Sure," he replied, still gripped by what he'd experienced.

Together, they rose and walked up the slope to the forest's edge. Neither said a word. And neither looked back at the darkening Lakes of Dreams.

# CHAPTER 7

# Two Separate Worlds

Neither of them slept well. Though they'd found a lovely spot—a mossy meadow beside a tumbling waterfall, the starry sky arching overhead—Atlanta and Promi tossed and turned the whole night. Like endless cries for help, their experiences at the lakes kept echoing in their minds.

Only Quiggley had no trouble sleeping. Curled inside a cupped oak leaf near Atlanta, he slept soundly for at least seven minutes—a full night's rest for a faery. For the remainder of the evening, he explored the forest in moonlight, one of his favorite times to be with the woods and its creatures. By dawn, he was halfway across the forest, so he decided it was time to return to Atlanta.

Meanwhile, morning light touched the companions' mossy meadow. The waterfall grew brighter, until it looked like liquid sunshine pouring over the rocks. A nearby spider's web transformed into golden threads. High in the branches of a mahogany tree, a nest of young bluebirds awoke and started chirping hungrily.

For Atlanta and Promi, though, this wasn't a time to enjoy their surroundings. Bleary from lack of sleep, they rose and gathered a bit of breakfast—some licorice roots, a few walnuts, and a kind of miniature melon often found near waterfalls.

Sitting next to Atlanta on the moss, Promi sliced the melon with his dagger. He handed half to her. Together, they ate the succulent fruit as juice dribbled down their chins.

"Mmm," said Promi with a smack of his lips. "Good melon. Almost as sweet as the sugarmelons that grow in the spirit realm. Just last week I found some growing on the banks of a river of honey."

"Too bad you don't have a sweet tooth," Atlanta teased. "Otherwise you might actually enjoy those things."

He grinned. "You might enjoy them, too, if you'd let me take you there sometime."

Chewing her last bite of melon, she shook her head. "You know it's against the law for mortals to visit the spirit realm."

"I suppose," he said with a shrug. "But by the same token, immortals aren't allowed to visit Earth. And that's never kept me from coming to see you."

Her blue-green eyes looked at him worriedly. "How difficult is that journey? I mean, are you putting yourself at risk by coming here?"

"No," he said, pausing to wipe his sticky hands on the moss. "The only risk is getting caught. And my *specialty* is never getting caught."

"It's really that easy?"

"All I need to do is catch a good wind and fly here, now that I know how. I'll never be as fast as a wind lion like Theosor, of course—but it's still a fairly quick trip."

"I mean, it's easy not to get caught?"

"Child's play. I've always been good at escaping pursuers! And there's really no harm in it. My father keeps telling me that my travels here are tearing holes in the veil between the worlds. But I don't buy it."

She leaned closer. "Why not? Sammelvar, the great spirit of wisdom, wouldn't lie to you."

Bitterly, Promi asked, "Really? You're saying I should trust the same man who has always treated me as just a pawn in his grand plans?"

Atlanta peered at him, guessing he was still struggling with yesterday's vision at the Lakes of Dreams. Or could there be something else going on, something he wasn't telling her?

Or maybe, she wondered, was there more to his vision than he'd revealed? Just as there was really more to her own?

Trying to comfort him, she suggested, "Maybe your parents just want you around more. It must be nice for them to have you back."

"Are you kidding?" Promi scowled. "That's the last thing they want! Especially after that fight."

"What fight?"

"Just before I came here. My father berated me for going through the veil. Made a big fuss that my visits to Earth are tearing so many holes that the veil could collapse."

Atlanta stiffened. "Promi . . . what if he's right?"

"But he's not! Not once, in all my travels, have I ever seen or felt the veil. And I've certainly never felt it tearing."

"But, Promi—"

"Don't you see what he's doing? Trying to control me, as always!

He thinks I'm selfish—but my parents are the selfish ones, still using me for their own purposes."

He paused, looking into her eyes that sparkled with green, expecting her sympathy. Instead, she said the last thing he expected.

"Listen, Promi. Your father could be *right* about the veil. And if he is . . . this whole world is at risk."

"What? It's a lot more likely he doesn't want me to see you! He's probably cooking up this whole thing just to keep us apart."

Atlanta shook her head. "Even if that's true, the veil matters more. The possibility it's in danger outweighs the desires of just two people."

Stunned by her response, Promi asked, "Even if those two people are us?"

Atlanta frowned. "Yes."

He reached for her hand. "There's something else you need to know."

He hesitated, trying to find the right words. "Time is, well . . . *different* in the spirit realm. It moves much more slowly than on Earth. Just a few minutes up there could be days or months—even years—down here. So by coming here often to be with you, and by spending lots of time on Atlantis, I'm . . ."

"Keeping us close to the same age?" Touched, she gave him a soulful look.

"Yes," he said softly. "I don't want you to get a whole lot older than me."

Atlanta drew a long, slow breath. "I see. But, Promi, you *still* can't put our needs ahead of the world's."

"What are you saying?"

"That you should trust your father on this."

"No!" Promi released her hand and stood. Angrily, he strode over to the waterfall. Then he spun around and declared, "He's just trying to stop me from doing what I want. Like he's *always* done. And what I want is to see you!"

He paused, trying to calm his voice. "He's just putting up barriers, don't you see? And I've *never,* in my whole life, believed in barriers."

Something about the way he said that sounded wrong to Atlanta. Dangerously wrong. She walked over and confronted him.

"I'm worried about the veil, even if you're not! There are evil spirits, too, as you know—spirits who would do terrible things down here if they could. And, Promi . . . I'm also worried about *you.*"

Angrily, he clenched his jaw. "What are you saying? That I'm evil? Or stupid?"

"No!"

"Or that you don't *want* me to come visit?"

"No, Promi!"

"Then what kind of idiocy *are* you saying?"

"You sound like you're still a pie thief! Like you can just sneak into the mortal realm any old time you want—as if it's somebody's kitchen. And," she added, her heart pounding, "I'm *not* just another dessert for you to steal."

Taken aback, he objected, "I never said anything like that."

"No? No? You said you love never getting caught and you don't believe in barriers. Sounds like a pie thief to me! Then you just toss aside any worries about the veil."

"Sure, but—"

"Listen," she said coldly. "That veil is protecting my world! My forest. My home. And if you don't understand that—*how can I ever trust you?*"

"Trust me?"

"Not to . . ." The words caught in her throat.

"I'm just trying to be free!" he shouted. "To make my own choices for a change!"

"Even if those choices put my whole world in danger?" She scowled at him. "Maybe you really *like* having us live apart, pulled by two separate worlds. That way you never get too close to any-body—and never have to change your ways."

"What do you mean?"

"That you're being selfish! Just like your father said. The veil matters more than any one person, Promi!"

Hearing her words, so close to Sammelvar's, was more than he could take. "No," he insisted. "You're wrong!" He stepped back-ward, almost falling into the pool beneath the waterfall.

Just at that moment, Quiggley flew back to the meadow. It didn't take his keen instincts as a faery to feel the anger and fear in the air. He sensed immediately that, even as this new day had begun . . . something else had ended.

# CHAPTER 8

# A Dream of Destiny

Somewhere in the sea east of Atlantis, a lone ship fought to stay afloat. Mighty waves crashed against the wooden hull, soaking the deck and everyone desperately clinging to the rails. Waves struck the ship with such force that towers of spray swallowed the entire mainsail, obscuring its design of a blue dolphin.

Several men and women, certain of death, lay prostrate before the carved image of the Greek god Poseidon that rose above the ship's prow. Frantically, they prayed to that ruler of the sea, his brother Zeus, and any other deity who might be moved to spare their lives. One woman, her black hair so drenched by seawater it looked like a mass of writhing snakes, clung to the stern rail and sang chants to the goddess

Athena. But her voice was drowned by the constant roar and crash of the waves.

Only one person on board remained steadfastly calm: Reocoles, the ship's captain. Standing behind the captain's wheel, his heavy-set body planted on the deck, he looked as immovable as the mainsail's mast. Even as the ship rocked dangerously from side to side, with seawater cascading off his brow, he stood firm, hands clasping the wheel's wooden knobs. All the while, his eyes scanned the horizon.

Reocoles seemed so firmly rooted to the deck that it would have been hard to believe one of his legs was badly lame. Since birth, that leg had troubled him. But now, propped against the wheel, he seemed oblivious to any such weakness. Only the shape of the heavy iron brace under his wet leggings revealed the truth.

Besides, something far stronger than a brace supported him—his indomitable will. Despite the raging storm that threatened to tear his ship apart and drown everyone aboard, his eyes gleamed with the certainty that a great new discovery awaited him. And with that discovery, all the power he'd ever dreamed of wielding.

An island of vast riches, ready for him to claim.

Surrounded by sheer cliffs, this undiscovered island rose out of the sea with a mighty façade. Though he couldn't see it through the violent waves, he felt sure it was there. For he'd seen it clearly in a dream the night before.

A dream he could still recall in vivid detail.

A dream that promised him his true destiny—all the power that life had, until now, denied him.

A dream that had been sent to him, he felt absolutely certain, from the gods on high.

"Sir!" shouted a bedraggled sailor, struggling to keep his balance. "I have important news!"

"Say it, then," commanded Reocoles, without turning his head away from the horizon.

The sailor, whose name was Karpathos, tugged nervously on one end of his very long (and very wet) mustache. "I have checked all the charts, sir. And there is absolutely no island in the direction we are heading!"

"No island, you say?"

"That's right," shouted Karpathos over the endless roar of the sea. "No island at all!"

Reocoles turned just long enough to shoot the sailor a furious glance. "*Of course* it's not on the charts, you imbecile! We haven't discovered it yet."

Karpathos blinked in confusion. Tugging worriedly on his soggy mustache, he protested, "But, Captain, sir—"

A cry interrupted him. It came from a young sailor who had volunteered to be lashed to the mast to see greater distances. Though the sailor's voice was barely loud enough to be heard above the din, his words rang out like a harbor bell.

"An island! I see an island!"

Sure enough, an imposing island was starting to take shape through the spray. Its sheer cliffs jutted out of the ocean; from its center rose a mass of thickly forested hills. A beam of sunlight fell directly on that forest, making it shine like a crown of luminous green.

"Exactly as my dream foretold," Reocoles muttered to himself. "The island whose riches I am destined to control."

Suddenly, the ship lurched sideways—so forcefully that Reocoles lost his grip on the wheel. He tumbled backward, landing on top of Karpathos. Before they could untangle themselves, another great wave crashed over them, sending them skidding across the deck.

The wheel, meanwhile, spun ceaselessly. For a powerful current now gripped the ship, spinning the craft in ever-tightening circles. A ring of waves lifted all around, surging skyward, blocking out any view of the island.

It was then that the sailor lashed to the mast raised his voice again. He shouted just one word—a word feared by sailors across the ages:

"Whirlpool!"

# CHAPTER 9

# Jaladay's Vision

Much had happened on Earth since Promi's abrupt departure from his family. But for those he'd left behind on the dome-shaped cloud . . . only a few minutes had passed.

Sammelvar, Escholia, and Jaladay traded anguished glances. None of them spoke. What was there to say after those angry outbursts?

Kermi, still asleep at Jaladay's feet, snored soundly. Other than that, and the rustle of the wind moving across the purple honeyscent flowers covering the cloud, there was no sound. Until, at last, Sammelvar raised his voice.

"I never thought," he said as he gazed at his wife, "that when we regained this realm . . . we would also lose our son."

Escholia's eyes widened. "We haven't lost

him. He just needs to find himself. And then, I believe, he will find us."

"I agree." Jaladay adjusted the band that covered her eyes. "Right now, what I feel most in Promi is *longing*. It's even stronger than his rage or pride or resentment."

"What is he longing for?" asked Escholia.

Jaladay inhaled slowly. "He just wants to be free . . . and loved. Same as all of us."

The elders traded glances, then Sammelvar said, "He deserves both. I only hope that he grows . . . bigger. True freedom means a lot more than just doing whatever you please. It means helping your world be the very best it can be."

"He will," declared Jaladay. "I'm sure of it."

At that moment, Kermi woke up. Opening his big blue eyes, he stretched all four furry limbs, as well as his long tail. With a sleepy sigh, he gazed up at the others and asked, "Did I miss anything?"

"No," answered Jaladay as she bent to pick up the blue ker- muncle. Cradling him in one arm, she added, "Just a huge family fight."

Kermi nodded knowingly. "So I take it Promi was here?"

Jaladay smiled sadly. "He was."

"I wonder," mused Sammelvar as he scanned the thousands of flowers surrounding them, "whether the creatures on all these little worlds have the same sorts of problems we have."

"I'm sure they do," replied Escholia. "And I'll bet they seem equally daunting."

Gazing at the luminous purple bridge connecting two flower worlds, Sammelvar said wistfully, "Someday I would like to walk upon that bridge and see where it leads."

"Maybe," offered Jaladay, "you will—"

She halted suddenly. Catching her breath, she froze, standing as rigid as a slab of vaporstone.

Her parents looked at each other worriedly. For they knew what this meant: Jaladay the Seer was having a vision.

Seconds passed. Jaladay didn't move, nor even breathe. Then abruptly—she jolted, with such force she dropped Kermi. But the little fellow's quick reflexes enabled him to catch hold of her robe. He scampered up to her shoulder and perched there.

Clearly shaken, Jaladay drew a deep breath. She pulled off her turquoise headband and stared at her parents with eyes as green as a forest at dawn. "It's about Promi."

"What about him?" asked Sammelvar.

Jaladay hesitated, then said, "He's gone back to Earth. To see Atlanta."

The elder spirit winced, knowing that yet another hole had been torn in the veil.

"That's not the worst of it," Jaladay added grimly.

"Is he in danger?" Escholia pressed.

"Yes," she answered. "Not only him, but the new island of Atlantis."

She swallowed. "And more than Atlantis! The whole mortal world is at risk—and in a way I don't understand, so is ours."

Sammelvar touched her forearm. "Tell us."

"There isn't much to tell. All I know is that soon a ship will come near Atlantis—too near. Having sailed from a land called Greece in the Aegean Sea, it will have a blue dolphin on its sail. But just when it comes within sight of Atlantis, the ship will be swallowed by a terrible whirlpool! Every last person on board will drown."

"Tragic indeed," said Sammelvar.

"But that's not the worst outcome," explained Jaladay. "That's what is *meant* to happen. What will happen. Unless . . ."

"What?" asked both her parents.

"Unless Promi saves them. If he saves that ship—or any of those sailors—something horrible will happen."

"I don't understand," said Sammelvar.

"How," asked Escholia, "could saving those poor sailors be bad?"

"I don't know." Jaladay peered at them. "But unless Promi is warned, unless he is told *not* to help those people . . . a terrible chain of events will begin. It will lead to the end of Atlantis—and maybe more!"

Sammelvar shook his white locks. "So if we are going to warn Promi of your vision, we must send someone else through the veil to find him."

Jaladay nodded.

"Then we can do nothing," he declared. "I cannot condone you piercing the veil, Jaladay—not even for this."

"But," she protested, "it could lead to disaster!"

"Destroying the veil would be a far worse disaster! No, I will not allow this." His gaze bored into her. "I forbid you to go."

Trying to comfort her, Escholia reached over and brushed her cheek. "Besides, we all know how unreliable visions and prophecies can be. They seem to mean one thing . . . but often mean another."

"I know, believe me." Jaladay shook her head. "Remember that phrase *the end of all magic* from the Prophecy? And how many different meanings it could have had? But you must hear me! This vision is different. It seems *crystal clear.*"

"All the more reason," said Sammelvar, "to doubt its clarity."

Sadly, Jaladay hung her head. She stroked Kermi's tail, which was dangling down from her shoulder.

At last, she raised her head and admitted, "Perhaps you are right."

"So," her father asked, "you promise not to go?"

Fixing her gaze on him, she said, "I promise."

"Thank you, my dear. Let us hope that, even without your help, Promi will do what's best."

"Yes, let us hope."

Sammelvar turned to his wife and said, "Time for us to go, I'm afraid." Glancing one last time at the luminous purple bridge between the flowers, he added, "May we come back again to this place someday."

Escholia nodded, then touched her daughter's hand. "Will you be coming with us?"

"No. I'd like to stay here a while longer." Jaladay gestured at the shimmering flower worlds that surrounded them. "Just to savor this place."

"A wise choice," said Sammelvar, his face careworn. "Let the wonders of this place soothe your heart, as they did mine—at least for a while."

Holding hands, the elders shifted their positions, making sure not to disturb any of the miniature worlds. Then they leaped, flying skyward with only a faint ripple of wind. Seconds later, they vanished in the curling mist that flowed throughout the spirit realm.

Immediately, Kermi hopped down to Jaladay's forearm. His blue eyes met her green ones and they gazed at each other for a long moment.

"So," she asked, "will you do it?"

He scowled, scrunching his little face. "The things I do for you! Not to mention for your idiot brother."

She almost grinned, knowing that was her ever-grumpy companion's way of saying yes. After all . . . she had promised not to go. But she'd said nothing about Kermi.

Her expression turned serious again. "You will find him? And tell him everything you heard me say? Every detail is important."

Rolling his big eyes, the kermuncle growled with annoyance. "Yes, yes. Imagine someone as clever as Sammelvar saying, 'Let's hope Promi will do what's best!' Ha! Since when has he *ever* done that?"

She tickled his ears affectionately. "Only when you or I were around to help."

"Precisely." Resigned to his fate, Kermi blew a thin stream of bubbles from the side of his mouth. "I just knew I shouldn't have joined you today."

"Even with so much at stake?"

"By agreeing to go talk with that buffoonerous manfool . . . it's my *sanity* that's at stake."

# CHAPTER 10

# Radiant Wings

After Kermi departed, carrying the warning to Promi, the cloudfield felt different to Jaladay. More empty. And maybe . . . more isolated.

*I'm always outside of big events,* she mused, *never in the middle of them.*

Scanning her surroundings, Jaladay noticed one especially intricate flower world. From its center, towers made of purple glass rose from a miniature city. The towers gleamed like a cluster of amethyst crystals, but revealed nothing about the tiny creatures who had built them. Other than vague, shadowy movements she glimpsed within the buildings, she was cut off from the world and its people. What were their struggles? Their toughest choices? Their highest ideals?

"I'll never know," she said glumly to herself. "All I can do is watch from a distance."

She sighed. *The life of a Seer.* She could see what others could not, but she couldn't really join in the action. For if she did, her presence alone would disrupt any visions she might have to offer. Always one step removed—that was her lot.

A sound of beating wings made her look skyward. A family of turquoise-scaled dragons was flying right above her head! She watched them—one adult and two young ones, with golden eyes shaped like diamonds, jagged wings, and enormous claws.

Their flashing turquoise wings, she realized, were the same color as her headband. She had removed it to look her parents directly in the eyes—a ploy that hadn't worked—and she now held the headband in her hand.

Watching the dragons fly overhead, she locked gazes with the largest one. The dragon, a female, regarded Jaladay with the same curiosity as the young woman was feeling about this creature. For a timeless moment, they observed each other.

To the dragon, Jaladay sent a simple thought: *Wish I were as big as you and could fly with such radiant wings.*

The dragon's wings slowed for a beat, gleaming in the misty light. In a rich, melodic voice, she spoke into Jaladay's mind. *And I wish, young woman, that I werrrrre as small as you arrrrre . . . so I could nestle among those flowerrrrr worrrrrlds without crrrrrushing them.*

*My name is Jaladay.*

*And mine, young flowerrrrr watcherrrrr, is Ulanoma.*

Jaladay smiled. The dragon and her family soared into a mountainous cloud, disappearing from view.

Suddenly, from right behind her, Jaladay heard a new sound—an ominous crackling she recognized instantly. Her blood froze.

Mistwraiths! Two of them were rising directly out of the cloud, their shadowy forms crackling with black sparks.

She leaped to her feet and started to jump into the sky. Pushing hard with her legs, she told herself desperately, *Fly now! Fly!*

Too late! The mistwraiths released a cloak of black sparks that completely covered Jaladay. The more she struggled, the more the cloak tightened around her. In seconds, she could hardly breathe, let alone escape.

The mistwraiths crackled triumphantly as they floated over to their helpless prey. More black sparks sprayed from their shadowy folds. Each flower that happened to be struck by one of those sparks perished instantly in a blaze of black fire, leaving only a sizzling stem where there had once been an entire world. The luminous purple bridge between the two flowers that Sammelvar had so admired vanished in black flames.

Hovering over Jaladay, the mistwraiths shuddered with pleasure, their dark folds rippling. More black sparks flew, destroying dozens more flower worlds.

But the mistwraiths didn't care. They felt only satisfaction, for they knew their master would be pleased.

Quite pleased.

# CHAPTER 11

# Solid Night

Darkness.

That was all Jaladay could perceive. Utter darkness in every direction. Hard as she tried, she couldn't see anything but that.

Worse, this darkness felt *thick* somehow— so fulsome it pressed against her, held her captive. Like a kind of solid night.

*Where am I?* she puzzled. Sitting up, she realized the mistwraiths' terrible net was gone. She was in some sort of room, a prison cell— that much she could guess.

She laid her hands on the floor beneath her and felt its cold, smooth surface. *Vaporstone?* she wondered. But if it was only that, why couldn't she see into its essence, reading the story of its construction? *For that matter, why can't I see—*

She caught her breath in the middle of her

thought. For its consequences were alarming beyond anything she'd ever experienced.

*Why can't I see,* she finished, *beyond the stone itself? Beyond the floor and walls of this prison?*

Panic swelled inside her. Jaladay's chest tightened and beads of sweat rolled down her brow. *My inner sight is gone! I am blind—truly blind.*

Desperately, she willed herself to calm down. She was still alive. And she had to be *someplace.* Which meant it was possible somebody could find her . . . unlikely as that might be.

*This isn't as bad as it seems,* she tried to convince herself. That vision she'd had about Promi and the ship full of sailors—*that* was serious. And the mission she'd given to Kermi, to warn Promi not to save them—*that* was serious.

By contrast, she told herself firmly, this situation here was just . . .

*Horrendous.* She was locked in a prison—sightless, helpless, and alone.

Taking a deep breath, she started to crawl across the floor. Moving cautiously, she advanced—but where, she couldn't tell. Nor could she shake herself of the most frightful fact of all: for the first time in her life, she couldn't see *anything.*

Her fingers touched a wall. Cold and smooth like the floor, it rose straight up from the seam. Glumly, she leaned against the wall, trying to stay calm.

No windows.

No cracks.

*No way to see.*

All at once, she heard a scraping sound like a heavy bolt being slid. In the wall opposite her, a thin line of light appeared. And another two lines, perpendicular to the first. A doorway!

Jaladay's heart leaped. She rose to her feet and stumbled toward the door. It started to open, flooding the cell with light.

She dashed toward it, even though her eyes throbbed to adjust and her mind raced to understand. She felt new strength coursing through her veins. For with every little bit the door opened, her inner sight revived.

She burst through the doorway, blinking in the brightness all around her. Then she stopped cold. For right in front of her was the very last person she expected—or wanted—to see.

"Narkazan!"

Hearing the astonishment in her voice, the warlord almost smiled, though it looked more like a predator baring his teeth. He sat back in his gray chair of woven vaporthreads and stroked his long, pointed chin. The fiery centers of his eyes, which were a brighter shade of red than his tusks, glowed with satisfaction.

"So," he rasped, "you recognize me. How nice."

Jaladay's forest-green eyes narrowed. "Not nice at all."

"Whatever you say, my jewel. Welcome to my new residence—considerably less windy than my last one."

Casually, he gestured at the room, whose high ceiling held two narrow windows. Through one of them, she saw jagged black clouds that looked like dark icicles. The only furniture was a cot, a chest made from some kind of metal, and the chair where he sat. Another doorway opened into an unlit hallway. And in the darkness of the hallway, something stirred—shadows within the shadows.

Jaladay froze. Mistwraiths!

"Ah yes," rasped Narkazan. "You recognize my servants. The same pair, in fact, who brought you here to be my guest."

Straightening up to her full height, she said coldly, "I am not your guest, but your prisoner."

Thrusting his ax-thin face toward her, he replied, "You are right about that." With a wave at the dark room from which she'd emerged, he asked, "How do you like your accommodations?"

She didn't answer.

"I had that room made especially for you, so you should be grateful. Every detail . . . right down to the rare ingredients I added to the vaporstone to deaden your second sight."

Jaladay shuddered, remembering how truly blind she'd felt in there.

"Ah," gloated the warlord, "you noticed. How lovely. It's nice to have one's labor rewarded."

He leaned forward. The scars on his face ran like poisoned rivers on a dead landscape. Peering at Jaladay, he said, "Now I have a simple question for you. Would you like to remain in that room for eternity? Except, of course, when I let you out to be tortured for my entertainment?"

Though she said nothing, she couldn't keep herself from cringing.

"I shall take that as your answer," he rasped. "Fortunately for you, there *is* a way to avoid that fate. All you need to do . . . is help me. Use your gift of second sight to guide my warriors as they conquer this realm!"

Ignoring how she recoiled, he declared, "You shall be my Seer. My greatest weapon! And to show you my noble intentions—if you cooperate, I shall spare your entire family."

Jaladay fixed him with her gaze. Trying not to reveal how scared she really felt, she spat her response. "I will never help you. Never!"

His fiery eyes seemed to sizzle. "Well then, my jewel, I shall have no choice but to target your family for extinction. I know how to make them suffer, believe me, I do! They will experience unrelenting agony . . . until their only escape will be to end their lives as spirits. To vanish *forever* from the universe."

He leaned back in the chair, tapping one of his gruesome tusks. "The first to go will be . . . your mother. While I'd much rather torture your father, after all the *inconvenience* he has caused me— it would be a true pleasure to watch him agonize over her fate."

"You monster!" Jaladay clenched her fists. "How could you do such a thing?"

"Very easily," he replied. "Next I will deal with your father directly. And trust me, I have some very special tricks in mind for him! Then finally . . ."

Narkazan's voice lowered to a growl. "Your brother, the young man of the Prophecy, will come last. Yes, my treasure, I have discovered his real identity. And I can assure you, I shall spare no pain or punishment for him—regardless of how much he screams or pleads for mercy."

Stunned by the warlord's cruelty, Jaladay remained silent. But her mind continued to race, trying to find some way to foil Narkazan's plans.

"Don't try any tricks," he cautioned. "Or I shall be forced to put some of my shadowy servants in that room with you. To give you company."

Seeing Jaladay shudder again, he chortled in satisfaction. At last, he leaned forward, jutting his chin toward her.

"What is your decision, my jewel? Will you help me—and save your whole family, as well as yourself? Or will you condemn everyone you care about to whatever tortures I can devise?"

Feeling certain of triumph, he gazed around the room. "Before long, I shall reclaim my old castle, Arcna Ruel. I miss its elegant towers and polished white walls, as well as its ready access to my servants."

The thought of his vaporstone castle made his predator's smile return. "Best of all," he continued, "I shall soon gain the limitless power I have so long sought . . . and so rightly deserve."

Jaladay swallowed hard. With great effort, she said, "I will help you."

"Good," the warlord rasped. "I suspected you would. Now, for your first task, I want you to use your remarkable gift to tell me—"

"I will help you," she interrupted, her voice growing stronger, "to plunge back into the Maelstrom! So deep you will never, ever come out again."

Narkazan's expression darkened. "Then you will rot away to nothingness!"

"Better to do that," she declared, "than to help you in any way."

He snapped his fingers. With an ominous crackle, the two mistwraiths emerged from the shadows and floated toward Jaladay. Black sparks sprayed everywhere, sizzling on the floor—then darkness enveloped her.

# CHAPTER 12

# Fresh Pastry

The day after he and Atlanta had argued, Promi wandered the cobblestone streets of the City of Great Powers. He assured himself that he'd come here just out of curiosity—to visit his old haunts. But he knew in his heart that he'd really come to get away from Atlanta and her forest home. To distract himself with a change of scene.

And what a dramatic change it was! This bustling human settlement was practically another world from the ancient woods. Besides, the City looked different now than it did in the days before Atlantis became an island—mainly because of all the broken walls and collapsed roofs from that tumultuous event.

Mostly, though, he noticed how much the City looked, sounded, and felt the same as ever. This was, after all, the place where he'd grown up. The place where he'd learned how to steal a pie, throw a knife, and disappear into the shadows.

He stepped into a narrow alley whose mud-brick walls pressed close together—closer than most alleys, thanks to all the flower boxes in the windows. Red geraniums, deep blue lilies, and spiral-stemmed roses filled the alley with the sweet aromas of a mountain meadow. By contrast, the pile of rags someone had left in the alley gave off a very different odor . . . more like a huge, unwashed armpit.

Passing quickly by the pile of rags, he followed the dimly lit alley. All at once, he burst into sunlight—as well as a noisy din he knew well. It combined the shouts of peddlers and bargain hunters, the ring of blacksmiths' hammers, the bleating of goats, and the chants of monks who sang to the beat of their prayer drums. Plus many more sounds that made a cacophony found in only one place on Atlantis:

The market square.

Promi strolled into the market where he'd found so many free meals growing up (not to mention new knives to replace the ones he'd lost in the course of his thievery). Just for old time's sake, he stealthily plucked a fresh green apple off a passing cart.

He bit into the apple, hearing the crisp *crunnnch* he liked almost as much as the taste. Moving deeper into the market, he weaved around a grumpy-looking camel being led to a leather-worker's stall for a new saddle—just before the camel bit his plump owner's bottom. The man shrieked and threw his armload of wheat and barley into the air. The camel, meanwhile, immediately started munching on the grains, gobbling them up before a pair of honking geese could claim them.

Promi took another bite of his apple, negotiating the crowded rows of fish vendors, paper merchants, and tool makers. As well as craftspeople selling handmade jewelry, rugs, tunics, pottery, and musical instruments.

He stepped around a circle of women wearing brightly colored robes and beads, dancing to their bone flutes. A herd of goats flooded past, pushing Promi so hard he collided with a monk selling strings of prayer leaves. After apologizing to the monk, he realized the leaves were being sold to raise money for the temple's new bell tower.

*The bell tower I destroyed,* he recalled. *Too bad about that. But it takes a serious earthquake to create an island!*

Glancing over his shoulder, he could see the gap against the sky where the bell tower had stood. As well as the crushed roof in the Divine Monk's temple and the smashed archway where the immense structure came down. He bit into the apple, remembering the time he had leaped into the air from the top of that very tower—as well as the face of the astonished temple guard who watched helplessly as he escaped.

Promi chuckled. *Those were fun days.* Tapping the silver dagger he now wore on his belt, he thought, *At least now I don't lose knives anymore.* As if hearing his thought, the dagger's magical string curled and tickled his wrist.

He tossed the apple core to a sheep whose wool changed colors depending on the weather, one of many wondrous creatures who had been captured in the Great Forest and brought to the marketplace. Seeing him do this, a three-tongued toad with the ability to speak human languages started roundly cursing.

"You blithering bumblebrain!" cried the toad. "I'll bet you stole that apple and dozens more meals, too."

*More like thousands,* thought Promi with a smirk.

Most of those meals, of course, had been desserts. Many were the days when he ate a freshly baked fruit pie he'd stolen, still steaming, from someone's kitchen window. Or one of the pastries, cakes, or cookies he'd grabbed off the shelves of the City's many bakeries. Or, best of all, the most delicious—and dangerous—theft he'd ever made: that smackberry pie, with its purple juices bubbling out of the sugary crust.

Of course, to get that pie he'd needed to work a bit harder than usual. He'd climbed unseen into the Divine Monk's private dining room, broken at least a dozen holy laws, evaded both the wicked priest Grukarr and his superior Araggna, and completely destroyed the temple's grand feast of Ho Kranahrum while escaping. And putting aside the small matter of being hurled by Grukarr into the dreaded Ekh Raku dungeon, getting beaten senseless, and almost dying . . . it was the sweetest pie he'd ever tasted.

Recalling that remarkable theft reminded him of Grukarr and Araggna—two thoroughly unsavory people. Their bodies had been found amidst the City's wreckage, giving a sigh of relief to everyone who lived here. Except perhaps the Divine Monk, whose nose for treachery was significantly less developed than his nose for his next meal.

*Now, there's something else that has changed. No more will those two cling to power . . . or torture their prisoners right here in this square!* Dangerous as they had been, the only way to grab that smackberry pie was to risk getting captured by them. *But,* Promi concluded with a smack of his lips, *it was totally worth it for that pie.*

Adeptly, he dodged a group of seven or eight children who were chasing after a puppet maker. One of those children, a girl with carrot-colored hair, made him think of Shangri. That bright-eyed girl had taken a liking to Promi after he saved her from a herd of stampeding goats. Which proved especially useful when her father, a baker, caught Promi stealing his pastries. If Shangri hadn't intervened at the very last moment, her father would have pounded Promi into something that resembled cookie dough.

*Good Shangri,* thought Promi, wondering how she was doing. *Maybe I'll stop at her father's pastry shop just to say hello. And maybe,* he decided, *stay long enough to try one of his amazing cinnamon buns.*

Passing the stall of a paper merchant, he saw a stack of leather-bound journals, beautifully crafted, along with elegant feather pens. His own journal, his constant companion for years, hadn't been nearly so handsome. In fact, it was just an old book of recipes for desserts that he'd taken from an unsuspecting pastry chef. Using worn charcoal pencils, he'd written in that journal almost every day—filling its margins with his scrawled entries.

*I miss that old journal.* He patted the empty pocket of his tunic, wondering whether he should get a new one. Maybe a real journal instead of a tattered old recipe book? Or maybe even a journal made from cloudpaper, so light yet durable, the same as Jaladay used?

He shook his head. *No, too fancy for me. I'll stay with old recipe books.*

A sudden gust blew through the market, scattering a family of ice sparrows, birds who made beautiful ice sculptures in winter-time. Tugged by the wind, a string of prayer leaves, each one inscribed with a blessing, broke off a monk's drum and flew into the air. Like a ragtag kite, it sailed over the marketplace.

"Look there!" shouted a boy, pointing at the prayer leaves. "They must be on their way to the spirit realm!"

"Yes," called a girl nearby. "They're being carried by tiny, invisible wind lions."

"Really?" asked the boy, wide-eyed with amazement.

*Well, not really.* Promi grinned, remembering when he'd first discovered the truth about wind lions. Not by hearing about it from someone else . . . but by landing on a lion's furry back after leaping off a rickety bridge.

*Now, that was a surprise,* he recalled with a chuckle. And, as it turned out, it was only the first of many surprises to come.

*Including that I'm an immortal, like Jaladay. That what I'd thought was my home all those years was really just my hiding place.*

*And that my real home is—well . . . nobody but me is going to decide where that is.*

Grabbing a handful of dates from a food merchant's cart, Promi chewed on one thoughtfully. The changes he could see in the marketplace and the City, he realized, weren't nearly as huge as the changes somewhere else. *Right here inside me.*

He swallowed the date. But he didn't taste its sweetness, for a crop of sour thoughts had sprouted in his mind. Thoughts about Atlanta—and how he'd treated her.

Why hadn't he told her his whole vision at the Lakes of Dreams? What had held him back? Was there something about her that he didn't trust? Or, much worse, was there some part of *himself* that simply wouldn't trust anyone?

Suddenly not hungry, he tossed the dates into a pen of squealing young pigs. Maybe, as Atlanta had warned, he was condemned to live his worst dream. Never to have a real home. A real family. A real friend . . . or someone who might become more than a friend.

He sighed, leaning back against a mud-brick wall at the edge of the marketplace. *Sure, Atlanta can be difficult sometimes. And there's more going on with her than she has been telling me. But the real problem for us isn't her. No . . . it's me.*

He rubbed one foot against the cobblestones. *I'm just a loner. Always have been, always will be.*

"Promi!"

He turned to see a young girl carrying a tray loaded with huckleberry tarts, still steaming hot from the oven. But as tasty as those pastries looked, he was even more pleased to see who held them. He couldn't mistake those carrot-colored braids, even though they were dusted with flour.

"Shangri!"

She smiled, showing her missing front teeth. "Good to see you,

Promi!" She nodded so vigorously that a cloud of flour rose from her braids.

Walking toward her, Promi pointed at the tarts. "You, too! And how nice of you to bring me breakfast."

She giggled. "Yer such a teaser. Papa says yer a rascally scala-wag—but a virtuous one."

"He's right about the scalawag." Promi tousled her hair in greeting, sending up another puff of flour. "But not the virtuous part."

"Mmm, methinks Papa's right. Anyways, I'm takin' these over to our stall here in the market. Want to come an' say hello to him?"

"Sure, if you'll let me carry that tray. Looks pretty heavy."

"Aw, I can handle it." She winked at him. "But it would sure lighten the load fer me if you'd take one."

He chuckled. "Well, all right. If you insist."

Choosing an especially fat one, Promi plucked it off the tray and took a big bite. The flaky, sugared crust crunched in his mouth, and his eyes opened wide with the sudden burst of sweet huckle-berries. Without even waiting to swallow, he took another bite.

Shangri giggled. "Guessin' you like it?"

"Mmmff," he replied through his mouthful of pastry. "Ipff weewy goob!"

"Come along, then." She tilted her head toward a row of food stalls. "Papa will be gettin' worried that I got lost."

"Or that you ran into a thief."

She shot him a playful glance. "Right. Ye've got to watch out fer them thieves."

Promi swallowed his last bite of the tart as they started to walk. He grinned, glad that they'd run into each other. A little time with Shangri had pushed his concerns aside . . . at least for a while.

Placing his hand on her shoulder, he said, "That was excellent. The only thing sweeter is one of your father's cinnamon buns."

"And o' course," she said brightly, "those sugary streams they say are up there in the spirit realm."

"Those are nice to drink from," he replied casually. "But there's nothing like fresh pastry."

She stopped and peered at him. "Have ye really been there to the spirit realm? The way ye said that—"

"No," he lied, feeling stupid for speaking so openly. Even though Grukarr wasn't around any longer to enforce punishments, it was still the law in the City that only priests, priestesses, and the Divine Monk himself could speak about the immortal realm. And the last thing he needed was to get Shangri into trouble. "I just made that up."

She peered up at him, her brown eyes full of doubt. "I'm not so sure."

"Really. I make up silly things all the time. Why, I filled a whole journal with them. Well, not really a journal—an old recipe book whose margins I crammed with notes."

"Show it to me?"

"Sorry, Shangri. I lost it."

She frowned at him.

"Come on," he coaxed. "There's your father over there."

Shangri turned and led him over to the baker's stall. "Papa, look who I brought."

The baker, as burly as ever, looked up from decorating a tray of cinnamon buns. Recognizing Promi, he smiled and wiped his hands on the apron that covered his ample belly. Fruit stains, flecks of dough, and lots of sugar decorated the apron.

"Well now," he bellowed, "miracles never cease! A visit from our fav'rite rascal." He winked at Promi. "Ye must be hungry."

"Always," Promi replied. "But really, I just came to say hello."

Choosing one of his freshly baked cinnamon buns, the baker

handed it to him. "Do me the favor of a taste. Jest to make sure I got the mix o' ingredients right."

Gladly, Promi took a big bite. An explosion of sweetness filled his mouth, every bit as good as he remembered. "Mmm," he said with satisfaction. "You definitely got it right! Maybe you should think about becoming a baker."

The big man laughed heartily, even as he took the tray of tarts from Shangri and set them on the counter. "That decision's already been made, lad." He patted his belly. "Many cakes an' pies ago."

Leaning toward Promi, he added in a whisper, "Though thanks to a certain young rascal . . . I don't have to work for me livin' anymore." He tapped the small bulge under his apron—which, Promi knew, was the sapphire-studded belt buckle he'd stolen from Grukarr and given to the baker.

"I'm glad," said Promi as he finished off the bun. "So why do you keep baking?"

"Fer the simple pleasure of it, lad! Not so much fer the eatin' as the watchin'. I do love seein' others eat what I bake."

Shangri, who had been searching through a box at the back of the stall, declared, "Found it!"

"Found what?" asked her father.

She held up a tattered old book. "That old recipe book you gave me way back when I was young."

The baker chuckled. "Unlike now."

Ignoring him, she pranced over to Promi and slid the book into his tunic pocket. "There," she told him. "Now you can keep a journal again."

"But . . ." Promi's words trailed away. There simply weren't the words for what he wanted to say. Or if there were, he didn't know them.

"And here, take this, too." She handed him a small charcoal pencil from her pocket.

The grateful look on his face said everything Shangri had hoped to hear.

With a nod at his cinnamon buns, the baker asked Promi, "Want another?"

"Well, sure. But if I eat too many more, you won't have any left to sell."

"A good thing," announced the burly fellow. He wrapped his meaty arm around Shangri. "Seein' how I was fixin' to quit fer the day, close up the stall, an' go fer a picnic with me daughter."

"Really, Papa?" squealed Shangri. She jumped with delight, making her braids bounce.

"Yes, really." Turning to Promi, the baker added, "Will ye join us, lad?"

"Please do," begged Shangri.

Unsure, he asked, "Won't I get in the way of your time together?"

"No," Shangri answered. "Ye'll jest add to the fun."

"What's the matter?" teased the baker. "Got some important thievin' to do?"

"Only when I'm hungry for pastry. And right now, I'm feeling just fine. Thanks to . . ."

He hesitated, surprised to hear himself start to say such words. But knowing they were true, he went ahead and said them. "Thanks to my friends."

# CHAPTER 13

# A Warning

Now I know why you invited me to come along, Master Baker."

Promi paused, adjusting the heavy sack he was carrying up the trail. Steep and sandy, the trail seemed to climb endlessly. "You invited me so you wouldn't have to carry all this food up here yourself."

The baker, huffing beside him on the trail, laughed. "Yer right, lad." Patting his ample belly, he added, "I learned long ago it's much easier to carry yer food *after* a meal than before."

"The hardest part isn't the weight," Promi replied. "It's the smell of all those cinnamon buns you packed. I'm ready to eat the whole sack just to taste them!"

"'Twill be worth all yer trouble, lad. We're almost there."

Shangri, jogging to keep up with them,

tugged on her father's apron. "Shouldn't we stop an' give him a rest, Papa?"

"No, me little sugarcake. As soon as we reach the picnic spot I have in mind, we'll give our rascally friend plenty o' rest. I promise."

"An' plenty o' food, as well?"

"Plenty, Shangri. Including cinnamon buns."

Promi shifted the sack's weight on his back. Despite what he'd said, it was indeed heavy—and feeling heavier with every step. *Wherever that picnic spot is,* he grumbled to himself, *it's easier to fly there from the spirit realm than to walk there with this load.*

"By the way, lad," said the baker as he flung a meaty arm over Promi's shoulder, "it's time ye called me somethin' besides Master Baker."

"How about Master Trickster? Or Master Loadmaker?"

"No, lad, ye can jest call me Morey."

Promi breathed a sigh of relief—not because he now knew the man's name, but because the hefty arm had finally come off his shoulder.

"Ye'll like this place," the baker promised. He reached over and toyed with one of Shangri's braids. "Yer ma an' me used to come here."

"Why, Papa? It's so far outside the City."

"Fer the views, mostly. She liked the sight o' such big grandeur. An' I," he added with a wink at Promi, "liked the sight o' *her.*"

Promi was just about to ask what grandeur—since, with the heavy sack making him bow his head, all he could see was the sandy hillside beneath his feet. But before he could pose the question, a new scent tickled his nose. Salty, rich, and briny, it contrasted starkly with the sweetness of cinnamon. Right away, he knew what it was.

The sea.

At that instant, a strong gust of wind, full of that briny smell, struck his face. Lifting his head, he realized that they were almost at the top of the hill they'd been climbing. A few steps later, the gust swelled to a steady ocean breeze—and an expansive vista opened up before them.

Promi dropped the heavy sack and gazed at the endless sweep of dark blue waves. He'd never seen the ocean look so vast, so uninterrupted. But for the few traces of clouds in the distance, it was hard to draw any line between sea and sky.

At his feet, the ground dropped sharply into a sheer cliff. At its base far below, powerful waves crashed against the rocks with thunderous explosions of spray. Beyond the cliff, white-capped waves rolled without beginning or end, while pelicans, silver-winged gulls, and cormorants wheeled over the water's surface. The seabirds' cries, shrieks, and whistles rose above the pounding waves—a wild melody sung to the ocean's deep and enduring drums.

Shangri slipped her hand into her father's. "Now I understand, Papa."

"So do I," said Promi.

The baker blew a long breath. "'Tis even more wondrous than it was last time I came. Fer then we wasn't yet an island, way out in the middle o' the sea."

"How," asked Shangri in a voice as small as a young waterbird's, "did the island ever happen? I mean . . . one day we're a part of that place called Africa, then snap yer fingers, an' the next day we're not. Now we're not part o' anythin' but water an' sky."

Morey shrugged his beefy shoulders. "By the wings o' the immortal spirits, lass, I wish I knew."

Shangri turned her gaze on Promi. "Do ye know how such a wonder could happen?"

"Me? No." He, too, shrugged . . . though there was a faint gleam of satisfaction in his eyes.

Catching that gleam, Shangri peered up at him. "Ye know more than yer sayin', methinks."

"No, Shangri," he protested, a bit too strongly. "You're wrong! I don't know much of anything . . . except how little I really know."

Morey nodded, stooping to open up the sack. "Knowin' how little we know is the start o' wisdom, lad."

"I don't believe you, Promi," declared Shangri. Placing her hands on her hips, she gazed at him. "There's somethin', well . . . *special* about you. I'm sure of it!"

Brushing her freckled cheek with his finger, he said, "The most special thing about me is how *much* I love a good cinnamon bun."

She peered at him skeptically.

"Speakin' o' that," the baker announced as he pulled a clump of cinnamon buns from the sack, "here ye go."

Eagerly, Promi took them. While they didn't look as appetizing as they had when freshly baked—especially since four or five had melded together from being jostled around in the sack—they still smelled as enticing as ever. And when he took a big, gooey bite, he could tell they hadn't lost any of their sweet flavor.

Before he even swallowed that first bite, he took another. Through his doughy teeth, he smiled at Shangri. "Goob av ebber!"

She giggled, putting aside her suspicions for the moment. Then, feeling hungry herself, she plunged into the array of picnic treats. There were pies (two each of strawberry, orange cream, and cherry—plus one lemon meringue), three large trays of apple crisp, persimmon tarts, a big bowl of double-sweet pudding, licorice and ginger cookies by the dozen, a box of coconut macaroons, three loaves of honey nut bread, and, of course, another huge clump of cinnamon buns. Not to mention three good-sized flasks of lemonade.

While Shangri and her father feasted and watched the rolling waves that stretched endlessly, Promi turned away from the sea to look at the view behind them. As he munched on the cluster of cinnamon buns, he surveyed the City. Even from this distance, he could pick out the market square and the Divine Monk's temple, as well as one of the huge prayer wheels at the settlement's big oaken gates. He spotted the deep gorge of the Deg Boesi River at the City's southern edge, impossible to miss with all the clouds of mist rising skyward.

Then he saw the faint outline of something he knew well: the rickety, half-built bridge that started at one side of the gorge and disappeared into the swirling mist. The Bridge to Nowhere, he'd called it—before discovering that it did indeed lead somewhere remarkable. For though it seemed unfinished and hopelessly dilapidated, that bridge stretched all the way to the spirit realm.

Chewing thoughtfully, Promi opened his inner ear and listened. He could hear, beyond the crashing surf and screeching gulls, a gentle, rhythmic sound that came from the bridge. It was the flapping of prayer leaves strung from the bridge's every post. And with each flap, a prayer for a loved one or a lost soul would be carried to the realm of the spirits, borne by a wind lion—the only immortal creatures with the special magic to cross between worlds without tearing the veil.

*Or so we've been told,* thought Promi. *Maybe we all have that magic, and the rest is just my father's attempt to scare off travelers between the realms.*

He took another bite. *Well, I'm not so easily scared.*

Lifting his gaze, he viewed the deep green expanse that stretched south and west. The Great Forest looked immense, as well as mysterious, filled with more wondrous and bizarre creatures than anyone knew. As well as the precious Starstone, whose power permeated the whole forest and deepened its magic. And that place also held someone he was missing more than he cared to admit.

*Atlanta.* Thinking of her, Promi stopped eating. He peered at the wide swath of greenery, wondering where in that forest she might be right now. More than that, he wanted to know how she was faring after their horrible fight. It had been a full day ago . . . but the feelings were still so raw that it seemed only a few seconds had passed.

*What a complete idiot I am!* Promi dug his toes into the sand atop the cliff. *Sure, she's difficult sometimes. And what a temper! But . . . she deserved better from me.* Why couldn't he have listened to her more openly? And responded more honestly?

He swallowed hard around a lump in his throat that had nothing to do with eating pastry. *For the same reason I couldn't admit that she was right. I'm still a loner. Still . . . afraid.*

Promi shook his head. *Still an idiot.*

"Some things never change," declared a sassy voice at his feet. "But at least you are starting to realize it."

"Kermi!" Seeing the blue kermuncle, Promi jumped. "How the . . . what—how?" he sputtered. "How did you ever . . . ?"

Playing with one of his long whiskers, Kermi looked up at the bewildered young man. "If you spoke your mind, you'd be totally speechless."

"Wheee!" squealed Shangri, spying their new visitor. She put down the slice of lemon meringue pie she'd been eating and started to approach Kermi. "What a thumpin' adorable creature!"

Promi, regaining his composure, muttered, "You don't know him like I do."

Kermi just waved his long tail and blew a stream of blue bubbles. "Most people live and learn, manfool. But *you*—well, you just live." Before Promi could even begin to reply, the kermuncle added dryly, "You'd need twice as much sense just to be a half-wit."

Shangri kneeled beside Kermi. As she gazed at him, fascinated, she was joined by her father, who had reluctantly set aside what remained of a cherry pie. Gently, Shangri reached out and stroked the creature's tail.

Kermi watched her for a moment. Then, with no trace of the sassiness he'd heaped on Promi, he said, "You are rather adorable yourself."

She blushed, even as she grinned from ear to ear.

"By Sammelvar's beard," said the baker. "It speaks! Jest like you an' me."

"Better," replied Kermi. "And I'm not an *it*. I'm a *he*."

"More like a he-demon," corrected Promi. Glaring at Kermi, he demanded, "Why are you here? All the way from the sp—"

He caught himself, hoping Shangri or her father hadn't heard his gaffe. "I mean, from the spot where we last met."

Kermi shook his little head, making his ears flap. "Don't worry, manfool, brains aren't everything. In fact, in your case . . . they're nothing."

"Why," Promi repeated angrily, "are you here?"

Releasing a pair of wobbly bubbles, Kermi waved at the ocean that stretched as far as they could see. "If my life were saner, I might have come here just for the view. But alas, I came because I needed to find you."

"Why?"

His expression suddenly serious, Kermi announced, "Jaladay sent me. With a warning."

Promi's brow furrowed. "What sort of warning?"

"You must not, under any circumstances, do anything to help save—"

"Look!" shrieked Shangri. She jumped up and pointed frantically at the waves below the cliff. "A ship! In trouble!"

# CHAPTER 14

# Disaster

*P*romi spun around to see what Shangri was so frantic about. The sight froze his heart—a ship, fully loaded with people, was foundering off shore!

Suddenly, the ship lurched sideways. Terrified cries erupted from its passengers. The doomed craft started to spin around and around in ever-tightening circles. *A whirlpool.*

Already tilting precariously, the ship began to flood as waves crashed over it. One of its three masts buckled and broke off. The mast smashed onto the deck, ripping right through the mainsail that showed a design of a blue dolphin.

While all Promi's instincts told him he must help, he couldn't do anything but watch. What could possibly stop a whirlpool? Besides, even if the ship somehow wasn't swallowed by the sea, there wasn't any place it could land. The entire coastline of Atlantis rose straight up from the sea; not a single beach or cove broke the line of impassable cliffs.

"What can we do?" shrieked Shangri, watching in horror.

"Nothin', lass." Her father hugged her tight to his apron. "That ship is doomed."

"Guess I didn't need to come all this way, after all," grumbled Kermi. He bounded over to the edge of the drop-off. *No way Promi could save those people,* he told himself, *even if he was foolish enough to try. And even he isn't that foolish!*

Meanwhile, Promi shuddered as the spiraling waves surged higher and higher around the ship. Some people dived overboard to escape the whirlpool, but it caught them anyway and dragged them downward. All the while, a bottomless hole opened in the sea—steadily swallowing the boat and everyone on it.

"'Tis a curse," the baker whispered in horror. "As if that ill-fated ship should never be allowed to land."

Kermi glanced at the baker. *Truer than you know, mortal.*

"How terrible!" wailed Shangri. She started to cry, holding tight to her father. "What I'd give fer a way to stop it."

"There be no way, dear lass. No way at all."

Promi continued to watch. Unlike the others, though, he hadn't yet abandoned hope. His mind raced, searching for some way—any way—the ship could be saved. But only seconds remained.

Desperately, Promi closed his eyes to avoid distractions and turned his inner ear toward the sea. Then he listened—not to the shouts of the drowning people, nor the roar and crash of the waves, nor even the groans of the ship's crumbling beams.

No, he listened for something much more distant and difficult to hear. Far below the spiraling waves, deeper than he'd ever thought possible, he listened for a voice.

The voice of the sea itself.

*Speak to me,* he called with his thoughts. *Speak to me, great ocean!*

No reply came. All Promi heard was the endless sweep and swoosh of currents, the constant tremble of millions of fins, and the distant echo of whale songs.

*Speak to me, please! I am only one small person and you are so vast . . . but I am that person who caused this island to be born.*

Still no reply.

*Speak, I beg you!*

At last, out of the darkest depths came a voice. Echoing from a bottomless abyss, it sounded as fluid as water yet as solid as ice, rising and retreating like the tides.

"I know who you are, Prometheus. *Swissssshhhhh.* And do you, *swisssshhhhh,* know who I am?"

The young man caught his breath, just as surprised to hear the voice as he was to hear his own name. His *full* name, no less— which no one had called him since childhood.

*You are,* he answered, listening with all his senses, *O Washowoe-myra, most ancient goddess of the sea.*

"True, *swisssshhhhh.* And why do you call me on this day when I have so many swells and stirrings to share with the world?"

At the edge of his awareness, Promi heard the shrieks of people drowning. He replied, *To save that ship! You must help, O Wash-owoe-myra.*

Currents surged in the depths, bearing her answer: "I cannot."

*But if you don't, all those people will drown!*

"I cannot, Prometheus. *Swisssshhhhh, hhhisshhh.* Much as I might want to . . . I cannot."

*Please, you must!*

"Even if those people are fated to die? Even if their survival might cause, *swisssshhhhh,* far greater damage than you can imagine?"

*Yes,* pleaded Promi. *No one should die that way. Do save them, if you can!*

A long pause ensued before the goddess of the sea spoke again. This time, her voice sounded more distant, moving away like a bird on an ocean breeze. "If I tried to save them, *swisssshhhhh,* then I could not save *you.*"

*But . . . ,* protested Promi. He stopped, sensing she could no longer hear him. Thoroughly dejected, he knew that he'd failed.

He opened his eyes. To his dismay, he saw the last shreds of the ship's sail disappearing into the whirlpool. Only a few of the people could still be seen, thrashing wildly to escape. Grimly, he turned away—then noticed something else.

Shangri was staring at him. Despite the tear stains on her face, she scrutinized him with sharp clarity. "I know you was doin' somethin' there, Promi. With yer eyes closed and all. But what?"

He sighed. "Nothing that matters. Whatever I tried . . . I failed."

Kermi, who had been listening, breathed his own sigh. But his was one of relief.

Suddenly, Morey gasped. "What in the name of everlastin' life is *that?*"

In the distance, a new wave was rising. No ordinary wave, it grew swiftly, lifting high above the surface like a hill, then a mountain, then a whole range of mountains. Powerful, gigantic, and as broad as it was tall, the wave rose skyward.

Stunned, the group on the cliff watched the mountainous wave swell. Then, all at once, they realized it was moving. Straight toward Atlantis!

With gathering speed, the great wave raced toward them. It towered above the waves, casting the whole island into shadow.

"Run!" cried Promi. He grabbed Shangri's arm and pulled.

"Wait!" she shouted, refusing to budge. "It's changin' shape!"

Promi and the others halted. Sure enough, the wave was condensing, drawing itself together into a new shape—one they immediately recognized.

A great, watery whale's tail.

While they watched in awe, the enormous whale's tail arched gracefully, shedding rivers of water onto the surface of the sea. Then, dipping downward, it swept into the very place where the ship had vanished. With an unstoppable surge of power, the whale's tail scooped out the ship and all its people and hurled them on top of the cliff.

Water cascaded down on Promi and the others, more than any rainstorm they'd ever experienced. Though it didn't last long, it drenched them all completely.

Just as the downpour abruptly ceased, something heavy fell from the sky. A body! It landed right on top of Morey and knocked him flat.

"Oof!" cried the plump baker, struggling to sit up. Beside him, a boy around twelve years old moaned and also tried to sit up. Rubbing his head, the boy blinked at Morey in disbelief.

"But . . ." said the boy, mightily confused, "I thought . . . I drowned."

"Ye *did* drown," said Morey, no less amazed. "Then ye rained down out o' the sky, right on top o' me."

The boy's forehead creased in concern. "Did I hurt you?"

"No, lad." The baker released a rumbling laugh and patted his belly. "Got me plenty o' paddin' right here. Enough fer both o' us."

Pushing the wet blond hair off his face, the boy smiled.

"Look!" cried Promi. He pointed down the hill. Strewn across the drenched slope lay pieces of the wrecked ship, along with seventy or eighty people. Not everyone, it appeared, had survived. But most of them were starting to move, even if they were coughing up seawater or had suffered broken limbs and bruised heads. That so many of the ship's passengers remained alive was nothing short of miraculous.

Quietly, Promi whispered, "Thank you, O Washowoe-myra."

Shangri clucked her tongue at him. She gave her soggy braids a shake, then said sternly, "Whatever ye do, don't ever tell me again yer not someone special."

He gazed at her. "All right. But Shangri . . . let's keep this whole thing our little *secret,* all right?"

She pursed her lips, considering his request. Finally, she said, "All right, it's our secret. But only if ye'll tell me everythin'! I want the truth, now—yer whole thumpin' story."

Knowing he was beaten, Promi gave a nod. "Fine, Shangri. I know I can trust you."

"That ye can. I'm good with secrets."

Promi glanced anxiously over at Morey and the boy. "Come over here, then. Where we'll be out of earshot."

Together they walked a bit down the hill where no one— including Kermi, who was moping on the cliff's edge—could hear.

Shangri squeezed the water from her braids, all the while scrutinizing Promi. "All right, now," she commanded. "Spill yer story. Startin' with this here island! Ye really did have somethin' to do with how it got created, didn't ye?"

Promi paused to watch a silver-winged gull soar past the cliffs. "A little something," he confessed.

"Maybe more than jest a little?" she asked brightly.

He grinned. "You don't miss anything, do you?"

Shangri blushed, which momentarily hid her freckles. "Papa says I could find a missin' speck of flour from a whole sack."

With that, Promi began to talk. He told Shangri the truth about the creation of Atlantis—including his rescue of the Starstone, the final battles with Narkazan and Grukarr, the surprising truth of the Prophecy, and his ultimate sacrifice. As wide as her eyes grew at that tale, they grew even wider when he described the sugary streams, honey cascades, and sweetfruit trees of the spirit realm.

Then he told her about the Bridge to Nowhere, revealing how blessings and prayers are transported to the spirit realm. When he described Theosor the wind lion, she begged him to tell her that part again. And when he did, she closed her eyes and tried her hardest to imagine sinking her fingers into the lion's fur, feeling his warm breath on her hand, and riding on the back of such a majestic creature.

He explained how he discovered his real identity, and that he was in fact immortal—though he didn't mention his lingering anger and troubles with his parents. He shared the origin of his magical dagger. The story of Kermi. The secret of Ekh Raku dungeon. The truth of the great whale's tail of water that had rescued the doomed ship.

Finally, he told her about Atlanta. Calling her "a true nature spirit" and "the most deep, most honest, and also most frustrating person I've ever known," he described her life in the Great Forest. Her beauty, both inner and outer. Her playful love of adventure. Her gift of magic.

Shangri listened carefully, then said, "Ye really do love her, don't ye?"

"I do," he answered, his voice just a whisper. "She's the only person who has ever—could ever—make me feel this way." He blew a long breath. "But I don't know if we can ever be together. Or if she even wants to, now that . . ."

"Now that what?" she pressed.

"Now that I've ruined everything." He told Shangri about the different ways time works in the spirit and mortal realms. About his last visit with Atlanta, a visit that started so promisingly and ended in disaster. Last of all . . . he told Shangri about his deepest fear, revealed at the Lakes of Dreams, that he could never really love anyone.

Shangri's forehead wrinkled with concern. "But ye really want to, I can tell!"

"Maybe. I don't know." Promi shrugged his shoulders. "Like I said to you before, I really only know how little I know."

She frowned and started to say something—when her father and the boy approached.

"Well, well," boomed Morey. "Looks like yer discussin' the fate o' the world over here!"

"No," said Promi, trying to sound lighthearted. "We're just talking about our favorite pastries. Right, Shangri?"

"Right," she said with a twinkle in her eyes. "An' a few other little somethin's."

"Good," replied the baker. "Well, I've been havin' a nice chat meself with this young lad who fell out o' the sky."

At that, the boy stepped forward. With an awkward bow, he said, "I am Lorno." Though he spoke with a strange accent, it was clear that his language was quite similar to that used by Atlanteans. "I came," he added, "from the port city of Athens in Greece."

"Good to meet you, Lorno. I'm Promi."

"And I'm Shangri." She nodded at Morey. "His daughter."

Lorno glanced at the baker. "Ummm . . . I've already, er, met your father."

The burly fellow grinned. "And he made, ye could say, a strong impression! Right on me head."

"Are ye hurt, Papa?"

"No, my sugarcake. I'm jest fine."

Shangri gestured at the many survivors from the ship. "So are they! Can ye believe it?"

"No," said the baker. "'Tis a miracle."

"Yes," agreed Lorno. "A miracle."

"I agree," said Shangri with a sly wink at Promi. "A miracle."

Kermi, who had padded over from the cliff just in time to hear this exchange, shook himself, spraying water everywhere. *It's no miracle,* he told himself grumpily. *It's a whopping disaster.*

# CHAPTER 15

# Etheria

**D**arkness settled on the Great Forest, dimming the bright colors of day and painting everything with the palette of night. Shadows deepened, between roots and along branches, within canopies and under leafy boughs. Many creatures, active all day until dusk, withdrew to the safety of their dens and nests—while just as many, invisible after sunrise, began to roam and fly on silent wings.

This darkness surrounded Atlanta as she walked home on pathways so familiar she didn't need to see them. Even in the thickening night, her bare feet knew exactly where to go. She turned corners without any visible signs, stepped over a cluster of orange-speckled mushrooms now hidden in shadow, and heard the quiet breathing of baby falcons in their nest above her head.

Dark as the forest was, though, it wasn't nearly as dark as her thoughts. In the day since she and Promi had parted so bitterly, those thoughts had multiplied, growing into a shadowy forest that filled her mind. And in those woods so thick and impenetrable, she felt completely lost.

*What an idiot he is!* she railed. *And what an idiot I was to let him into my life.*

She turned into a dark corridor lined with spruce boughs. But she hardly noticed the sweet scent of those needles as they brushed against her face. *He's acting so selfish, so ignorant. Imagine disregarding his father's command to protect the veil! He's endangering us all—and he just doesn't care.*

Losing her concentration, Atlanta stubbed her toe on a sharp rock. She yelped, frightening away an owl in the tree beside her and a family of river otters on a nearby stream bank. The throbbing of her toe only worsened her mood.

*So he'd like to be free, would he?* she grumbled. *Well, I've set him free! No more time wasted with him. Now he's free to steal pies—or other people's time—as much as he likes!*

A faint whirring of wings told her that Quiggley had returned from his early evening travels in the forest. The faery circled her once, releasing a wave of compassion, then settled lightly on her shoulder.

Even in the darkness, she knew just where to stretch out her finger to touch his antennae. They tapped her finger gently, and that subtle drumming deepened her feeling that the faery truly cared.

*You're someone I can trust, little friend.* She chuckled sadly. *Guess you're going to be the only man in my life.*

As she entered a different grove of trees—mostly acacias, with a few monkey puzzles and cedars—her thoughts, too, changed terrain. They entered a darker and fiercer part of her mind.

*Promi is a selfish dolt. Losing him won't be nearly as bad as the other losses I've had.*

A new wave of compassion flowed into her, and she knew Quiggley understood. Yet even his constant, loyal presence wasn't enough to heal the open wound in her heart.

*Fortunately,* she told herself, *I still have Etheria in my life. Whatever happens, I can always depend on her!*

She crossed a meadow of sweetstalk fern, the soft fronds brushing against her feet. The ferns' aroma wafted up to her nose, mixing with the scent of the lilac vines she'd woven into her gown. Then, in the trees ahead, she saw the golden glow she'd been expecting.

Following a well-worn path into the trees, Atlanta watched the glow steadily brighten. At last, she ducked under a mesh of branches and stood before her forest home—the comfy little place where she was always welcome, regardless of her mood.

As always, when she returned after dark, the home radiated light. Atlanta knew that the same golden glow shining through those small square windows also filled each room inside. And that a warm pot of mint tea, with plenty of wildflower honey on the side, would be waiting to greet her—timed to the exact moment she arrived.

*All thanks to Etheria,* she thought gratefully. Already the welcoming light and the smell of her favorite tea were helping to brighten her mood. Quiggley, noticing the difference, nodded his tiny head vigorously, making his cotton hat slip to the side.

Approaching her home, Atlanta marveled at its simple, symmetrical shape. That hadn't been difficult to accomplish, mind you. For the whole structure was really a hollowed-out acorn that had grown to enormous size—at least three times the height of a fully grown person. The acorn, from one of the magical oaks near Highmage Hill, just happened to have been dropped by an unsuspecting squirrel very near to the Starstone, whose power greatly magnified the acorn's size, as well as its own magic. As a result, the acorn was already almost a house when Atlanta had found it. All it took was the help of a few friends to do the rest— beavers to hollow it out, woodpeckers and termites to carve the windows and door, and a sturdy team of centaurs to haul it to this spot.

Even as Atlanta reached for the latch, it lifted and the door swung open. Grinning at Etheria's affection for a dramatic entrance, Atlanta stood in the doorway and bowed deeply. The faery on her shoulder fluttered over to the teapot that sat waiting on the small pinewood table in the kitchen.

"Etheria," called Atlanta, "I'm home." Then, with genuine appreciation, she added, "And I'm so very glad you are in my life."

Without waiting for any response, she strolled over to the table. Eagerly, she poured herself some tea into her favorite mug, carved from the burl of a fallen oak by Honya, the most skilled wood-carver among the chimpanzees who lived in the Spirit Hills at the southern end of the forest. After stirring in some honey, she leaned back in her chair and took the first sip.

Fresh mint and honey truly tasted like relaxation in liquid form. And this particular tea always soothed her mind. So did the sight of all the beeswax candles in the house, which Etheria had lit only moments before. All in all, Atlanta felt better than she had all day.

She winked at Quiggley, who had stretched out on the tea cozy she'd made from strips of moss. "Well, little friend . . . it's good to be home."

Raising her voice, she called, "Did you hear that, Etheria? I hope so!" Taking another sip, she added, "I never should have let that pie thief into my life—but now that's over and done. And I'm back here with you."

At that instant, all the candles glowed brighter. In the cupboard, plates and bowls clinked against each other merrily. And in the bedroom, the downy cover fluffed up with satisfaction. It was almost as if the house itself was celebrating Atlanta's return.

Which, in fact, it was. Because the house *itself* was Etheria.

The acorn's magic, magnified enormously by the Starstone, had given Atlanta a home with plenty of intelligence. As well as plenty of personality. And a highly independent streak.

Now, sometimes that worked well—as it did this very evening. When Atlanta had returned home and needed a warm, comfortable welcome, she got it. However, sometimes Etheria's independent ways made life truly *un*comfortable.

Atlanta was still, months after the incident, trying to apologize to the family of centaurs (including a pregnant mother) who had stopped by for a friendly visit. Before they even knocked on the door, Etheria sprouted thorns all over her outside walls and produced an odor of horse manure so strong it was practically suffocating. Not only that, when the centaurs didn't take the hint and go away, Etheria suddenly shrank herself down to the size of a boulder—which nearly crushed Atlanta, who was baking bread in the kitchen.

Though the centaurs did finally gallop off, the poor mother was so upset that she gave birth several weeks early. And while the young centaur was basically healthy, he developed a terrible allergy to manure. (This is rather inconvenient for someone who is half horse.) To this day, the sight of manure makes him sneeze violently. And the smell of the stuff causes him to break out in hives—and, even worse, to feel an overwhelming urge to defecate.

While Atlanta had tried to talk with Etheria about this kind of thing, she hadn't made much progress. After all, if a house doesn't want to talk with you, it will simply shut all its windows and doors tight and lock every cupboard drawer. Even though Atlanta guessed that Etheria really hadn't wanted to feel like a barn, with all the cleaning that would have been necessary after the centaurs' visit, that didn't justify such behavior. Yet so far, Etheria hadn't allowed any discussion of the incident. If Atlanta even so much as mentioned the word *centaur,* the whole house started shaking as if there had been a sudden earthquake.

On this evening, though, such troubles—*house problems,* as Atlanta called them—seemed very far away. She relaxed into her chair (which was padded with soft bubblereeds she'd gathered from the ponds near the Waterfall of the Giants), sipped her mint tea, and enjoyed the quiet of home.

Just then, the top drawer of the cupboard popped open. A furry brown head emerged, followed by a plump body and a truly massive tail. The squirrel, Atlanta's longtime housemate, peered at her with beady black eyes.

"I don't suppose you brought any food for *me,*" he grumbled. "I'm nothing but a lowly squirrel, after all."

From his resting place on the tea cozy, Quiggley shook his antennae scoldingly.

"What's up with you, Babywings?" snorted the squirrel. "*You* don't have to eat anything but dewdrops."

Quiggley scowled and jumped to his feet. His antennae waved vigorously, and he seemed ready to fly right into the squirrel's face if Atlanta hadn't intervened.

"Now, now, Grumps." Atlanta set her mug down on the table and glared at the squirrel. "If you're going to share this house with us, you've got to be nice to everybody."

Looking like he'd just swallowed a rotten acorn, Grumps frowned. "Even Babywings?"

"Even him. And his name is Quiggley."

"Oh, all right then." The squirrel waved his bushy tail like a flag of surrender. "I will call him by his proper name."

The faery relaxed and started to sit down again.

Then the squirrel added, "Is that all right with you, Baby-wings?"

Quiggley jumped up again, his wings whirring angrily.

"Fine, fine," grumbled the squirrel. "If you don't have any sense of humor, Quiggley, then I can't help you."

Atlanta traded glances with the faery, who shrugged his little shoulders. Both of them knew that they weren't going to get any better manners out of the cantankerous squirrel. Maybe his sour disposition had something to do with having to live inside an acorn that he could never eat. Or maybe he'd fallen out of a tree as a youngster and struck his head. In any case, Grumps had always lived up to his name.

Turning back to the squirrel, Atlanta said, "That's an improvement. As a reward, I just happen to have something for you."

"Better be good," he muttered.

She reached into her robe's hip pocket—the very same pocket where she'd carried Quiggley during those days when he'd been so badly injured that he nearly died. And she smiled to know that the faery had so fully recovered that he was completely ready to fly into battle to defend his honor from such rudeness. Then, from the pocket, she pulled three fresh acorns and tossed them into Grumps's drawer.

Without a word of thanks, he dived down after them. But the satisfied wave of his tail, protruding above the lip of the drawer, told Atlanta that her gift had been gladly accepted.

Suddenly—a harsh knock struck the door. The whole house started to shake. Atlanta jumped off her chair, but the quaking grew so strong she could barely stand.

# CHAPTER 16

# Gryffion's Tidings

S top that, Etheria!" commanded Atlanta. She grabbed hold of the table for support against the violent tremors shaking the acorn house. "Right *now.*"

After a few grudging creaks and moans from the floorboards, Etheria settled down to a constant tremble. Rolling her eyes, Atlanta grabbed her mug of tea (which was just about to slide off the table) and moved it away from the edge.

She strode over to the door. Before opening it, she cast a withering glance around the house, as if to say, *Behave yourself.* Then she lifted the latch.

Facing her in the doorway stood an elegant unicorn, his silver coat tinged with white and his prominent horn shimmering with subtle radiance. Atlanta recognized him immediately: Gryffion, the oldest and wisest of the unicorns. Yet while they had talked occasionally near his home on the Indragrass Meadows, she never expected to find him at her door.

"Gryffion. What a surprise to see you!" For the benefit of Etheria more than the unicorn, she added, "This is a great honor."

The unicorn nodded in greeting. "Apologies for the loud knock," he said in his rich baritone voice. "I'm just not used to rapping on doors with this horn of mine."

Atlanta grinned. "And my apologies to you for Etheria's little earthquake. She gets, well, carried away sometimes."

Gryffion's lavender eyes glittered with amusement. In a voice loud enough that Etheria would be sure to hear it, he said, "You are fortunate indeed to have a house so protective and devoted to your well-being."

Etheria's trembling grew noticeably quieter, though the house continued to rumble.

"And I might add," he said with a wink at Atlanta, "that I take great care to keep houses clean whenever I visit. Besides . . . unicorn manure is much more fragrant than that of horses and other creatures."

Instantly, Etheria's trembling ceased. Atlanta could hear the sounds of a new place being set at the table and something being prepared in the kitchen.

"Your manners are impeccable," she told the unicorn with a smile. "As is your understanding of, shall we say, *tricky* personalities."

Gryffion chuckled, rustling his white mane. "You can thank my mate for that! She's given me lots of practice over the years."

"Please come in." Atlanta stepped over to the table, where a large bowl sat next to her mug. The teapot had been refreshed and the woodstove was baking something that filled the house with a delicious aroma.

"Ah, fresh banana bread," observed Gryffion as he walked in, hooves clomping on the floorboards. "Only a supremely talented house could provide such a treat."

Every candle in the kitchen flared brighter.

Atlanta almost laughed. "Some tea?" she offered.

"Lovely," he answered. "With plenty of honey. But," he said good-humoredly, "no need to fetch me a chair."

"Then I'll stand, too," offered Atlanta.

"Gracious of you, my dear." Seeing the faery on the tea cozy, Gryffion gave him a respectful tip of his luminous horn. In return, Quiggley nodded and clapped his antennae together, a faery's sign of high esteem.

Turning to Atlanta, the unicorn remarked, "I see you have a quiggleypottle in your life. Very good luck."

"Most of the time, at least," she replied, remembering her big fight with Promi. "But even he can't protect me from my own stupidity."

"Our fate as mortals," said Gryffion with a flick of his tail.

Quiggley promptly flew over and landed on the collar of Atlanta's robe. As he perched there, she could feel the gentle brush of his wings against her neck . . . as well as the wave of understanding he sent to her.

Pouring some tea into the bowl, as well as her mug, Atlanta asked, "Are things going well with the unicorns?"

"We are blessed. A healthy new colt was born only last week."

She stirred in the honey. Just then, the woodstove jumped slightly off the floor—just enough to toss a steaming loaf of banana bread onto the table. It landed with a thud and the bread knife slid over to join it.

The unicorn swished his tail in delight. His silver coat gleamed. "Thank you ever so much."

The walls and floor of the house sighed with satisfaction.

"You are most welcome," said Atlanta as she sliced some banana bread for her guest. "So what brings you here today?"

"Tidings," Gryffion replied. He took a swallow of tea from the bowl, then frowned. "Not good ones, I fear."

Atlanta caught herself just before taking a bite of banana bread. Setting the bread back down on the table, she peered at her guest. "Tell me."

Gryffion's lavender eyes looked suddenly sad. "A new unicorn is born only rarely, every thousand years or so. And when that occurs, we have a tradition of reading its placenta for signs of the future."

On Atlanta's shoulder, the faery stiffened. Even his antennae seemed frozen.

"What did you see?" Atlanta asked.

"Destruction." He sighed grimly. "The signs, repeated over and over, predicted *a terrible day and night of destruction.*"

Atlanta caught her breath. "Those were the same exact words the centaur Haldor said in his prophecy for Atlantis! Until now, I thought that was probably just one of his pessimistic ramblings. But—"

"Now you know otherwise," completed the unicorn gravely. "As do I. Any prophecy deserves attention—but a repeated prophecy, all the more."

The kitchen candles quivered, making all the shadows in the room tremble.

"What else," Gryffion asked, "did the centaur say?"

Atlanta took a long, slow breath, trying to recall that night on Moss Island when Haldor had spoken. "He said this island—he predicted that, too—would touch the wider world. Not through its wondrous creatures and places, or even its magic. And not through its buildings and great inventions."

She paused, gazing at Gryffion. "No, he said the lasting power of this place would come from its *stories*. The tales of Atlantis, he promised, would long survive and be cherished by people all over the world."

"But the land itself?"

"Would be lost forever. He said it would sink deep into the sea and disappear. After 'a terrible day and night of destruction'— Atlantis would perish."

The candlelight dimmed further, making the room almost as dark as the forest outside. For a long moment, no one talked. Finally, the unicorn took another sip of tea, then spoke again.

"Something tells me that this will happen soon. And that humans will be at the center of it all."

"That's true too often," said Atlanta glumly. "How can the same species be capable of so much good and so much evil? Create such beauty and powerful tools—and also cause so much damage and suffering?"

The old unicorn shook his head, tossing his mane. "We have a saying about the human soul:

> *More tangled than the vine,*
> *More mysterious than the sea;*
> *Bright and dark, large and small,*
> *Imprisoned yet free.*"

He touched Atlanta's arm with his horn, sending a warm, renewing tingle through her body. Even the faery on her collar felt it and fluttered his wings. Then, in a voice no less warm, Gryffion explained:

"The tools people make can be powerful, indeed. But what is *truly* powerful are their choices about how those tools will be used. After all, a hammer can be used to build a neighbor's home—or to crush that neighbor's skull. As a gift . . . or as a weapon. And the difference lies not in the hammer, but in the choice."

Atlanta swallowed. "What then can I do? I'm just one person . . . and the times are so dark."

"You can be a candle," offered Gryffion. "Bring some light into the dark."

He looked at her with compassion. "And try to make the best choices you can."

# CHAPTER 17

# One Great Story

As they walked through the cobblestone streets of the City of Great Powers, Promi, Morey, and Shangri grilled young Lorno. Eager to know more about the boy's shipmates and home country, especially since they'd never met anyone from another land, they peppered him with questions. Lorno would barely finish answering one when his companions asked him another.

Except for Kermi. While the others tossed a stream of questions at Lorno, the kermuncle sat in silence on Promi's shoulder, his long blue tail draped down Promi's back. He barely moved, except occasionally to blow a few bubbles or stroke his whiskers. Despite the continuous chatter around him, Kermi just sat there, too glum even to make his usual snide remarks.

"Are ye sure," the baker asked, "ye don't want to stay with the monks at the temple, like the rest o' yer shipmates?"

"No," Lorno replied. "I want to find something more . . . well, independent. Where I can come and go as I please."

Promi grinned. "That I understand."

Chewing on his last slice of apple crisp, Morey offered, "Well then, lad. Why don't ye stay with us? We have a nice little room above the bakery, which ye can have at least till ye find somethin' better."

The boy's whole face brightened. "Really?"

Shangri nodded so energetically that her braids flapped like wings.

"Yes, lad. We'd much enjoy yer company."

"Thank you. To think that I fell out of the sky onto such a generous family!"

Shangri giggled, hopping over a dog who was fast asleep on the cobblestones.

"Always choose with care who you fall on," said Promi jauntily. "That's my motto in life."

Kermi rolled his eyes, but said nothing.

"I thought yer motto," said the baker as he elbowed Promi, "was to find whatever pastry's jest come pipin' hot out o' the oven— and eat it."

"That's my *other* motto." Promi took another bite of the clump of cinnamon buns in his hand. "Especially if the pastry is covered with cinnamon."

"That's another spice we don't have in Greece," said Lorno through his own mouthful of pastry. "But I'm sure glad to discover it now."

"You really came all that way to find cinnamon?" asked Shangri.

"Well, it was supposed to be a voyage of discovery," Lorno explained. "That's why the ship was loaded with so many of our best scientists, architects, engineers, and inventors. Why, even our captain, Reocoles, is a master machine builder. He told us many times that our goal was simply 'to find nature's bounty and make the best use of it all.'"

"Includin' good pastries," joked Morey.

"*Especially* that," the boy replied. Then, midway through a bite, his brow furrowed. "We just didn't expect to get lost at sea, run out of supplies, and then almost drown in a huge whirlpool."

Morey patted him on the shoulder. "Yer here now, lad."

He nodded. "And I'm glad of that! But I sure do wish I knew how we happened to get saved."

Shangri shot a knowing glance at Promi.

"Just one of those fluke waves," said Promi casually, thinking of the watery whale's tail of the sea goddess. He smirked at the pun, doubting anyone else would get it. But on his shoulder, Kermi groaned painfully.

"Amazin' things happen sometimes," added Shangri, giving Promi a wink. "Ye jest never know what'll happen next."

"Story of my life," said Lorno as the group turned down another street, this one lined with windows with colorful flower boxes.

"What was *your* reason to be on that ship?" asked Promi. "You're not old enough to be one of your country's great scientists or inventors, are you?"

"Not at all. My job on the ship was, well . . . not so highly skilled. I was the apprentice to the assistant deck mopper."

Promi grinned. "You were very good at it, I'm sure."

"Terrible, actually."

"So tell us . . . what do you *want* to be?"

Lorno hesitated. "Well, someday, if I'm lucky, I'd love to . . ."

"What?" pressed Shangri. "What do ye really want to be?"

He took a deep breath. "Well . . . a bard. A storyteller of great fame."

Frowning, he shook his head. "Trouble is . . . I haven't found the story I really want to tell. Somewhere out there," he said wistfully, "it exists, I keep hoping. *My one great story.* But I don't have any idea where."

Shangri sidled up to him and took his hand. "Ye'll find it, Lorno. I jest *know* ye will."

He managed a small smile. "Thanks. And by the way, my name isn't Lorno."

"What?" she asked, perplexed.

The baker chimed in, "I heard ye meself say that's yer name, jest after ye landed on top o' me."

"That was then," answered the boy, "and this is now." Seeing the bewildered looks all around him, he explained, "Every great writer needs a pen name, you see. And I haven't found the right one yet. So I keep changing my name, trying new ones on for size."

Promi laughed out loud. "So what's your name right now? Quick, tell us—before it changes again."

The boy, not seeing the humor, said crustily, "It's Vasto."

Shangri scrunched her freckled nose at him. "I liked Lorno better."

"Really? Well, I guess then I could try something else. How about . . . Tello?"

She just shrugged. "Whatever ye like, I s'pose."

Trying to keep a straight face, Promi asked, "How can you have a name that's famous and celebrated as a bard if you keep changing it?"

"Someday, I'll find a name that *everyone* will remember!" the boy answered. Suddenly, looking confused, he turned to Shangri. "What was that last name I told you? I, um . . . forgot it."

Kermi, unable to resist a barb, finally spoke up. "Before you find a name everyone will remember, you'll need to remember it yourself."

Tello, formerly Vasto and Lorno, blushed almost as red as the awning of the shop they were just passing, a provider of herbs and spices. He ran his hand through his blond curls. "I guess," he admitted, "you have a point."

"Kermi *always* has a point," Promi observed. "And believe me, it's never dull."

The kermuncle's tail reached up and batted Promi's ear. "You're the only one around here who's dull, manfool."

"Now that's another amazing thing about this island," said the boy. "Animals who talk! We don't have anything like that in Greece."

"My sympathies," grumbled Kermi. "So you have no choice but to listen to people like this manfool all the time."

Tello winced as he glanced at Promi. "I see what you mean."

"Oh, he's just getting started," Promi said, rubbing his earlobe. "You should see him when he's not in such a happy mood."

Though Kermi's eyes narrowed, he said nothing. He merely blew a stream of bubbles.

Shangri pointed at the bubbles and exclaimed, "I jest love it when ye do that."

Instantly, Kermi stopped. He turned away and pretended to be sound asleep.

"Here we be," announced Morey as they strode up to his bakery. "This is where I make all the food ye've been eatin'." He pointed at the floor above the awning. "And that's yer new home, lad."

"Thank you again."

"No trouble," the hefty fellow replied. "Come settle yerself inside, Lorno—er, no, Totto."

"*Tello.* For now, anyway."

Shangri faced Promi. "Will ye be comin' in, also? Ye must be hungry for another pastry er two." Her eyes glowed with their shared secret—and also a look of mischief. "I mean . . . after all the *hard work* ye've done today."

"You're referring to that heavy sack I carried up the hill, right?" he replied with an equally mischievous look.

"Right, Promi. What else?"

He grinned. "But, no, as much as I love your pastries, I'm totally full."

"At least," added Morey, "fer an hour or two."

Shangri tapped Promi's tunic pocket, which she knew held the journal she'd given him. "Guess ye'll have a few new things to write 'bout after today."

"Just a few." He tousled her red hair. "You really do know how to make an amazing picnic."

Looking up at him, she grinned. "Anytime."

# CHAPTER 18

# Invisible Wings

After parting with the others, Promi continued to walk down the street. Thinking about the day's remarkable events, he didn't pay any attention to where he was walking, merely padding along the cobblestones. He even forgot about the sullen little passenger who was riding on his shoulder, pretending to snooze.

Abruptly, he halted. For he was standing, he suddenly realized, in the very same alley where he'd first met Atlanta months before. He stared at the spot where he'd found her, looking as bedraggled as any beggar after being chased out of the Great Forest by Grukarr. What was it about her that had prompted him to talk with her—and, much more amazing, to offer her his newly stolen lemon pie?

*Her eyes*, he recalled. A rich shade of blue-green, they reminded Promi of a springtime forest and an impossibly deep lake, brought together by some alluring magic he couldn't describe.

He bit his lip. *I miss her. Curse the stars and moon above, I do!*

A wave of regret flowed over him, as overwhelming as any real wave sent by the sea goddess. *How could I have ruined everything?*

He kicked a pebble down the cobblestones, walking aimlessly, feeling more glum with each step. Even if she did say those awful things . . . she did have one good reason.

*She could be right.* He heaved a sigh. *Well, now I know exactly what I need to do! I'm going to march back out to that forest and tell her I'm sorry.*

It may not do any good, he knew. But he felt real determination to try. *I'll go first thing in the morning,* he vowed. *And nothing will get in my way.*

"Do my senses deceive me?" said Kermi from his shoulder perch. "Or is something troubling my dear manfool?"

Promi winced. The last thing he wanted to do was talk with Kermi about all this. But he couldn't very well deny everything and pretend to be just fine. Deciding to tell the truth but keep it short, he grumbled, "I was an idiot to Atlanta."

The kermuncle's tail thumped against his back, as if applauding. "You? An idiot? Why, that is the single most intelligent thing I've ever heard you say."

Shaking his head, Promi demanded, "Why did you ever come down here, anyway? Can't you do something better with your time? Aren't there enough people you can torment up in the spirit realm?"

Kermi's eyes narrowed to blue slits. "Since you asked . . . I came only because Jaladay begged me. So I could give you a warning."

"What sort of warning?" he asked suspiciously.

"Oh, nothing too important," said Kermi in a bland tone of

voice. "Just a little advice to you about how to avoid destroying Atlantis, the mortal world, and the entire spirit realm, as well."

Promi stiffened. "What advice?"

Enjoying the moment, Kermi yawned and sent a few bubbles floating lazily up to the sky. "Maybe I'll tell you tomorrow."

"Tell me now!"

"All right, but you don't need to get so rude about it." He cleared his little throat. "Jaladay had a vision of a Greek ship approaching Atlantis—a ship loaded with passengers and a blue dolphin on its sail."

"All right. So what was her advice?"

"She insisted, manfool, that you absolutely must *not* save that ship! That if you did . . . a great catastrophe would follow. A catastrophe big enough to destroy everything."

Stunned, Promi tried to digest this. "But . . . you never told me before it happened."

"You never gave me a chance, manfool!"

"And you—" started Promi. But he halted abruptly, having just heard a sound that always stopped him short. A sound he knew well. A sound that, the first time he'd heard it, transformed his life forever.

The distant roar of a lion.

*Theosor*, he knew instantly. But why was the wind lion here?

Only then did Promi realize that, in his distracted wandering through the streets, he'd come very close to the Bridge to Nowhere. The structure, stretching partway across the canyon, disappeared into billowing clouds of mist. It looked, as always, so flimsy that it could barely support the weight of all the prayer leaves that covered its planks like a flock of silver-winged butterflies.

Yet he knew well this bridge was anything but flimsy. It spanned two worlds, one mortal and the other immortal. For those brave enough to walk upon it—or, as Promi had done that first time, to leap off it—this bridge reached amazingly far.

Drawn to the sound of the wind lion's roar, Promi stepped closer to the bridge. Kermi, who had also heard Theosor's call, stayed perfectly still. Clouds rose from the rapids in the gorge, swirling and churning, making Promi's hair and Kermi's fur sparkle with mist.

Just as Promi placed one foot on the first warped plank of the bridge, the wind lion's magnificent form appeared out of the clouds. Theosor's silver-hued mane rippled like water, as his huge paws strode closer. Somewhere near the lion's massive shoulders, invisible wings vibrated in the mist. But his most striking attribute was his eyes—huge brown eyes that could see from one world into the next.

"Theosor!" exclaimed Promi, peering into those eyes. "It's good to see you again."

Then, speaking to the wind lion by thought, he added, *I hope you're not angry at me for flying between the worlds without you.*

"No, young cub," Theosor replied in his deep, rumbling voice that rolled like thunder. "I am not angry, though you cannot fly as fast as I can."

"That I know! Only you could have outraced Narkazan and his entire army."

Theosor nodded, rippling his great mane. "Nor can you fly through the veil without tearing it, for only wind lions possess the magic to do that."

At the mention of the veil, Promi frowned. He started to ask the wind lion about Sammelvar's claims, but before he could, Theosor spoke again.

"No time for that now, young cub. I have been sent here to find you—and bring you to your parents at once."

Promi's frown deepened markedly. He rubbed his foot into the plank. "Last time I saw them . . . it wasn't exactly a happy reunion."

"No matter," boomed the wind lion. "Your sister Jaladay is missing."

The young man jolted, and Kermi released a screech. "Missing?" they both asked at once.

Theosor nodded. "She may be in grave danger."

Immediately, Promi leaped off the bridge and landed squarely on the lionsteed's back. A *whooooshhh* of invisible wings—and they vanished into the clouds.

# CHAPTER 19

# Mist Fire

The instant he leaped, Promi felt time slow down. The sound of prayer leaves flapping slowed to a steady drumbeat, each beat sending a cherished prayer to the spirit realm. Even the rush of cold, wet air on his face seemed to happen in slow motion. As did the sensation of landing on Theosor's sturdy back.

*Already*, Promi thought, *time is moving faster for everyone on Atlantis than for me.*

Suddenly, everything returned to what seemed like a normal pace, telling him that he'd adjusted to spirit time. For a moment, he just opened his senses to the experience of flying, once again on his old friend. He felt the flexing of Theosor's powerful shoulders, saw the vibration in the mist from invisible wings, smelled the moisture on the lion's fur, and heard his own heart pounding with excitement.

And he also felt the squeeze of Kermi's tail wrapped securely around his neck.

Promi grabbed hold of the wind lion's mane as they plunged deeper into the clouds. Theosor bounded vigorously, turning this way and that, following a path only he could see into the billowing mist. All the while, the lionsteed's silver fur glistened like moonlight on a flowing stream.

As always, the spirit realm changed continuously. Mountains of mist rose higher and higher before they melted away into lush valleys or rolling plains. Oceans of clouds suddenly opened into canyons so deep they had no bottom, before a new mountain rose right out of the abyss. An endless procession of vistas melted into each other, ever evolving.

At the same time, Promi glimpsed an infinite array of places within places, scenes within scenes. Sometimes he'd see a brilliant rainbow forming in the heart of a peak; other times he'd find hints of forests or deserts within oceans. And for every place he could identify, many more remained a mystery.

The wind lion veered one way and then another, leaping over an emerging cloudscape here and plunging straight through one there. Some places felt like windy tunnels, with hordes of misty creatures racing past. Others, by contrast, seemed utterly still—until a flock of cloud-winged birds bubbled out of its surface and rose into the sky, or a single gigantic head appeared and swallowed the place entirely.

"Young cub," rumbled Theosor, "I am worried about Jaladay. And about what this could mean."

"So am I," answered Promi.

"Me too." The kermuncle's small body shuddered. "I should never have left her side for that fool's errand."

Theosor vaulted upward, landing on a vertically flowing river of mist that carried them swiftly higher. Seconds later, he leaped off the rising river and plunged into a cloudscape where everything glowed different shades of green. A deep green ocean swelled with tides, as a blue-green mountain twirled above the water. Veering again, the wind lion loped across a vast, stormy scene where lightning and thunder exploded on all sides.

Between blasts, Theosor said, "You once told me, young cub, that *impossible* challenges were your specialty."

"Still are," declared Promi.

The wind lion turned his head just enough to fix his gaze on the young man. "Good. Because my inner sense tells me that this involves much more than your sister . . . and could be your greatest challenge yet."

Promi clenched his fingers more tightly in the lion's mane.

Just then, Theosor dived into a lightless tunnel. Like a drum, it echoed with the thunder claps they'd left behind, until at last they had traveled so far the storms faded entirely away. In a sudden burst of light, they flew out of the tunnel and into a place of blue sky and wispy shreds of mist.

Straight ahead, in the middle of a revolving ring of mist, stood Sammelvar and Escholia. Both of them turned toward the approaching visitors. Sadness and worry showed on both their faces.

Entering the ring of mist, Theosor landed on a tuft so airy it was almost invisible. Gracefully, he padded over to the elder spirits. As Theosor came to a stop, Promi jumped off. With the wind lion by his side and the kermuncle on his shoulder, he faced his parents.

"Something gravely serious has happened," said Sammelvar.

"Jaladay is missing?" asked Promi. "For how long?"

"Since we last saw her on the purple cloudfield of Orquesta," said Escholia, her voice trembling. "Right after you left us."

Promi tensed. "No sign of her at all?"

"Nothing," answered Sammelvar. "Save this." He held up Jaladay's turquoise headband. "It was left on the cloudfield."

Promi reeled at the sight of the cloth that he'd only seen on his sister's face or in her hand. Kermi growled angrily.

"There is more," continued Sammelvar. "On the spot where she'd been sitting, we found the unmistakable evidence of *mistwraiths*."

Escholia nodded grimly. "Their black sparks do so much damage. Especially to such a delicate place."

"Mistwraiths!" Promi blew some stray hairs off his face. "I thought they all went into hiding after Narkazan disappeared."

"So did I," rumbled Theosor. "How dare they show themselves?"

Gazing at the wind lion, Sammelvar said, "That is indeed the right question. I can only surmise that something significant has happened—something that gives those dreadful beings the protection they need to abandon their hiding places."

"Not—" began Promi.

"Yes." The spirit of wisdom grimaced as he spoke. "Narkazan, I fear, has returned."

"No!" shouted Promi. "That's not possible!"

"But it is," declared Theosor, nudging the young man with his enormous head. "Just because no one has ever escaped the Maelstrom before doesn't mean it isn't possible. And if anyone burns with vengeance enough to do it, that would be Narkazan."

A gust of wind buffeted the ring of mist, scattering some lacey shreds. But nobody moved. All eyes remained fixed on Sammelvar. He drew a long breath and then spoke again.

"We have no way yet to know if my suspicions are true. But if indeed they are, then Jaladay is truly at risk." Glancing at his wife, he added, "He will try to make her turn her powers against us—and when she refuses . . ."

Silence fell over them. For everyone knew that Jaladay would never cooperate with the immortal warlord.

"Do you think," asked Promi at last, "he will kill her?"

"Yes," replied his mother, her eyes shadowed with worry. "Any spirit—even one as strong and brave as Jaladay—can die from pain that's just too intense or prolonged."

"Like drowning," rumbled Theosor. "Or being skinned alive."

Sammelvar clenched his fists. "Both of which Narkazan has used in his tortures. And I am certain he's found other methods, as well."

He drew a deep breath and faced his son. "On top of that, we have another problem. The veil is close to failing entirely. We—"

"*If* that's really true," interrupted Promi. He locked gazes with his father. "Why worry about something no one can prove, when we need to focus on saving Jaladay?"

Sammelvar answered frostily, "I know that you would rather not believe it's true, Promi. That way you can visit Atlantis anytime you like."

"But—" Promi objected, his rage rising.

"I have not finished," declared Sammelvar firmly. "What I was starting to say is something that you of all people should consider."

*Heed him, young cub,* Theosor said silently to Promi. *This is a time to listen, not speak.*

Grinding his teeth, Promi remained quiet.

"We must remember," Sammelvar went on, "that if Narkazan discovers the weakness of the veil, he will use that to his advantage. Right now, I'm afraid, it would take only a small band of his warriors to destroy whatever remains. Then there will be no way to stop him from invading the world of mortals, whose magic and resources he has long coveted."

Trying to keep his voice calm, Promi asked, "But how do you know the veil is so weak? *What makes you so sure?*"

Sammelvar and Escholia traded glances, understanding that Promi's question was only partly about the veil.

Reluctantly, Sammelvar admitted, "You are right that there's no way to be sure, because the magic of the veil repels all the normal ways of perceiving it."

"So," said Promi with more than a touch of smugness, "you really *are* just guessing."

"I suppose that's true, my son. But over the years, I've developed a keen understanding of the veil—a feeling for it, you could say."

"But you still have no proof! And you want us to stake so much of our plans—and our lives—on some undefined *feeling*?"

Theosor growled quietly at this rudeness. But Promi didn't seem to notice. His resentment was just too strong.

"Yes," answered Sammelvar. "That's right." He took a step toward the young man. "I am asking you, just this once, to trust me."

Promi studied his father for a moment before speaking. "Well," he answered, "I *can't*."

Once more, Theosor growled.

"Don't you see why?" asked Promi. "Now that I'm old enough to think for myself, I just don't buy this."

To Promi's surprise, his father nodded in agreement. "Yes, I do see. It seems . . . I must prove this to you."

"If you can."

Escholia looked at her husband with growing concern.

"When I told you we couldn't be sure," Sammelvar declared, "I said that was true in 'all the normal ways.' There *is* one other way. But it comes with a great risk."

Escholia sucked in her breath. "Not . . ."

"Yes," said her husband with a grim nod. "We could use *mist fire*."

Peering at Promi, he pledged, "I will do this for you. But as I said, there will be a cost. Calling up mist fire to show us the veil will leave a faint residue—an afterglow—for at least a few days' time. If, by some chance, Narkazan sees what the mist fire reveals . . . he will know our great weakness."

"But," protested Escholia, "is this wise?"

"No," replied Sammelvar. "But it's necessary." He gazed at her, then added, "If only to regain the trust of my own son."

"You shouldn't," she insisted.

"I must." The elder then turned back to Promi and asked, "Knowing what I have told you, do you still want me to proceed?"

Theosor's deep brown eyes watched his friend. *Think carefully, young cub.*

But Promi was still too full of anger to do that. All he could think about was how sick and tired he was of being told what to do with his life.

"Yes," he declared. "Proceed."

"So be it." Sammelvar reached up and twirled a small shred of mist around his finger. Focusing on the mist, he spoke an ancient chant:

> *Flame now, mist fire—*
> *Burn bright and rise higher.*
> *Show me secrets I must know,*
> *Hidden where I cannot go.*

Stretching out his hand, he commanded, "Show me the Veil of Peace that divides the mortal and immortal worlds."

Instantly, the wisp of mist flared into a blazing red flame that reached from Sammelvar's hand up to nearly twice his height. As the elder spirit removed his hand, the flame hung in the air. At the same time, it flattened and took the shape of a trembling piece of red cloth.

Promi, along with the others, gasped. For the cloth had been torn almost to shreds. Some sections were connected by just a single thin thread. Overall, it looked so weak it could simply disintegrate from a gust of wind.

Swiftly, the vision began to fade. Like the embers of a dying fire, it quivered and glowed for a few final seconds. Then it disappeared completely.

Theosor turned his head, scanning the surrounding clouds. "I can see a subtle red glow in the most distant mist. And it was not there before."

"The afterglow," said Sammelvar grimly. "Let us hope our enemies don't notice it before it, too, fades."

Promi swallowed. Looking straight at his father, he said, "I'm . . . sorry."

"So am I, my son. I wish that it hadn't been so."

"As do I," added Escholia.

"But it *is* so," Promi declared. "And I'm going to do the only thing I can to lessen our troubles."

"What," asked Sammelvar, "is that?"

"I will find Jaladay! Whatever it takes, I will find her."

"Wait," pleaded Escholia. "If there are mistwraiths—"

"Then I will face them." Promi straightened his back. "And Narkazan, too, if I must."

Sammelvar reached for his son's arm. "You don't need to do this, you know."

"I know."

"Please, Promi," said Escholia. "We don't want to lose *both* of you to Narkazan."

Theosor shook his mane and rumbled, "I would like to go with Promi."

"Me, too," piped up Kermi, thumping his tail on Promi's back.

Sammelvar frowned. "I cannot let you go, good Theosor. Now

that we have revealed the true state of the veil, I need you and your most trusted wind lions to patrol the entire perimeter of the after-glow—and to capture any allies of Narkazan you may find. You must stop them from reporting back to him."

Theosor gave a nod. "As you wish." Then his huge eyes moved toward Promi. "I am sorry not to join you, young cub."

"That makes two of us," Promi replied.

"Three of us," added Kermi.

Sammelvar peered at his son. "Since I cannot, alas, give you the help of a wind lion . . . I can at least give you some advice. About mistwraiths."

"What advice?"

"Mistwraiths," said the elder spirit, "are rightly feared in every corner of the realm. They are malicious, brutal, cunning, and mer-ciless. They are Narkazan's most dangerous creations, raised from birth to terrorize and destroy anything alive. They devour the life, as well as the magic of other creatures. And they are totally loyal to their master because they fear his wrath."

On Promi's shoulder, Kermi shuddered.

"But they do," Sammelvar continued, "have one weakness. Only one."

Promi's eyebrows lifted. "Tell me."

*"They have never known love."*

"What?" asked Promi, confused.

"Just what," Escholia asked her husband, "are you suggesting?"

Sammelvar scowled. "I'm not really sure." He locked gazes with Promi. "But I suspect . . . the best thing you can do, if attacked by a mistwraith, is somehow to give it your love."

Promi recoiled, backing away. "Are you completely crazy?"

Escholia stared at her husband in utter disbelief. Kermi looked horrified. Even the ever-loyal Theosor shook his mighty head.

"That's not advice," said Promi. "That's idiocy! Suicide! Even if it made sense, which it doesn't—it's impossible."

"No," corrected Sammelvar. "It's not impossible. Just very, very difficult."

"And crazy!" Promi frowned at his father. "First of all, there's no possible way to love something so horrible—so it really can't be done. By anyone. And second, even if I could find some way to do that . . . what would happen? Would love kill the mistwraith? And if it did, would that also kill me?"

Sammelvar ran a hand through his hair. "I just don't know. All I can say is if you do try this—you must truly give it your all. And you must hold on *long enough* that you won't be destroyed."

Promi scowled. "Thanks for the advice. But there's no way I'm going to take it."

Sammelvar merely sighed. "Then go, my son. With our blessings . . . as well as our hopes."

# CHAPTER 20

# Faith

Unwilling to wait even a minute before setting off to find Jaladay, Promi refused his parents' invitation to spend the night with them in their ring of mist. As lacey shreds floated by, darkening toward the end of the day, he felt only increased urgency to find his sister.

Even if that meant dealing with mistwraiths.

Promi's parting from his parents was hurried, as well as awkward. Though they didn't speak any words, their expressions said enough. Promi knew he'd never forget his mother's misty blue eyes, so full of worry, and his father's careworn face, weighed down by everything that had struck his world, as well as his family.

Saying good-bye to Theosor was no easier. Promi gave the wind lion a hug, burying his face in the thick mane. He breathed in the rich smell of Theosor's fur, which reminded him of all they had done together. And he couldn't help but wonder whether he'd ever smell that again.

Looking into the lion's deep brown eyes, Promi said telepathically, *Travel far and stay safe, my friend.*

"It will be hard for either of us to stay safe," Theosor replied.

"Are you saying," asked Promi with a hint of a grin, "that it will be impossible?"

"Our specialty," rumbled the wind lion. But there was no joy in his words.

"Well, manfool," said a grumpy voice on Promi's shoulder. "We can keep on delaying or we can get going. Your choice."

With a sigh, Promi said, "You really don't have to come, you know."

"Of course I do, you bumblebrained idiot! Why . . . you could get *destroyed*."

Promi raised an eyebrow, surprised to hear such an unusual expression of concern for his well-being. Touched by the kermuncle's kindness, he started to say thanks—when Kermi finished his comment.

"And what fun would that be, if I'm not around to see it?"

Promi clenched his jaw.

"Besides," Kermi continued with a rap of his tail on the young man's back, "the whole point of this exercise is to rescue Jaladay without getting her killed. And I sincerely doubt you can do that without my help."

"Let's go, then."

As Kermi settled into position, wrapping his tail around Promi's neck, Promi felt strangely comforted. In a way he didn't want to admit, he actually felt grateful to have some company on this mission. Even the company of a little blue demon he'd often wanted to strangle.

With a last glance at his parents and Theosor, Promi leaped. Up into the swirling mist he soared, knowing only his goal—but utterly unsure how to accomplish it. Where could Jaladay be? And how could they find her?

"Where is our first stop, manfool?" asked Kermi in his ear.

"Well, um, I . . ."

"Good. I'm so relieved. For a moment there I was worried you might actually have a plan! And then I might have fallen off in shock."

Ignoring him, Promi announced, "We'll go to that cloudfield where she was last seen. To see if we can learn anything about those mistwraiths."

"Fine, fine," grumbled his passenger.

"One thing I can tell you for certain," said Promi. "Despite what my father said, there is *no way* I'm ever going to touch one of those shadowy monsters on purpose. And I'm definitely not going to give it any love!"

"For once, manfool, I must agree with you."

Considering his thorny relationship with his father, Promi thought, *He may have been right about the veil. But how can I possibly trust him when he gives me such crazy, suicidal advice?*

"That problem," said Kermi, who had heard his thoughts, "could be tougher than rescuing your sister."

Through the billowing clouds they soared. Even though the dim light at this time of day cast many of the clouds in shadow, Promi saw glimpses of life—whole civilizations, even—within their darkening vapors. As always, the spirit realm's mysterious ways intrigued him. How many worlds existed here among the clouds? What endless varieties of shapes and sizes did they take?

Plus one more question that haunted him as they flew through the darkening mist: would all those worlds survive whatever was to come?

Promi's thoughts turned to Atlanta. Would her precious forest be one of the places that didn't survive? He knew from his encounters with Narkazan and his henchman Grukarr that seizing the sources of magic in the Great Forest would be a top priority. Fortunately, Grukarr had died in the earthquake that created Atlantis . . . but it seemed Narkazan was still around. And if so, he'd be more dangerous than ever—as well as more determined to conquer the Earth and plunder its treasures.

*It was wrong,* he told himself sadly, *to tear more holes in the veil. But it wasn't wrong at all to visit Atlanta.* He saw, in his mind, her face. She was really extraordinary, despite her flaws. Not to mention smart, adventurous, and beautiful.

Frowning, he thought, *Whatever chance we still had is gone now.* Despite his vow earlier that day, he wouldn't be going back to find her and apologize.

Atlanta, he knew, had faith in him—at least she did, before he destroyed it. And even if he couldn't ever regain it . . . that faith had been a gift.

As Promi soared through the cloudscape, he realized, *Nobody has ever had that kind of faith in me before. Except maybe Shangri. And Bonlo.*

He smiled sadly, remembering the brave old monk with the white hair who had saved his life in the dungeon of Ekh Raku. At the cost of his own life, Bonlo had protected Promi. And the monk also taught him some valuable history of the mortal and immortal realms—as well as the Prophecy. Although Promi had been a captive audience—in more ways than one—Bonlo had filled their time in the dungeon with tales of wonder, tragedy, glory, great losses, and even greater hopes.

*Bonlo. You gave me so much . . . even at the end.*

Even as he banked a turn through the clouds, heading toward the spot where Jaladay had disappeared, Promi thought about

Bonlo's most unexpected gift. *That belief in me. He kept telling me that I was better than I seemed, that I was destined for great deeds— even though he had no evidence at all.*

Sure, Promi knew that he had, in fact, done a few things right. But he'd also done several things massively wrong. Like tearing holes in the veil as if nothing mattered but his own desires . . . which had also wrecked his chances with Atlanta. All considered, he still didn't deserve that faith from the old monk. Yet he knew that, if Bonlo were still around, it would still be there.

Why, Bonlo had even believed, long ago, in Grukarr! Before Grukarr became a monstrous, power-mad priest who served Narkazan, he'd been a confused, damaged orphan boy. Bonlo took him under his wing, sheltering and mentoring Grukarr for many years, hoping to bring out the best in him. But that best, if it ever existed, had been buried much too deep to find.

Promi sighed. *I just hope that someday, somehow, Bonlo's faith in me will turn out to be justified.*

Spotting a dome-shaped cloud in the distance, Promi glided toward it. Even in the growing darkness, the cloud glowed with a purple hue from all the flowers. And he could smell their delicious aroma, as sweet as honey itself, from a good distance.

Yet Promi knew that this cloud's most amazing quality wasn't its rich color or sweet scent. It was the cloud's array of miniature worlds, each one distinct from the rest—an entire field of worlds.

Promi landed, taking care not to crush any of the honeyscent flowers. Instantly, Kermi jumped down and bounded over to the spot where he'd last been with Jaladay. Following the kermuncle over to the spot, Promi reached his hand in his pocket to touch his journal. Writing journal entries was a favorite pastime for both him and his sister, something they'd done together as small children and still enjoyed.

He stopped. Right before him, in the midst of the cloudfield,

sat a blackened spot that stank of incinerated worlds and the creatures who had lived there. A few of the destroyed flowers still
smoldered, sizzling as their remaining stalks and petals burned
slowly down to nothing. But most of what remained was just emp-
tiness—devoid of life or landscapes.

Kermi, standing in the middle of the scorched spot, growled
angrily. "Mistwraiths," he said, "no doubt about it."

"How could they do this?"

"Very easily," Kermi answered. "Mistwraiths live to devour
magic and destroy life. They thrive on fear. And they—"

A sudden burst of crackling made them both whirl around.
Right behind them, a pair of dark shadows was rising out of the
cloudfield—shadows that vibrated with black sparks.

Mistwraiths!

# CHAPTER 21

# The Chase

*I*n a flash, Kermi leaped onto Promi's shoulder, and the young man jumped into the air. Just as they left the cloudfield, black sparks, sizzling and crackling, sprayed the spot where they'd been standing.

Both mistwraiths shrieked angrily and leaped after them. Hurtling through the swirling mist, they rippled with rage, leaving two black swaths behind. Like a pair of dark comets, they pursued their intended prey.

Promi soared through the clouds, feeling Kermi's tail wrapped around his neck. He weaved and swerved, zipping through mountainous clouds and under darkening rainbows. Yet nothing he did gained any distance from the mistwraiths. In fact, they seemed to be drawing closer.

"Er, manfool," whispered Kermi into his ear. "This would be a good time to show some speed if you've got any."

"I'm trying!"

"Then try harder. Or else we'll end up like those flower worlds back there."

Promi swerved sharply and plunged into a cloud tunnel of howling winds. The winds jostled them furiously, making Promi's long black hair fly in all directions. Kermi's whiskers flapped against his face, while his round ears fluttered against his head.

They shot out of the windy tunnel. Right behind them came the mistwraiths, crackling with sparks. Behind them, twin trails of blackness blotted out the waning light.

Promi careened into an especially dark cloud. All around them, vapors pressed as thickly as seawater. Both Promi and Kermi held their breaths.

The companions streaked past thousands of glowing bubbles that were floating through this watery realm. Each bubble held a luminous world of its own, full of colorful places and bizarre creatures. Despite floating in the same waters, though, each bubble was destined to remain always separate, always apart.

Bursting out of the dark cloud, they flew into a wide expanse of brightly colored, cube-shaped crystals. Even as night fell across the spirit realm, shrouding all its worlds in darkness, these crystals radiated yellows, greens, purples, and reds. Wherever they came together, new colors appeared, tinting everything around them.

From each crystal came a strange sound, like a note from an airy flute, but more rich and resonant than any flute Promi had ever heard. Weaving together across the cloudscape, those sounds made a wildly unpredictable symphony—sometimes loud and cacophonous, sometimes quiet and melodic, always surprising.

*One day,* thought Promi, *I'd like to come back and explore this place.*

"First you'll have to survive *this* day," Kermi reminded him.

Glancing behind, Promi saw the mistwraiths were still there—and gaining. Putting on a new burst of speed, he vaulted upward into a spiraling storm cloud. Lightning flashed all around, while thunder boomed.

*Zzzzappp!* A searing blast of lightning sliced past, barely missing them. Then another zapped even nearer—so close Promi felt it singe the hair on his head.

He veered to the side, bursting out of the storm. Now they were flying over a dark blue sea of clouds, a region where liquid worlds washed over one another constantly. From the waves below, a pair of golden eyes shaped like diamonds poked above the surface and watched them pass. Then the eyes rose higher, revealing a huge head covered with turquoise scales.

But neither Promi nor Kermi noticed. All their attention was on the sound of crackling sparks that was pressing closer by the second. Desperately, Promi tried to fly faster—but the mistwraiths continued to close the gap. Now they were right behind!

A black spark glanced off Promi's left foot, searing his skin. He knew only seconds remained before their shadowy pursuers incinerated them completely. So he did the only thing he could think of—he flipped over backward, spinning a circle in the air.

"Manfool!" shouted Kermi, almost losing his grip.

The maneuver gained them a little distance from the mistwraiths. But only a little. As fast as Promi was flying, the deadly beings pressed closer.

And closer.

And closer.

The mistwraiths, rippling with rage, were now just a hair's breadth from Promi's feet. He could almost kick them—but to do that would cost him dearly in flesh and bone.

The mistwraiths swelled, already savoring the taste of conquest.

Their shadowy folds rippled, spraying more sparks. Then, in unison, their heads opened into cavernous black mouths.

The mouths opened wider. They salivated streams of darkness, for these mistwraiths were most eager to devour their prey. At the very instant the mouths started to close on Promi and Kermi—

A huge creature flew at them from the side. Looking like a giant squid with leathery black wings, the creature opened its own enormous mouth—and swallowed Promi and Kermi whole.

The two of them tumbled down the creature's throat. They rolled along the ribbed gullet and finally came to a stop in a dark, cavernous belly. A harsh creaking sound echoed all around them— the creature's breathing, perhaps? Dazed and bruised, they knew only that they were, miraculously, still alive.

Outside, the enraged mistwraiths shrieked crazily. They hurled themselves against the creature, assaulting it with black sparks. But there was nothing they could do now, for this creature's thick hide seemed impervious to their sparks, as well as their power.

"That was rough," said Promi, rubbing his sore head. "But I'd rather be in here than out there."

"That depends," grumbled Kermi, "on exactly where *here* is."

"Wise words," declared a voice that reverberated ominously.

The companions both started—not just because someone was in there with them, but for another reason, as well. Both of them, especially Promi, had the uncomfortable feeling that they had heard that voice before.

Just then a thick net fell over them. Made of fibrous vaporstone, it held them securely. And the more they flailed and struggled, the tighter it wrapped around them.

"Lights," commanded the voice.

All at once the creature's entire belly flooded with light. Astonished, Promi and Kermi realized that they were not in a living creature at all, but in some sort of machine—a flying ship made of vaporstone panels that gleamed with a gray metallic sheen. All around the ship's hold were arrayed lights, switches, meters, levers, dials, and screens flashing endless streams of numbers and symbols. Round portals revealed the world outside, as well as the leathery wings whose constant beats made the creaking sound.

*A flying ship,* thought Promi, thoroughly amazed. *I wonder if any more of these exist in the spirit realm.*

Operating all the gadgetry, about a dozen men scurried around the hold. All of them wore heavy brown robes with deep hoods that hid their faces. They worked busily and efficiently, pausing only to inspect a screen or adjust a dial.

Only one of the robed men wasn't actively tending to the machinery. Taller than the others, he stood in the center of the room next to a chair clearly designed for the ship's captain. He strode toward the entangled captives, chortling from under his hood.

Placing his hands on his hips, he declared, "Well, well, won't my master be pleased to see you."

Promi's mind raced. Where had he heard that voice before?

"Before I take you to him, though," the captain continued, "I have some plans for you. Plans that I will find quite amusing— while you, alas, will find them excruciatingly painful."

He chortled again. Then, from under his hood, he whistled the first few notes of a jaunty tune.

The blood froze in Promi's veins. "No," he said, horrified. "It's not possible!"

"You are mistaken," declared the captain. Throwing back his hood, he proclaimed, "It is I, your old friend Grukarr."

# CHAPTER 22

# Unending Agony

Y ou're no friend of mine," growled Promi, struggling without success to break free from the vaporstone net.

"Or mine," added Kermi—though his voice sounded muffled because his contortions to escape the net had stuffed a good portion of his tail into his mouth. And his struggles had only jammed the tail in deeper.

Grukarr's face, still as pallid as ever but with the silvery sheen of people in the spirit realm, flushed with anger. Yet his voice remained calm as he replied, "Whatever I say is so."

Studying his prisoners, he stepped closer, his bootsteps echoing in the metal hold of the flying machine. Meanwhile, the hooded crew continued to monitor and adjust the gadgets, screens, and dials that covered the walls of the hold. Outside, visible through the round portals, the leathery wings beat relentlessly, making a harsh creaking sound that sometimes rose to a shriek.

Savoring the sight of his helpless prisoners, Grukarr chortled with satisfaction. "How lovely you are so surprised to see me! I did not enjoy dying, mind you. But that experience will never come again, now that I am an immortal spirit."

He took another step closer so that he stood right in front of Promi. "I suppose," he said while stroking his chin, "that I ought to *thank* you for killing my mortal self. Otherwise, none of this glorious new adventure would be possible."

Without warning, he kicked Promi hard in the ribs. As the young man convulsed in pain under the net, the former priest smiled. "There. You have now been thanked."

Grukarr glanced out the nearest portal in time to see the pair of wrathful mistwraiths departing. "Too bad for you, shadowy ones. This prize was never meant to be yours."

Promi stiffened. Ignoring the throbbing of his ribs, he asked, "You mean this was all a trap?"

Grukarr whistled some more of the jaunty tune, taking his time before answering. Playful notes tumbled forth, reverberating in the ship's hold.

At last, Grukarr said, "The trap was perfectly executed, I might add. I guessed you would start your search for your sister—Jaladay, is that her name?—on the spot where she'd been captured. The fact that those mistwraiths were also in the area played right into my plans. And tracking them wasn't difficult. Alas . . . they are the only ones to be disappointed by the outcome."

He stroked his chin again. "But I can assure you, their frustrations are greatly outweighed by the pleasure that my master will take in your demise."

Grukarr's voice lowered. "You see . . . death doesn't come easily to an immortal. But it does come—oh yes, it most certainly does!"

He glared at Promi. "And my master has ways of ensuring that you experience both agony and death."

He licked his lips, as if he was just about to eat a tasty treat. "First, though, I have some *presents* to give you—presents I've been saving for just this occasion."

"I'm surprised Narkazan took you back again," growled Promi. "After how badly you botched his plans for the Starstone and the invasion."

"Some people never learn," said Kermi in his muffled voice.

Grukarr scowled. "Narkazan knows that I am more ready than ever to serve him. And to torment *you*.

"Six! Eleven!" barked Grukarr. Two of the hooded men snapped to attention and faced him, while the rest of the crew continued with their tasks. "Ready the hatch—but don't open it until I command."

Spinning around, he called to another pair of men. "Number five! And you—nine!" Like the others, the men jumped to attention. From under their hoods, they watched their captain with full concentration.

Grukarr waved at a vaporstone crate beside his chair. "Fetch the blades," he ordered. "Attach them now."

Under the net, the prisoners exchanged glances. *Whatever he's planning*, thought Promi, *we're not going to like it.*

Kermi's eyes grew even bigger than usual as he saw the men pull from the crate a long line of rope fitted with daggerlike blades. *That's obvious, you idiot! So what are you going to do to get us out of here?*

Promi's mind raced, searching for an answer. Yet none came to him. He wriggled, trying to grab his knife from its sheath, but the net held him too tight to budge. And there wasn't anything nearby—not a single stray tool or weapon—he might be able to use.

Meanwhile, the first pair of men twisted a large valve and raised several levers. The dark outline of a hatch appeared on the floor, ringed with tiny silver lights. In unison, the men marched over and stood on either side of the hatch.

But Promi and Kermi weren't watching. Their attention remained focused on the deadly blades. The men carefully stretched out the line on the floor so the blades, hundreds of them, lay flat, gleaming dangerously.

"Now," ordered Grukarr, "apply the treatment. Don't forget your gloves, you vermin!"

Donning heavy gloves, the men lifted a small black bottle from the crate. Carefully, they carried the bottle over to the blades, opened it, and affixed a pointed top. Kneeling over the blades, they prepared to pour whatever potion the bottle held.

"Just one drop for each blade," snarled Grukarr. Turning to the captives under the net, he added, "That is all it takes for endless misery."

He glared at Promi. "When this potion touches your skin, it will boil and bubble. That's right—your skin will melt away! Not all at once, mind you. What fun would that be? No, all this will happen with agonizing slowness."

Promi tried to show no emotion, determined to deny the priest any more satisfaction. But his heart was galloping. And the skin on his chest started to prickle with heat, something that happened only when he felt most afraid.

"But that," continued Grukarr, "is truly *mild* compared to what will happen when it enters your bloodstream." He grinned wickedly. "That is when you will wish you'd never been alive."

Though he kept his face expressionless, Promi's chest grew hotter. The mark over his heart felt ready to burst into flames.

Grukarr turned to watch as the men applied one drop of the black potion to each blade. At the instant each drop fell, that blade would start to hiss and sizzle noisily. As the men finished, they delicately closed the bottle and returned it to the crate.

At a nod from their captain, the gloved men clasped each end of the line and started to drag it over to the prisoners in the net. Slowly, they wrapped the still-sizzling blades around the captives, making sure that many gleaming edges were very close to touching Promi and Kermi—who stayed utterly still, barely breathing.

It took several wraps to use the whole line. All the while, Grukarr watched intently, humming a merry folk song he'd learned as a youth. Finally the men finished, secured the ends, and backed away.

"Good," declared Grukarr. "All we need now is a bit of motion. Just to stir things up." He nodded to the men standing by the hatch.

Immediately, one of them pushed a button on the nearest console. A whirring sound erupted—followed by a sudden gush of air as the hatch opened. The men stepped back so they wouldn't be sucked outside.

"At last," declared Grukarr, raising his voice to be heard above the din of air rushing outside the hatch. "The time has arrived."

Facing the prisoners, he smirked. "I will enjoy what happens next. You, however, will not."

Then, to the crew, he commanded, "Hook them up! And you, number seven—engage the winch."

The men scurried about the hold. Several of them carried sturdy hooks attached to ropes that led to a massive winch on the ceiling. They connected the hooks to the net holding Promi and Kermi, being very careful not to touch the poisonous blades.

Meanwhile, man number seven flicked several switches and engaged the winch. A blue light started to flash. Satisfied, the man turned his hooded face toward his leader, awaiting the next command.

"Now," Grukarr explained to his prisoners, "is the moment I have long desired. You will be dragged over to the hatch. If the process is a bit uncomfortable, I do humbly apologize."

"Nothing about you is humble," said Promi through gritted teeth. He wanted so badly to leap up and pummel this madman—but he couldn't move even a little bit without touching the blades.

Grukarr glared at him. "Soon you will know only one thing—unending agony! For I will throw you outside the ship, where you will slam and bounce against the hull for the rest of this night as we fly to Narkazan's lair. Blades will slice you, poison will devour you. And then, whatever remains of you and your furry pet, my master will give you his most special welcome."

Kermi growled angrily—not just to hear about the painful torture to come, but to have been called someone's pet. The very idea!

Triumphant, Grukarr strode over to the hatch. Positioning himself right next to it so that he could see out the opening—and, he hoped, hear every scream of terror—he chortled. Then he turned his head toward the man at the winch controls, who was standing just behind him.

"Proceed," Grukarr commanded.

CHAPTER 23

# Dark Waves

s Grukarr's command rang out, man number seven nodded eagerly. Though he was much shorter than his captain, he drew himself up to his full height to show how proud he felt about what he was going to do.

Standing by the open hatch, Grukarr smirked. He watched triumphantly as the man reached his hand toward the winch controls.

*I have waited so long and suffered so much for this,* thought the former priest. His eyes darkened like a stormy sky. *Now it's their turn to suffer.*

Grukarr turned around to view the prisoners, helpless under the net. No matter how many times he had envisioned this scene, the reality was going to be better. Much better.

Promi and Kermi glared at him. Though

they couldn't do anything to prevent the horrible torture awaiting them, they could at least deny their enemy any show of fear. Yet both of them knew they'd soon plunge into the worst misery they'd ever known. Promi's whole chest prickled with heat.

Then man number seven, standing behind Grukarr, did something unexpected. He pulled back the hand that was reaching for the controls—and suddenly charged at Grukarr, hurling the full weight of his body into his leader's back! Both of them tumbled to the edge of the hatch.

"What—?" bellowed Grukarr. Purple with rage, he caught himself just before falling through the opening.

With one hand, he grabbed the throat of his assailant. The man's hood fell back, revealing a white-haired man with a kindly face—a face that Grukarr had never expected to see again.

Promi gasped, just as surprised as Grukarr. If not for the poisonous blades surrounding him, he would have leaned forward to make sure his eyes hadn't deceived him.

*Bonlo!* He blinked, astonished by the sight of the old monk who had taught him so much in the terrible dungeon of Ekh Raku. And who had given his life to save Promi's.

"You!" shouted Grukarr, glaring at the elderly monk. "How dare you come here?"

The monk's eyes gleamed. Through his constricted throat, he said, "Did you really think an ogre like you could get to the spirit realm, but not me?"

"Why you mutinous, dastardly old fool!" Grukarr's free hand reached into the folds of his robe and pulled out a dagger. "You deserve to—"

Bonlo kicked with all his might, landing his boot right in Grukarr's crotch. The big man howled and doubled over, dropping his dagger. Bonlo jumped on his foe, even as he shouted, "Now, men!"

Immediately, three or four of the hooded men pounced on the

others, pulling them away from their controls. Two more men, meanwhile, donned heavy gloves and set to work freeing Promi and Kermi from the deadly blades wrapped around the net. But with no more crew flying the ship, the whole craft started to twist and spin—even as it veered down toward the roiling sea below. Vaporstone panels bent and buckled from the increased forces, while mechanical parts screamed.

"Hurry!" cried Promi as the men tried desperately to remove the blades.

Yet such intricate work couldn't be rushed. The men did their best to untangle the prisoners, but progress was slow—too slow. The ship was spinning out of control!

Then, to make matter's worse, one of Grukarr's loyal crew leaped at a man helping the prisoners. They fought brutally, slamming each other with blows. Kermi managed to stretch out his tail and smack that attacker in the eye—but the fight continued.

All the while, Grukarr and Bonlo wrestled on the floor, both groping for the dagger. Locked together, they rolled perilously close to the hatch. Grukarr was just about to grasp the weapon when the ship reeled, sending them both careening into a wall.

Finally clasping the dagger, Grukarr roared with rage. He leaped on Bonlo and waved the blade in his face. "Maybe I can't kill you, now that you're immortal. But I can certainly cut out your tongue, your eyes, and more! And if I can cause you enough pain . . . then perhaps you'll meet your true death."

Outside, one of the mechanical wings suddenly broke off. The ship lurched, spinning faster and faster as it dived toward the ocean. Grukarr was thrown sideways, which gave Bonlo a chance to wriggle free. But the wrathful servant of Narkazan stumbled after him, brandishing the weapon.

One of Grukarr's men, thrown backward by a blow, slammed

into the wall of levers and buttons that controlled the winch. He slumped to the floor, unconscious. But the impact had started the winch. Its gears grinded, then the winch started pulling the ropes attached to the prisoners' net.

Finally able to move one arm, Promi tried to extract himself without touching any of the blades that sizzled with poison. All at once, a sharp tug pulled on the net, nearly knocking his face into a mass of blades. The winch! Pulling the ropes!

All around the hold, people fought desperately. Grukarr, blind to anything but revenge, charged Bonlo. The ropes from the winch tightened, only seconds from dragging the net to the open hatch— with Promi and Kermi certain to be sliced. At the same time, the flying ship reeled and spun, plummeting toward the sea.

Just as the ropes fully tightened, Kermi broke free of the net. Like a bolt of blue lightning, he sprang over to the controls. Madly, he pounded every button in sight. The winch halted abruptly.

One of the buttons he'd pushed, though, turned out the lights. The furious battle continued—but in total darkness.

"Turn them back on!" shouted Promi. "I can't get out without some light!"

Kermi's ears swiveled in confusion. Which buttons should he push? With no time to decide, he hit them all.

The lights came back on. So did the winch. Relentlessly, it started to pull the ropes again.

Promi, meanwhile, could move enough now to reach his knife. He grabbed the hilt and started slicing through the vaporstone net. The blade flashed as it severed his bonds—but other blades, hissing with poison, also flashed all around him.

The remaining wing broke off. Now the ship plunged downward with even more speed, only heartbeats from crashing into the dark, brooding waters below.

"Got you!" crowed Grukarr. Seizing Bonlo by the shoulder, he locked gazes with his old teacher. "You've spoiled my plans for the last time!"

Grukarr thrust his dagger at the old monk's chest. At the same instant, someone plowed into Grukarr, sending him flying. Bonlo twisted to see the face of his rescuer. Promi!

Grukarr stumbled backward. He, too, saw Promi and released a vengeful roar. His eyes practically blazed with wrath. Then, without warning, he stepped right into the open hatch.

The roar morphed into a terrified scream as Grukarr plunged through the hatch. Promi watched him vanish, then crawled back over to Bonlo.

The old monk tried to rise—but groaned and fell back. His grateful expression suddenly turned grim. For he felt Grukarr's dagger embedded in his heart. Blood poured from the wound, soaking his robe.

Promi kneeled beside his old friend. Seeing Bonlo's wound, he cringed.

"Don't worry, lad," said the old monk weakly. "It was worth everything to see that look on his face just now!"

"That was nothing compared to his look when you first plowed into him." Promi tried to grin. "And when you kicked him where it hurts."

Bonlo brightened a bit. "Every monk should have martial arts training, you know." He winced at the pain in his chest. "Even if it hurts."

Suddenly grim, Promi asked, "What happens to you now? If your spirit body perishes and can't be renewed?"

"Don't know, lad." He coughed painfully. "I've never before died . . . after I already died!"

Bonlo coughed once more, this time spitting blood. "But you, good lad," he said with difficulty, "you *must* survive."

"I don't want to lose you again, Bonlo."

The white-haired monk gazed up at him. "I knew when I first met you, lad . . . there was something special . . . about you. That you were destined for . . . great deeds."

With a voice so weak Promi could barely hear, Bonlo added, "And lad . . . you still are."

Even through his misty eyes, Promi couldn't miss the love in the elder's expression. He held Bonlo close, so that their faces touched.

"Er, manfool," said Kermi, tapping Promi on the shoulder. "If you'd like to get off before we crash into that ocean, you'd better—"

Before he could finish, Promi scooped Bonlo into his arms and staggered over to the hatch. Kermi jumped onto the young man's shoulder just as he leaped.

A fraction of a second later, the ship smashed into the churning waves, exploding into thousands of pieces. Broken vaporstone panels, gadgets, wheels, glass, and bodies rained down on the sea. Everything from the ship disappeared into the depths.

Including Promi and his friends. No sign of them remained. Meanwhile, as if nothing had happened, the dark waves rolled on and on.

CHAPTER 24

# Darkness

In the deep darkness of her prison cell, Jaladay tried to keep exercising her mind. To keep it from being deadened by the oppressive blindness that weighed on her so heavily. That wasn't easy, given the sudden waves of panic she kept feeling, waves so powerful they wiped out any other thoughts and soaked her robe with sweat.

*Narkazan may have robbed me of my sight,* she reminded herself often. *But I can still use whatever senses I have left.*

Touch, for one. She could feel the cold, smooth vaporstone floors and walls of her cell. She'd even found subtle indentations, swirls, and notches in the stone. She tried to memorize them, assembling them into patterns. Not because that information could ever be useful—but because the activity might keep her from losing her mind completely.

Every once in a while, she caught the scent of something new—such as a crumb left on the floor from a meal that had been slid through the slot in the door. But those meals of tasteless, chalklike cake and water didn't have much scent. They served only one purpose: to keep her alive until the warlord was finished with her.

No, the main thing she could smell was her own urine and excrement in the corner. She hated that smell so much, it made her want to retch. But she couldn't do anything about it.

Hearing was her only other remaining sense. Yet she didn't have much chance to use it. On rare occasions, she heard Narkazan ranting in the room outside her cell. But none of his rants told her anything remotely useful.

Beyond that . . . all she could hear were the echoes of her own thoughts. And too often, her own panic.

How many days had she been imprisoned? She'd lost count. At least ten, she guessed. Though the days and nights—impossible to separate in this endless darkness—had begun to blend into one another.

Over and over, she asked herself the same questions. How much longer could she survive? Would anybody ever find her? Was there any way to warn her parents of Narkazan's plans for conquest of both the spirit and mortal realms?

And two more questions, as well. She was thinking of them right now while she sat in total darkness, twirling a strand of hair with her fingers. *Did Kermi deliver her warning about the Greek ship to her brother? And would Promi have the wisdom to heed it?*

Somberly, she gazed into the darkness of the cell—all the more impenetrable because she couldn't use her second sight. *I'm blind, totally blind!*

By itself, blindness was challenging enough. Even worse, though, was what it did to her mind. *My world is so much smaller, tighter. Closing all around me.*

Using her sleeve, she wiped some beads of sweat off her brow. Would she ever see, truly see, again? Ever touch the face of someone she loved? Ever—

The sound of a bolt being slid interrupted her thoughts. Then a line of light appeared in the opposite wall. The door!

She crawled eagerly toward the door. Her heart leaped to see the line of light joined by perpendicular lines. *It's opening!* she rejoiced.

Just as she reached the wall—the door slammed shut. The heavy bolt slid again. All the light disappeared.

"No!" cried Jaladay.

On her knees by the door, she beat on it with her fists. She kept pounding, even though her hands hurt and she could hear, through the narrow food slot, Narkazan and his henchmen laughing on the other side.

Finally, she slumped against the door—trapped, helpless, and alone. She hung her head and sobbed.

More days of quiet misery followed. Except for the moments when the tray of food came or went, there was no interruption. No answers to her questions. And no hope.

Then, one day, without warning, the door opened again. And this time, it wasn't a tease: the door swung wide, filling the cell with light.

Jaladay shouted in surprise. She rose and stumbled toward it, hoping to get through before it closed again. The pain in her eyes from such a sudden burst of light, the ache in her stiff limbs and neck—none of that mattered. She was getting out!

She stepped into Narkazan's chamber, blinking in the light. Right in front of her sat Narkazan in his vaporthread chair. He was flanked by mistwraiths, three on each side. As before, the windows revealed nothing but dense, icicle-shaped clouds.

The warlord leaned forward and jutted his narrow chin. His

fiery red eyes studied her intently, as his fingers drummed one of his tusks.

"How nice to see you again, my jewel," he snarled. "Though you look terrible. And smell worse."

He gave her a thin predator's smile. "Are your accommodations to your liking?"

Jaladay replied with a murderous look.

"Good. I am glad." Straightening in his chair, he pointed to a pile of scrolls on the metal chest beside his cot. "Do you know what those are, my treasure?"

Without needing to use her second sight, she guessed, "Maps? Battle plans?"

"Very good." Narkazan stroked his tusk. "I am nearly ready to commence my war of glory. All my preparations are coming together nicely. In a few more days, the conquest will begin!"

As if applauding, the mistwraiths crackled in unison. Their dark folds rippled with pleasure, casting black sparks onto the floor.

"Yes, yes," their master told them. "I know you are eager."

His voice dropped lower. "I, too, am eager! This will be my ultimate victory, my long-awaited triumph."

Tapping his narrow chin, Narkazan mused, "That reminds me. Perhaps the time has come for me to send another dream to my ally in the mortal realm. Just to *encourage* him."

At that, Jaladay raised an eyebrow. A mortal ally? Who could that be? And how does he fit into Narkazan's plan?

She continued to gaze at her captor. Not because she wanted to look at him, but because she wanted him to keep on talking, to take as long as possible with this meeting. She was savoring every second of seeing again. Of breathing clean air. Of experiencing even this small dose of freedom.

As Narkazan continued to boast about his coming conquests,

she thought desperately about what she could do to warn her parents, Kermi, Promi—anybody who could possibly try to stop this madness. But what? It was too late to save herself, she felt sure of that. Yet maybe there was some way to contact someone—maybe even to derail Narkazan's plans.

How, though? This hideaway must be somewhere obscure, far too hidden to be discovered by anyone loyal to Sammelvar and Escholia. And from such a great distance, she couldn't reach anyone she knew by sending a telepathic message.

*Wait.* She bit her lip. There might be one way! The message might not be understood. Or even intact. And it wouldn't go to any of the people she most wanted to reach, people she knew would try to help. Instead, if this plan somehow worked, her message would go to—

Narkazan pounded his fist on the arm of his chair, disrupting her thoughts. Immersed in his ranting, he fortunately hadn't noticed that his prisoner had been doing anything but listening. Now, however, he'd come to his point.

"Make your choice, Jaladay! This is your last chance. Will you help me by sharing your gift of second sight?"

He leaned forward again, probing her green eyes. "Remember this, my jewel. I am offering you this one last chance to assist me. There will be no more!"

He cackled quietly. "I almost hope you will refuse, so I can proceed immediately with my plans to torture your mother, your father, and most especially your meddling brother."

He scowled, making the scars on his face darken. "But that desire is merely a personal preference. I will set it aside forever if you will help me win the war."

The mistwraiths crackled with impatience. Narkazan demanded, "Now, what is your choice?"

Jaladay drew a deep breath, and replied, "Never. I will never help you!"

Even as Narkazan roared in anger and the mistwraiths swept toward her, sparks flying, Jaladay tried to send her message. But the mistwraiths cloaked her more quickly than expected. Marshaling all her strength, she formed her thought—

But she didn't have enough time. Before she could finish, darkness descended.

CHAPTER 25

# The Machines District

During the time Promi had been in the spirit realm, much had happened. He'd flown with Theosor, met with his parents, witnessed the mist fire, visited the cloudfield where Jaladay disappeared, tried to escape the mistwraiths, been captured by Grukarr and then—thanks to Bonlo—gained at least a chance to survive before plunging into a remote spirit realm sea.

Yet during that same time, much more had happened on the isle of Atlantis. For time moved faster in the mortal world—occasionally much faster. In this case, by the time Promi splashed into that sea with Bonlo in his arms, a full five years had passed on Atlantis.

In those five years since the ship of Greek

explorers had landed, some things hadn't changed. The City's market square continued to bustle with throngs of tradespeople, entertainers, makers of crafts, willing buyers, and all kinds of animals. The Divine Monk continued to celebrate religious festivals and feasts (especially the feasts). In his pastry shop, Morey continued to bake delicious treats just because he loved to do so, Shangri helped him for the same reason, and the lad from the ship still lived in the room upstairs.

Much more, though, had changed. Nothing showed that more dramatically than the graceful, bright-spirited young woman with flowing red hair who strode out of the pastry shop this morning. In her hands she carried a still-steaming rhubarb and cherry pie. Just as she stepped into the street, she glanced at the room upstairs whose window was wide open to the spring air.

Shangri grinned. *He's writin' right now,* she told herself. *I'm sure of it.*

More and more these days, her thoughts turned to that handsome young man upstairs. He still dreamed of becoming a famous bard, though he had yet to discover the story that would inspire his very best writing—what he continued to call his "one great story."

Today, however, her thoughts moved to someone else—someone she hadn't seen for five whole years. Even so, the memory of their last conversation seemed as fresh as if it had happened just yesterday.

Promi.

*Where is he now?* she wondered, though she felt sure he was somewhere in the spirit realm. Recalling what he'd told her about how time moved slower there, she guessed that he might feel that he'd left only recently. But for Shangri, it was a long time ago.

Yet she remembered the details of everything he had told her that day on the cliffs above the sea. The origins of Atlantis. The description of the spirit realm—especially its sweet rivers of honey. The way prayers from mortals could travel all the way to that far-away world, thanks to wind lions.

And most of all . . . the way he spoke about Atlanta. While Shangri remembered all the words he'd said about her, what she'd noticed most was that look in his eyes. A look so full of love.

A bit of hot cherry juice dripped onto her hand, jolting her back to the present. *No more dallyin',* she told herself. *I've got a pie to deliver before it's stone cold!*

Her well-worn sandals tapped the cobblestones as she walked toward the market square. But when she came to the alley she'd taken countless times to the square, she didn't turn. Instead, she just kept going and turned down a completely different street—one that led into the heart of the City's newest neighborhood, what most people called the Machines District.

As someone who had always been observant of people and her surroundings, Shangri's sharp eyes didn't miss much. She had certainly noticed how much the City had changed in the last several years. Especially in this neighborhood where the Greeks lived and worked.

Led by Reocoles, their ship's captain, they called themselves *the people delivered by Poseidon.* And they'd brought with them many new words and songs, ceremonies and skills. They even had their own array of gods and goddesses who lived in a part of the spirit realm they called Mount Olympus. But the most striking thing they'd brought to Atlantis was a great industriousness that produced all sorts of new machines—machines that had already changed everyone's lives.

Plumbing, for one. Every street in the City now had ducts and drains like the gleaming copper duct that ran beside Shangri, bubbling with water, at this very moment. Not to mention all the pipes that ran up the mud-brick walls into every home and storefront and stable, carrying water in and out. Cisterns, fed by pumps from the ducts, sat on the roofs of most buildings. So did little windmills that turned the frequent ocean breezes into power for the pumps.

Even more amazing, coal-fired boilers now sat on the roofs of homes belonging to the wealthiest merchants, as well as the Divine Monk. Their purpose? According to the rumors Shangri had heard—which seemed utterly impossible—those boilers made hot water available to everyone in the homes. *At any time.* So whenever the Divine Monk wanted a hot bath, all he needed to do was turn a valve and hot water flowed automatically into his tub!

Shangri shook her flowing red curls, sending up a puff of flour from her morning's work at the bakery. *That jest can't be true,* she told herself. *Though I've seen a few other things happen I never s'posed could be true.*

Like modern, coal-fired cookstoves that allowed some people to make three or four times the amount of pastries that her father could produce with his old one. And without any wood chopping needed. Sure, those stoves made the City's air more smoky and sometimes got so hot they caused fires . . . but most people didn't seem to mind.

Or like other examples she could think of easily. The tall torch lamps that now illuminated almost every street corner after dark. The machines (whose gears she could hear whirring and cranking in the building she was passing right now) that made new, cheaper tools for carpenters and blacksmiths, as well as parts for more machines. The strange new medicines, made by something called *chemistry,* which were starting to appear on apothecaries' shelves. The big vehicles with such screechy wheels that carried up to ten cartloads of wood, rocks, or coal—as well as the heavy boiler to make those wheels turn. And the much bigger vehicles used for mining all the coal needed to power so many machines.

Those mining vehicles stood so large they never came into the City. Like buildings on wheels, they moved very slowly and only came to the City's gates, where men unloaded the coal and moved it to vehicles that could fit on the streets. Most people didn't even know those mining machines existed. It was only last month, when Shangri decided to take a stroll outside the gates, that she'd seen one being unloaded. And the sight of such a huge, lumbering contraption had made her jaw drop.

As Shangri walked through the streets of the Machines District, she couldn't help but notice how busy everyone looked. Yet . . . their bustling seemed strangely different from when her father was busily making his latest pie or cake creation. No, these people seemed busy in an unsatisfied way, as if they were carrying invisible loads on their backs, loads they didn't like carrying.

On top of that, everyone here scurried about as if they were late for an important meeting. No one stopped to chat or even say hello. They just kept walking as fast as they could to wherever they were going, their minds elsewhere.

The most uncomfortable part of this neighborhood, though, was simply the air. Fumes from all the machines and vehicles hung in the high, narrow streets. Shangri's throat itched and her eyes watered. Around her on the streets, some people held kerchiefs over their mouths as they moved along.

Suddenly a pair of men hurried out from a door and knocked into Shangri. She barely managed to keep herself from dropping the rhubarb cherry pie. But the ceramic bowl of whipped cream she'd also been carrying smashed on the cobblestones, breaking into shards. Neither of the men paused to apologize.

She took a deep breath to calm herself—but inhaled so much of the fume-filled air, her throat burned. Slowly, she continued on her way. But now she watched every door carefully before she passed and tried to walk in the least crowded places she could find.

Of course, on some stretches she couldn't avoid the crowds, especially if one or more of those screechy-wheeled vehicles went hurrying past.

Finally, she saw a new building, larger than any others on the street. Three big chimneys belched black smoke from its roof. From the roof's peak waved a flag with a blue dolphin, the same design as the sail of the doomed ship. The whole building, covered in plaster, looked like it had been painted just recently. It shone pearl white except for the shadowy smudges of coal dust under the chimneys.

Shangri strode up to the building and read the copper nameplate:

## REOCOLES

## MASTER MACHINIST

Balancing the fruit pie on one open hand, she lifted the heavy knocker shaped like a trident. It slammed down, though Shangri wasn't sure how anyone inside could hear it above the street noise. But a few seconds later, the door opened.

# CHAPTER 26

# Nature's Bounty

A big, broad-shouldered man opened the door for Shangri. Wearing a brown tunic with sea blue arm bands and Greek symbols on the shoulders, he looked like a soldier in uniform—but not a uniform she'd seen before. He nodded, then turned to a heavyset, gray-haired man who was seated in the middle of several machines that filled the wide room.

In a voice loud enough to be heard above the clatter and squeal of the machines, he announced, "Master, the girl with the pie is here."

Right away, the heavyset man looked up from a table covered with machine parts where he was working. Putting aside a large gear and some sort of tool he was holding, he stood up and wiped his grimy hands on his apron—a rather wide one, given the size of his waist.

Shangri noticed that it resembled the aprons worn by her father and other bakers. Yet this one had lots more pockets and smudges from grease instead of fruit preserves and flour.

The man approached Shangri, walking with a pronounced limp that made him wobble like a misshapen gear. He smiled in greeting. "Welcome, my dear. I am Reocoles. And you are?"

"Shangri, daughter o'—"

"The most famous baker in the City," finished Reocoles. "A pleasure to welcome you, Shangri! As well as the pie I ordered."

With a glance at the uniformed man, he said, "Take this delicious-looking pie from the young lady and set it over there."

Nodding obediently, the man carried the rhubarb and cherry pie over to a table nearby. That table, unlike the other ones in the room, didn't hold any machine parts or other gadgets. Instead, the only thing on it was a large map. It looked to Shangri like a map of a forest, maybe the Great Forest outside the City. Yet . . . unlike the Great Forest, this one was crisscrossed by dozens of roads and bridges.

"I am delighted you came," continued Reocoles. "Having heard a great deal about your father's fruit pies, I decided to have one delivered. But I never expected it to be brought by such a lovely young woman."

Shangri blushed, her cheeks only slightly less red than her hair.

"Come," said Reocoles, extending his arm to her. "Let me give you a tour of my humble workshop."

Guiding her away from the table with the map, he brought her to a large brown lever that protruded from the wall. He grabbed the lever with both hands and pulled it down. Immediately, all the whirring and clattering ceased as the machines stopped.

"There," he said with a sigh, "it's quiet enough to talk." Without much feeling, like a bard saying a line that's been rehearsed too many times, he added, "I do so enjoy the quiet."

He pointed to a huge bellows beside the largest furnace Shangri had ever seen. "One of my earliest inventions, that bellows. It keeps my fires hotter for longer periods, which helps me mix the metals I need."

Sweeping his arm around that part of the room, he said, "See those shelves up to the ceiling? Various ores I use for different purposes. And there, next to the bellows, my area devoted to making stronger, lighter tools and weapons."

Creasing her brow, Shangri wondered, "Weapons? Fer what?"

"Oh," he replied, guiding her over to another part of the room. "You never know. Just in theory. What I meant to say was those are all experimental devices."

He stopped by a table arrayed with pieces of glass, as well as quartz crystals, plus half a dozen tools for cutting and polishing. Picking up a concave crystal, he handed it to her. "Can you guess, my dear, what that is for?"

Shangri felt the crystal's smooth edges and flat surface. "Not sure." Then, on a whim, she held it up to her eye. She caught her breath. "Bigger. Everythin's bigger!"

"Good for you, bright one. It's called a lens, capable of magnifying whatever you want to see."

"Amazin'!" Shangri looked around the room, seeing how the lens made all the machinery seem closer. Then, as her gaze fell on the table with the map, she froze. For she could plainly see, written on the map's bottom edge, the words *Great Forest Plan*.

Then she saw something even more strange. Under those words, in smaller lettering, was the phrase *Resources for the Empire*.

*What resources?* she wondered. *And what empire?*

"Right you are," said the master machinist. "Modern science is truly amazing."

Deftly, he snatched away the lens and put it back on the table. "This particular lens is going to be for a device called a telescope—something I can use to gaze up at the stars."

*But how,* wondered Shangri, *will ye be able to see them through all the smoke?*

"Now look over there." Reocoles pointed to a long table where two more men were working with slabs of metal and glass. "They are working on a different set of projects."

Shangri noticed that both men wore the same sort of uniform as the man who had let her in. That man, she also saw, had returned to his position by the door, standing as straight as one of the axle rods piled beside him. Why, she wondered, were uniforms needed at all?

"They are making," continued Reocoles, "the prototypes for more, shall we say, *futuristic* devices."

"Like what?"

"Like a new kind of torch lamp that won't need to be soaked in oil every day to burn through the night." Seeing Shangri's surprise, Reocoles explained proudly, "It will burn instead from a kind of gas I've been developing in my laboratory across the street. Gas that will someday be piped to every lamp on every street corner. And perhaps, into people's homes."

The inventor paused to chuckle. "Of course, such an amazing service would be expensive . . . as well as profitable."

"What's that?" asked Shangri, pointing at a complex mass of gears strapped together with wires and rods.

"That," he answered proudly, "is my astrolocator—a device to predict the motions of stars. It still needs a lot of work, but one day I will be able to tell you exactly when there will be a lunar or solar eclipse."

Gesturing at the workmen, he went on, "And I'm also developing an entirely new kind of game! Yes—a game that can be played by just one person."

Shangri cocked her head in puzzlement. "But games are meant fer *sharin'*. People come together jest to play them."

"Sure," said Reocoles with a gleam in his eye. "Yet this new game would allow you to play all by yourself if you ever chose! Why, you wouldn't need to speak to another person, or even see him, if you didn't want to. Isn't that wonderful?"

She scrunched her nose, not sure that was the word she would have used.

"Come see another marvel." Reocoles led her over to a table next to the far wall. As before, he limped badly. Shangri glanced down and saw that he wore an elaborate metal brace around his left leg, complete with a set of gears at the knee.

"You will be impressed by this," the inventor boasted. Waving at the table, he added, "My most ambitious project."

To Shangri's surprise, the table displayed at least twenty squares of grassy turf. On some of them, the grass looked green and vital; on others, yellow and withered—or completely dead. More perplexing still, one side of the table held a row of glass jars that looked a lot like her father's jars of baking spices, flour, and sugar. These ones, though, held very different items. They were crammed full of insects, ranging from tiny aphids to enormous grasshoppers.

"What," she asked, "is this?"

He beamed. "I'm developing something called pesticides and herbicides. So that farms and vineyards won't be invaded by unwanted insects and weeds. That way farmers can produce more. *If* they are lucky enough to have my products, that is."

"Wait," protested Shangri. "If those poisons kill the insects who eat the plants, don't ye s'pose they could also hurt the people who eat them?"

"Nonsense. These methods are perfectly safe."

"But how can ye know that?" Shangri shook her head. "Seems to me, people should leave nature alone, at least till they're sure that messin' with nature won't do somethin' bad."

Reocoles frowned. "Here, my dear. Let me show you something."

He led her over to a most unusual object—a large wooden wheel studded with knobs. Mounted on a pedestal by the building's largest window, the wheel glistened with flecks of white sea salt.

"The wheel from yer ship," said Shangri, amazed.

"That's right." Reocoles placed his hand on the wheel, gently touching its knobs like the face of an old friend. "My captain's wheel."

He pointed to a chipped brass plate affixed to the pedestal. Though the letters inscribed on the plate were Greek, Shangri looked at them with fascination:

## τον έλεγχο της φύσης

"The name of my ship," Reocoles explained. "It means '*the Control of Nature.*' For that is the highest and best use of the gifts we humans got long ago from Zeus, the king of our gods, as well as Hephaestus."

Confused, Shangri asked, "As well as who?"

"Hephaestus, the most clever god of them all—the god of making crafts, machines, and inventions."

She nodded. "Ye admire him 'specially, I see."

"True, my dear." He patted his leg brace. "Like me, Hephaestus was lame, though in my case it happened at birth and in his, when he fell off Mount Olympus."

He straightened his back. "Both of us overcame our difficulties through ingenuity and hard work. And both of us learned how to use nature for the benefit of others."

Leaning toward Shangri, he said, "That is why our ship's motto was the same as my own: 'to find nature's bounty and make use of it all.'"

Though she'd heard that phrase before, it had never given her the same pause as it did this time. But she said nothing.

"Poseidon, our god of the sea, saved my life and the lives of my shipmates for a reason," he declared.

*Poseidon didn't save you,* thought Shangri. *Promi did.*

"And that reason," he continued, "should be obvious to you now. So I could bring benefits untold and a richer life to you and all the people of Atlantis!"

"Ye sound like yer the king o' this island."

"No," he replied with a smirk, "though I could be if I chose. I am content to be just a humble craftsman. But mark my words: I can do anything I want on this island. And one day, perhaps, beyond."

A chuckle bubbled from his throat. "As long as the Divine Monk gets enough hot water for his baths, that is."

Her heart pounding, Shangri objected, "Yer motto sounds like everythin' about nature is here jest fer us humans—that the land an' trees an' all the other creatures are jest here to serve us."

"Well, they are."

"No! Every creature deserves our respect. They've jest as much right to live an' breathe an' survive as we do."

Reocoles clucked his tongue. "So naïve, my dear. Humans know what is best! And everything in nature matters only in relation to how it helps us or hurts us."

Shangri's face reddened, though this time it wasn't from blushing. But before she could reply, the master machinist spoke again.

"Here I am, babbling like an old fool! Please forgive me. Why, I haven't even shown you what I most wanted you to see."

Despite his ungainly limp, he set off briskly toward the other end of the room. With a last glance at the ship's wheel, Shangri followed. The master machinist led her over to a large iron contraption that she recognized right away—although it was far bigger than any other she'd seen.

"An oven," she said, wide-eyed. "An' a thumpin' big one."

"That's right, my dear. Did you know this stove can bake up to six times as many pies or cakes or loaves of bread as the old one your father uses now?"

"No."

"And that the first baker I convinced to buy one tripled his business overnight?"

"No."

"And yet," said Reocoles, scratching his head in puzzlement, "your father has refused to buy one from me."

"Well, he jest *likes* his old oven. They've worked together fer a long time, like a couple o' friends."

"How sweet," said Reocoles. "But wholly impractical. If anyone deserves to have one of my new ovens, it's your father, the most admired baker in the whole City of Great Powers. Why, if he got one, he'd be eternally grateful."

Shangri's eyes narrowed. "What ye really mean to say is, if he got one . . . ye'd sell a lot more to other bakers."

Reocoles gave her a wink. "You are just as smart as you are pretty." He stepped closer and put his hand on her shoulder. "Now, won't you help me convince him to change his mind?"

"But I told ye, he jest doesn't want one."

"I've solved that smoke problem," said Reocoles, speaking fast. "Now I provide a pipe that takes it all outside."

She backed away. "He *doesn't* want one, do ye hear?"

"What if I gave him one for a whole year free of charge? Just as a gesture of friendship."

Shangri clenched her jaw, then said, "Yer not actin' out o' friendship. Yer actin' out o' *greed*."

Reocoles made a sound like a rumbling furnace. "Show her out," he commanded the man by the door. "Never let her in here again. And spread the word to watch for her in case she tries to cause any trouble."

# CHAPTER 27

# To Be a Bard

In his room above the bakery, Lekko—his chosen name these days—wrote on a scrap of yellow-tinted paper. Though his job at the paper merchant down the street gave him a goodly supply of scraps (in exchange for half his pay), he still went through great quantities. And his room showed it: paper, crumpled or piled high, covered with writing or torn to pieces, lay everywhere.

Lekko sat in his chair by the window, scribbling with a charcoal pencil. The paper, sitting on an old book about the Divine Monk's temple on Lekko's lap, had lots more crossed-out words than legible ones. He'd been working on this page since before dawn, but several hours later he had very little to show for it.

Frustrated, he ran his fingers through his scraggly blond hair. *Getting up early to write is the easy part,* he told himself. *Especially when you live right above a bakery that starts making such fabulous smells before dawn.*

He chewed the end of the pencil. *The hard part is actually writing something decent.*

Right now the bakery smelled of fresh ginger cookies. He took a big sniff, enjoying the quiet thrill he always got from ginger in any form. And that was also true, these days, about a certain young woman with ginger-red hair.

Shangri would be back soon from her morning deliveries, he knew. In fact, she should have returned by now. Something must have delayed her.

*Probably just her love of talking with people,* he thought with a grin. He'd seen enough to know that many people ordered their pastries delivered not because they didn't like to come by Morey's shop—but because they liked chatting with Shangri even more. As Morey put it, "Who needs the sunshine when ye have the likes o' Shangri?"

Lekko put down the page and pencil. He stood up, paced across the little room, and grabbed his water jug and glass from a low table beside his sleeping pallet. Pouring himself a glass, he took it over to the window.

From this spot overlooking the street, he could watch the parade of people on the cobblestones below. Shepherds leading their flocks to the marketplace, craftsmen carrying leather goods or jewelry or woven shawls, monks beating their prayer drums while chanting in worshipful monotones, and many other slices of life passed by every day. Plenty of inspiration for writing—except he wasn't wanting to write about that.

Lifting his gaze, he looked over the rooftops to the smoky haze that always darkened a certain part of the City. The Machines District. The area where his fellow survivors from the shipwreck had settled five years ago. All except for him.

He could see, waving atop the roof of Reocoles's headquarters, the flag of the blue dolphin. Though it was often hard to see through the haze, he sometimes glimpsed one or two of his former shipmates up on that roof working on one of the master machinist's contraptions—either because that invention needed some wind to work or because there just wasn't enough room inside the building.

Lekko gazed intently at the neighborhood populated by his fellow Greeks. While he missed a few of them, the people on the ship he'd been closest to had died in the whirlpool. And he certainly didn't miss Reocoles, whose genius as an inventor was so often driven by his tyrannical urge to control everyone and everything around him.

*That lame leg of his,* guessed Lekko, *didn't just pitch him into plenty of ravines as a child. It pitched him into a life of craving power.*

Lekko took another swallow of water. The trouble was . . . Reocoles's unrelenting drive was destroying aspects of the City, as well as other people's lives. While his inventions were often beneficial as well, that destruction continued to spread like a subtle, creeping disease.

Though Lekko was only twelve years old when the ocean had miraculously spared him, he could clearly remember what the City had been like then. And see how different it was now. Torch lamps on every corner was a good improvement. So was better plumbing.

But what about the increasingly foul air that made people cough and gag? The wasted machine parts or packaging that now littered too many streets? The diminished connections between people who used to pause to greet one another but now hurried on by?

*Reocoles would say this was all nonsense,* Lekko felt certain. *Actually, he'd probably say it was heresy.*

The young man pursed his lips, thinking. *Which is why I want to write about those things. To be a bard who explores how societies can grow and change . . . yet still protect what deserves to endure.*

Wistfully, he scanned the rooftops. "Maybe," he said aloud, "that will be my one great story. The one I've been searching for all this time."

Even as he said the words, he knew that there was only one way to find out. To write! But that, he also knew well, was hard work.

*Almost as hard,* he thought with an ironic grin, *as choosing my permanent pen name.* Lekko, he felt, was close—but like so many other attempts, it wasn't quite right.

*Maybe I'll just end up going back to Lorno,* he wondered. *It's special, since that was the name I had when I first landed on Atlantis. And also on Morey's head!*

His grin widened, since that was the name Shangri still called him. She'd given up trying to keep track of whatever name he was using currently. So even if he didn't feel satisfied with that, she'd be pleased.

*And that,* he told himself, *counts for a lot.*

Footsteps! He heard someone climbing the narrow stairs up to his room. Stepping over to the door, he opened it, knowing he'd be seeing Shangri's joyful face.

It was Shangri, all right. But she certainly wasn't joyful. Her typically bright eyes were clouded; her hands that usually brought him a treat from the bakery were wringing anxiously.

"What's wrong?" he asked.

"Oh, Lorno . . ." She fell into his arms and they embraced for a long moment. Then she pulled away and shook her head, swaying her long hair across her shoulders.

"What's wrong?" he repeated.

"Everythin'! I jest came back from Reocoles's place. And what I saw makes me sick with worry fer our homes, our fellow creatures—our whole island." She drew a deep breath. "He has plans fer all o' us . . . and fer his own empire."

The young man scowled. "By the blood and bones of Zeus, it's as if our ship brought an invasion to Atlantis! We should never have been allowed to land."

She took his hand. "Don't say that. At least one person on yer ship was certainly supposed to land."

Meeting his gaze, Shangri added, "I am sure o' that. Totally sure."

# CHAPTER 28

# A Vivid Dream

eocoles was soaring, riding the winds high over Atlantis. Like a powerful hawk, he sailed through the sky, rising on the swells and circling the landscape far below.

Though he didn't have any wings or feathers, he rode the air currents with ease. His outstretched arms carried him wherever he chose. And with no need to walk upon the ground, he had left behind the clumsy metal brace for his leg.

*Flying!* he told himself giddily as the winds tousled his gray hair. *I am, for once, moving freely!*

*And I am also dreaming,* he thought lucidly. *This dream feels so real, so true . . . I am certain it must be another dream sent to me from the gods on high.*

Even as he flew into a cloud and out the other side, he smiled. *The last divine dream helped me discover this island called Atlantis—and begin my climb to greatness.* He banked a turn to the right. *What discovery, I wonder, will this new dream bring?*

Below him, he saw clearly the City of Great Powers, dominated by the Divine Monk's temple. He saw, too, the market square, the City gates—and his great accomplishment, the Machines District. Despite the layer of sooty haze that for some inexplicable reason hung over that section of the City, he couldn't miss seeing how it bustled with activity and industry.

*The true heart of this place,* he thought proudly. How these poor people ever managed to exist before his ship arrived, he could never understand.

The only irksome sight in the City was that dilapidated old bridge that the local folk had decorated with prayer leaves. Why, it didn't even go all the way across the river gorge! Just seeing the bridge annoyed him, since there couldn't be any purpose to having such a rickety, half-finished contraption.

*When I'm finished with my more pressing projects,* he reminded himself, *it's high time my men tear that bridge down and build a shiny new iron one in its place.*

He chortled, guessing that the Divine Monk might hear some resistance from the locals to this plan. In their ignorance, they seemed to be attached to such old, useless structures. *All I need to do to solve that problem,* he told himself, *is to name the new bridge after His Holiness the Divine Monk.*

Banking another turn, he flew southward across the river. Soon he was sailing toward the Great Forest, that mass of unused trees and waterways. On the open land just north of the forest, he saw with pride, was the industrial complex he'd created over the past several years. Pit mines, ditches, and roadways hummed with the business of resource extraction and refining.

Suddenly—the whole scene shifted. The industrial complex expanded, pushing across the forest's rim and deep into the thick mass of trees. As steadily as oil flowing over a body of water, the complex grew swiftly larger. Before long, instead of only a few mines, a network of dozens appeared, complete with new ditches and tailings ponds. The Great Forest, meanwhile, vanished under a maze of roads, dams, and clear-cut slopes, along with the rows of tenement houses to enable more workers to labor for longer periods.

*The future!* realized Reocoles. *Thanks to Zeus, I am being shown a glimpse of the future.*

Soaring overhead, the master machinist marveled at how completely the forest's resources were being utilized. Why, even from this altitude he could see piles of glittering gemstones that had been mined! And he also took pride in how many of the roads, bridges, construction sites, and refineries he'd already been planning to build—and which could be found on the map labeled Great Forest Plan that graced the building he humbly called his "workshop."

Yet there was much more going on in this vision of the future than he'd previously imagined. In particular, he could tell that some powerful new energy source was being extracted from the landscape. Though he couldn't tell exactly what it was, he felt certain it was not merely coal, oil, or timber. No . . . this new form of energy, being processed under large domed structures, seemed both immensely powerful and deeply mysterious.

*Just one of the many treasures that awaits my discovery,* thought Reocoles. He swooped lower, pleased at how much more of the land was now visible without the nuisance of all those trees.

Then, miraculously, he heard in his mind a voice. The voice, he felt certain, of Zeus himself.

"All this and more awaits you, Reocoles. And with this progress will come all the power you desire—as well as the empire you deserve.

"But lo," the godly voice intoned, "heed this warning! The future you have seen will come to pass *only* if you work much faster. For change is coming to your world—and you must be ready to seize every opportunity!

"Or else," the voice concluded, "you and all your works shall perish forever."

At that, Reocoles woke up. He wiped his face, drenched with perspiration, with his bedsheet. Though dawn was still several hours away, he strapped on his leg brace, dressed himself, and went straight to work.

# CHAPTER 29

# Triumph

itch me, you fools!"

At Reocoles's bellowed command, six of his uniformed aides reached for the bundle of straps connected to a thick rope. After considerable fumbling and tripping over one another, they secured the straps to their leader's waist and chest. Then, in unison, they backed away.

"Finally," he growled. "Now raise me up there so I can see."

The men started pulling on the rope, which ran through a pulley atop an observation tower, lifting Reocoles into the air. He scowled impatiently until they set him down on a wooden platform just below the top. There two more uniformed aides unfastened him.

Reocoles limped over to the railing at the platform's edge. He gazed out on his growing industrial complex. Before him stretched the vista he'd seen at the start of his recent dream—although not now, alas, from the height of a soaring hawk. While that dream had come to him over two weeks ago, its memory remained as vivid as ever.

He could see a vast network of open pit mines, ditches, piles of tailings, and buildings that spewed black fumes from their smokestacks. Directly in front of his tower sat a large waste pool that gleamed putrid yellow. Whatever toxic substances bubbled in the pool produced a stench like rotting flesh.

"Beautiful," he proclaimed.

Viewing the complex, he watched with pride as three huge mining vehicles, each the size of a house, tore at the rocks exposed in the pit mines. These machines, with jawlike scrapers protruding from their fronts, resembled giant, rock-eating beasts that constantly spouted black smoke. One of them worked at the edge of its pit, enlarging the mine by ripping out bushes and scraping away the rich brown soil.

Over the past several years, the mining complex had steadily expanded. Though still confined to the open plain north of the forest edge, the complex included three vast pits and a maze of ditches and dams, all gouged out of the land. To some, the aerial view might have looked like an open wound. But to Reocoles, it looked like a monument to human ingenuity and progress. He smiled at the sight.

Then, recalling the severe warning from Zeus he'd received at the end of his dream, the smile vanished. "As good as this is, it's not nearly enough! We must work faster and harder. We must push deep into the wasteland forest and turn it into what it can be—the hub of a new civilization. *The heart of an empire.*"

As Reocoles scanned the scene below, there was one thing he didn't notice. Though all this activity was happening near the border of the Great Forest, no birds or any other forest creatures came near. Except for one, apparently. The twisted carcass of a young bear cub lay beside the waste pool. Lured there by curiosity on a recent night, it had probably pawed the strange liquid, hoping to find a fish. Then, intrigued by the unusual smell, it must have taken a drink.

A small but plucky river, whose origins were deep in the forest, flowed out of the woods and into the complex. For countless years, it had cascaded northward to the Deg Boesi canyon, where it poured from the heights in a glittering waterfall. Locals who visited the place called it Rainbow Falls.

Today, however, not even a trickle poured from Rainbow Falls. Its entire supply of water had been dammed or diverted to help move tailings and other waste products into the pool. The river's disappearance did, in fact, annoy Reocoles—not because he felt any remorse, but because he needed more water for his expanding businesses.

"Have you done it?" barked Reocoles to his foreman who had joined him on the platform—Karpathos, who still wore a long, curled mustache. "Have you located another water source?"

Karpathos nodded. "Yes, Master. And you will be pleased to know—"

"I won't be pleased," interrupted the machinist, "until we no longer face such mundane obstacles to meeting our demands!"

Karpathos nervously pulled at one end of his mustache. "Nor will I, Master."

"So where is this new river?"

"As I was starting to say, Master, it lies only a short distance inside the forest. We found it during the expansion survey."

"Good. When can you start to build the dam and redirect its flow?"

Karpathos swallowed. "Well, er . . . Master, there is a slight problem."

Reocoles's glare could have ignited a torch.

"It's that cursed forest, Master. As you know, the survey is the first time we've actually entered there, going past the trees at the very edge."

"Get to the point, you fool!"

"Well," continued the foreman, "the trees in there are denser and taller than anyone expected, slowing our progress. And Master . . . there seems to be some uncooperative wildlife."

"What?"

"Animals, Master. Ferocious ones! They are resisting our efforts to do what needs to be done. Just yesterday, one of my men—er, sorry, *your* men—was gored by a wild boar. And our lead surveyor was attacked for no reason—by a flock of fierce little birds he likened to those fictional things called faeries."

"Zeus's thunderbolt!" cursed Reocoles. "That forest is my nemesis!"

He cast a steely eye on his foreman. "That, however, will soon change."

"How, Master?"

"The same way anything changes—through hard work and determination. As well as a good supply of weapons, tools, and machinery."

Reocoles limped over to the side of the platform nearest to the wide swath of green that stretched to the horizon. "The local urchins call it the Great Forest," he sneered, "as if it were a true place deserving a name."

Karpathos frowned. "But no one lives there."

"Correct. It's only an untamed mass of trees and whatever beasts inhabit them." Reocoles paused, gazing at the distant greenery. "And it is also something more."

"What?"

"A treasure chest," declared the leader of the Greeks. "Trust me, Karpathos! Once we cut whatever swaths are needed to open it up—to lift the lid of the chest, you might say—we will find resources beyond anyone's imagination."

He gestured at the mining pits. "Look how much coal and iron and gemstones we've already found just outside the forest. Why, I'll wager Apollo's chariot that there is more, much more, under all those trees."

Eagerly, Karpathos added, "As well as much useful timber."

"Correct. We can always use more wood." He lowered his voice. "Which someday we will use to build not just one ship, but a whole fleet of them! To trade those resources, as well as my inventions, throughout the world. And to extend the reach of what will one day be called the Empire of Atlantis."

"You will make this island rich and powerful, Master."

"Yes." He grinned slyly. "And it won't do me any harm, either."

Karpathos twirled the end of his mustache with mounting excitement. "I have also heard, Master—not from anyone reliable, mind you, just monks and other native folk—that there is also another kind of treasure to be found in those trees."

Reocoles raised an eyebrow. "What treasure is this?"

"Magic. The locals swear that—"

"Blast the locals!" said Reocoles dismissively. "There is only one kind of magic in the world. *Human ingenuity*. Yes, and only one source of that magic—the human brain."

"Of course, Master." The aide nodded anxiously. "I never meant to imply otherwise."

"Good, Karpathos." Reocoles tapped his fingers on his leg brace. "Because if I ever thought you did, I would have to demote you for such superstitions. You wouldn't want to spend the next several years working at the waste pool, would you?"

"N-n-no, Master."

"Then see that no more obstacles slow our progress. If you

meet animals, kill them. Trees, fell them. Boulders, move them. Do you understand?"

Karpathos bowed. "Yes, Master."

Glancing down at the yellow waste pool, Reocoles said, "If we are to open that new pit on schedule, and also accommodate our growing supplies of resources and the chemicals needed to process them, we will need to enlarge that holding pond. By at least three-fold, I estimate. How long will that take?"

Furrowing his brow, Karpathos calculated for a few seconds. "Six to eight months with the workers I now have."

"Too long!" fumed the machinist. "I want you to bring on more men and women—as many as you can handle. Scour the City for them! Offer them bonuses for beating your timetable. Make them taste the wealth that could be theirs if this project succeeds."

"Excellent plan, Master."

"I don't need your flattery, Karpathos. I need your success!"

"I understand." Karpathos tugged on both ends of his mustache. "We will succeed."

"No," countered Reocoles firmly. Seeing his foreman's surprise, he added, "We will *triumph*."

Quietly, the machinist added, "And our triumph will be felt across the world."

"Shall we lower you down?"

"Yes. Make it fast. I have too many projects back in the City to dally here any longer."

As the aides secured the straps, Reocoles looked gravely at the swath of trees that bordered the complex. *You shall not stand in my way,* he vowed.

Shifting his thoughts, he mused about the name he'd chosen for his ship: *The Control of Nature.* In ancient times, primitive times, those words meant that nature controlled man. But now, a new era had dawned. Thanks largely to his own superior talents!

"Soon," he muttered to the deep green forest, "it is *I* who will be in control."

Seconds later, the men lowered him down from the tower. As his feet touched the ground, he waited impatiently to be unstrapped, wobbling slightly on the uneven turf. Then he noticed one of his workers who, unlike everyone else, was not working hard at his assigned task.

No more than ten paces away, the man lay on his back in the dirt, wheezing loudly. Each breath he took was a labor. A wet rag covered his face. His hands twitched for no evident reason.

Reocoles gestured in the man's direction. "Why isn't he working?"

"Fell sick," an aide replied. "He's a digger at the waste pool. Been there several months now, but yesterday he started complaining about his head and his breathing, that sort of thing. Then this morning—he just fell over in a heap."

The aide shrugged. "Didn't want him tripping up the other diggers, so I just dragged him up here."

Reocoles scowled at the sick worker. "Weakling."

Turning to the aide, Reocoles commanded, "Put him in that supplies vehicle over there. Bring him back to town come nightfall and dump him somewhere. We don't want his bad example to spread among the others, do we?"

"No, Master."

"Good. Now get back to work."

As Reocoles limped to his waiting vehicle, one word kept echoing in his mind. It was a word that seemed closer to reality than ever before, a word that inspired him like no other.

*Triumph.*

# CHAPTER 30

# Poison

Shangri thought long and hard about what she should do after seeing Reocoles's map. The words *Great Forest Plan* alone would have been troubling enough, for all its underlying assumptions of aggression and domination of a place that had always been wild and sacred—as well as magical. But when she remembered, as well, that phrase about an empire, on top of Reocoles's penchant for control . . . she knew that she had to act.

But how?

Telling her father what she'd seen would surely spark his outrage. Yet without more hard evidence, it would simply be the word of a teenage girl against one of the City's most powerful men. And without that sort of evidence, they simply wouldn't be able to rouse the support of their fellow citizens—let alone the Divine Monk.

No, too many people (including His Holiness) were much too comfortable with their hot baths and big ovens to raise any concerns about Reocoles. They'd rather not rock the boat. Which was just what the master machinist was counting on.

The only thing that could change that balance, Shangri knew, was if she could provide some facts too compelling to deny. And the more she thought about it, the more she felt sure that those facts could be found out in Reocoles's mining area across the river canyon. Problem was, nobody who worked at the mines would talk about it. They'd been sworn to secrecy—or they'd lose their jobs.

*So if nobody will tell me the truth,* she concluded one morning as she walked back to the bakery after finishing her deliveries, *I'll jest have to go find the truth myself.*

She gulped, knowing it wouldn't be easy or safe: Reocoles wouldn't be pleased to have any intruders. *But,* she told herself, *it must be done.*

She chose a day when her father was planning to close the bakery so he could barter for new spices and other ingredients, which meant he wouldn't be needing her. Of course, she couldn't tell him about the dangerous plan she'd hatched for that day, since he'd surely object.

The other person she couldn't tell was Lorno. He, too, would object—and if he couldn't convince her to change her mind, he'd insist on joining her. But the last thing she wanted to do was to put him—and his whole future as a famous bard—at risk. No, this was a job for her alone.

On the chosen day, Shangri waited for her father to go to the market square. When she felt certain that he'd gone, and that Lorno was hard at work writing upstairs, she slipped away unnoticed.

She darted through the alleyways to one of the bridges across the Deg Boesi. As always, the river crashed through the chasm below, sending up towering plumes of vapor. But she was surprised to see that Rainbow Falls, which she remembered clearly from the last time she'd crossed that bridge, wasn't there at all.

On the river's southern bank, she faced an open plain that stretched to an endless swath of green hills—the Great Forest. On the plain, it wasn't hard to find the way to Reocoles's mines, since a wide and rutted road cut across the land, snaking around boulders and deep gullies. What few trees had once grown on the plain had been cut down, and the sight of those lifeless stumps made Shangri's heart sink. Much of the topsoil on both sides of the road had washed away, so hardly even a tuft of grass could be seen.

*This,* thought Shangri as she walked somberly along, *is what Reocoles is callin' progress.*

Suddenly she heard a loud, screeching sound. A vehicle! Hidden by a big boulder, the vehicle was fast approaching—and just seconds from turning the bend where the driver would certainly see her. But where could she hide?

Unable to get to the boulder in time, Shangri did the only thing she could. She dived into one of the muddy ruts on the side of the road. No sooner had she flung herself facedown in the rut, her long red hair splayed across her back, the vehicle appeared.

It was a heavy mining cart, powered by a coal-fired boiler, loaded with coal and iron ore. Concentrating on avoiding the deepest ruts, the driver barely noticed the unusual splash of color— something red—on the side of the road. He kept driving, splattering Shangri's back with mud as he passed.

Seconds later, after the vehicle had left, she lifted her head. When she felt sure the driver wouldn't look back and see her, she pulled herself out of the rut. Mud dripped from her hair, her freckled cheeks, and her bakery apron, which she'd forgotten to remove. But otherwise she was fine—and more determined than ever to see those mines.

Shangri crossed the road to the other side where the ruts looked deeper, in case she needed to dive for cover again. She rounded another bend and then—

Froze. The new vista almost knocked her over backward, as if a mining vehicle had rammed right into her.

As far as she could see stretched gigantic pits with enormous piles of rocks all around. Huge vehicles with metal jaws, spouting clouds of black smoke, dug the pits steadily deeper. Meanwhile, other vehicles, plus dozens of workers with shovels, toiled to rip out rocks and bushes around the edges to widen the mines. Several buildings jammed the area between the pits, belching more smoke from their chimneys.

People moved everywhere, like a colony of ants, carrying rocks and tools, pushing carts of ore or stoking bonfires of timber. Every worker was busy—except for the men who wore brown tunics with sea-blue arm bands, the same uniforms she'd seen men wearing at Reocoles's building. Hefting whips in their hands, the uniformed supervisors watched over groups of workers, shouting commands.

Then Shangri saw someone else—a woman crumpled by the edge of a rock pile. Hunched as she was, her face buried in her hands, she was either coughing or sobbing. It was hard to tell which.

Just then Shangri caught the scent of something horrible. It might have been the decaying body of a dead animal . . . but no single animal could possibly smell that bad.

Puzzled, she wiped a clump of mud off her nose and sniffed the air. *What in the name o' the Divine Monk's beard is that?*

Deciding the smell was coming from behind one of the huge rock piles, she darted off the road and up a huge mound of dirt where she could see better. Aware that the higher she climbed, the more visible she'd be to the supervisors, Shangri made sure to duck behind any stray boulders she could find. At last, she stood high enough to see the source of the putrid smell.

*A yellow lake.* She shook herself, unable to believe her eyes. The lake seemed unnatural—even poisonous. *How could somethin' like that happen?*

Then she saw, pouring into the lake, a stream of yellow liquid. It flowed out of one of the smoky buildings. Whatever they were doing in the building was producing that foul liquid!

By the side of the putrid pool, she glimpsed a strange shape. All at once, she recognized it—the carcass of a young bear. Poisoned by the lake!

Hovering over the carcass was a small flying creature. At first, Shangri guessed it was a blue-winged moth. Then, in a flash, she realized what it really was. A faery! Perhaps the faery had been a friend of the cub, and when it had gone missing from the forest, went to find it—only to discover that the bear had died a horrible death. Even from such a distance, Shangri could feel a wave of sorrow emanating from the grieving faery.

Shangri's mind spun. If that deadly pool had killed the bear, what were its fumes doing to the workers nearby? And what might its poisons do to the ground, to the neighboring forest, and maybe even to the water used by people in the City?

*I've seen jest about enough,* she decided. *All I'm needin' now is a quick look inside that place where the poison's bein' made.*

Stealthily, she started back down the mound. But as she descended, her foot kicked loose a small rock that rolled downward. Seeing it, she caught her breath, hoping no one else would notice.

The rock tumbled downward, gathering speed. Shangri watched, standing rigid. As the rock neared the bottom, it looked likely that it would fall harmlessly into a ditch. She breathed a sigh of relief.

Just above the ditch, the rock hit a lip of stone and bounced higher. It flew through the air—and smacked the shoulder of a supervisor who was facing the other way. He whirled around.

Seeing Shangri, he shouted, "Intruder!"

Several uniformed men bounded up the mound. Even as Shangri started to dash away, strong hands caught hold of her and threw her to the ground. Grabbing her clothes, as well as her hair, they dragged her down the hillside. Laughing and shouting in triumph, they dropped her at the feet of their foreman, Karpathos.

Hearing the commotion, the faery by the carcass looked over and sized up the situation. A whir of blue wings—and the faery flew back to the forest.

Karpathos, meanwhile, twirled one end of his mustache, chortling with delight. "Well, well," he said. "Look who has paid us a visit! The red-haired wench who recently insulted our leader so rudely—when all he was offering was kindness."

"He offered nothin' like that," spat Shangri. "He's a greedy monster! An' when people hear what he's really doin' out here—"

"That won't happen," declared Karpathos firmly. Smoothing his mustache, he explained, "People won't be hearing *anything* from you, my dear. Ever again."

He bent lower, so that his face was practically on top of hers. "I know exactly what to do with you, wench. There will be nothing left of you, no evidence at all."

Allowing himself a grin, he added, "The master will be very proud of me."

Though his words made her shudder, Shangri rose to her feet and faced him squarely. "You won't succeed," she said bravely.

"Really? Just wait."

Raising his voice, Karpathos commanded, "Take her to the waste pool! Tie rocks around her limbs. Then . . . give her a swim."

## CHAPTER 31

# Rising Wind

On the same day Shangri was captured, Atlanta sat on the front step of her home. As she sipped some fresh elderberry tea that Etheria had prepared, she watched a family of squirrels who sat poised in the branches of a nearby tree. The squirrels' dark eyes studied Atlanta's house with clear amazement, waving their tails and chattering among themselves— no surprise, since the house in question was a giant acorn.

"Yes, yes," said Atlanta softly. "I really do live here." Then, after a barrage of chattering, she added, "But you cannot."

Seeing their tails droop, she shook her head. "You can't eat it. Etheria would have an earthquake if you tried! And besides . . . my old friend Grumps, the squirrel who lives in the cupboard, wouldn't hear of it."

Several of the squirrels sighed sadly. Then, after another burst of chattering, the family scampered off.

Atlanta grinned, then took another swallow of tea from her burl mug. "See there?" she said in a raised voice. "It's not necessary to frighten our guests—or smell like a huge pile of manure, as you did for those poor centaurs—to protect our privacy."

The whole house, front step included, started to shake violently. The shutters on all the windows slammed in unison, scaring off a pair of larks who had just landed nearby.

"Go ahead and shudder," said Atlanta calmly, as she tried to keep from spilling her tea. "But I'd like you to try—just try—to be a little more friendly to strangers."

Etheria fell still for a few seconds—then suddenly shook one more time.

"Yes!" insisted Atlanta, now annoyed. "*Including* centaurs."

From inside the acorn house, all the floorboards sighed.

"Good." Atlanta shook some spilled tea off the sleeve of her gown of lilac vines. "Now I expect you to do better."

She took another sip of elderberry tea. "After all," she added, "you are quite simply the most intelligent and devoted house anyone could have."

The shutters opened with a merry round of squeaks. From the chimney came a proud little puff that smelled like fragrant cedar.

Atlanta couldn't resist a grin. "By the way, Etheria, do you have a slice of lemon? It goes so well with this elderberry."

From the kitchen came a loud rattling, followed by the sound of cupboard drawers being opened and closed. As well as Grumps's voice as he muttered, "Can't anybody take a nap in peace around here?"

Just then, with a soft whir of wings, Quiggley flew out from the kitchen. Holding a slice of lemon in his tiny arms, he wobbled in the air from the strain of such great weight. Yet he managed to make it safely to Atlanta. With a final frenzy of wings, he dropped the lemon in her mug, then promptly landed on her wrist.

"Thank you, little friend." She nodded at the faery as he shook some drops of lemon juice from his arms. "You are the best!"

Quiggley's antennae quivered. Atlanta felt a wave of pleasure flow through her, enough to make her beam. "What would I ever do without you?" she asked.

The faery shrugged his shoulders as if to say he couldn't imagine how she'd ever survive. Then he fluttered up to her shoulder. He settled close enough to her neck that she could feel the familiar brush of his wings on her skin.

Atlanta pulled the lemon wedge out of her mug and squeezed. As the juice drained into the tea, the air filled with the sharp yet sweet smell of lemon. She drew a deep breath, savoring the aroma, long one of her favorites.

All at once, the smell brought back a nearly forgotten memory: the freshly baked lemon pie Promi had given her on the day they first met. Hungry, lost, and huddled in a deserted alley, Atlanta had certainly needed that gift—more for the gesture of kindness than the pie itself. In that moment, she'd filled her nostrils with the aroma of lemon. Nothing had ever smelled so good.

*Promi,* she mused. *Where are you now? What's happened to you in the years since you left? And why, exactly, did you leave?*

She sighed, blowing on her tea. For she knew the answer to the last question. *You left because we fought.*

Sure, Promi had acted like a selfish, wooden-headed fool on that day. Imagine being so cavalier about destroying the veil! He simply disregarded all the dangers.

*Yet . . . I was just as much a fool myself.* Atlanta peered glumly into her mug. *If only you'd given us a chance to make amends. Or at least to try.*

She shook her head of brown curls. For she knew that would

never happen. Not now, after five whole years. Too much time had passed.

*What I know for sure now,* she thought somberly, *is that whatever we had—or might have had—just wasn't that important to you. Otherwise . . . you'd have come back at least one more time.*

Against her neck, feather-soft wings quivered. Compassion flowed through her, a big wave to have come from someone so small as a faery.

She heard, in her memory, part of the unicorns' saying about the human soul:

*More tangled than the vine,*
*More mysterious than the sea.*

Those words reminded her of Gryffion, the old unicorn who had paid her a visit not long after Promi's departure. The newborn he described that day had grown into a strong young colt, full of bounce and curiosity about the world. She'd seen the young unicorn only a few weeks ago, frolicking on the Indragrass Meadows, his luminous horn sparkling in the sunlight.

She sipped some elderberry tea. *Hard to believe,* she thought, *that such a joyful creature could have been born with such a grim prophecy.*

Despite Quiggley's trembling antennae, urging her not to think about the upsetting prophecy, she pondered those words. They'd been said both by Gryffion and the centaur Haldor. And no matter how many times she'd recalled them, they never lost their sting.

*A terrible day and night of destruction.*

Suddenly, a breeze rushed through the trees around her house. That, at least, was how it sounded. Yet no leaves stirred. Not a single tree bent with the rising wind.

For this, Atlanta knew, was no wind at all.

She set down her mug and stood. At that instant, hundreds of faeries—more than she'd ever seen in one place, even at the ancient Faery Glens—flew out of the forest. The sound of all their wings humming and whirring was so loud that Etheria slammed closed her shutters. Meanwhile, the air in front of the house glittered with vibrating little bodies.

Some wore translucent cloaks like Quiggley, while others sported purple vests, rust-colored leggings, or streaming green ribbons in their hair. Many wore hats made from cotton or flakes of bark, made with tiny holes so their antennae could protrude. But none of this colorful garb was nearly as striking as the faeries' unadorned wings, which glowed like shimmering rainbows.

Atlanta watched, amazed by this whole experience. "What does this mean?"

Quiggley leaped off her shoulder and plunged into the flock of faeries. His antennae waved frantically as he communicated with the others—especially one blue-winged faery who seemed very distraught.

Seconds later, he buzzed back to Atlanta. Hovering before her wide eyes, he sent her a sharp pang of danger, urgency, and panic—all caused by something that was happening in the forest.

"Show me," she demanded. "Take me there!"

# Devastation

As fast as she could, Atlanta sprinted through the forest. She followed the flock of faeries, trying her best to keep up with them. On her shoulder rode Quiggley, his antennae trembling anxiously.

Unlike the faeries' flock—which moved like a shimmering cloud through the trees, hundreds of pairs of wings humming—Atlanta couldn't just float through the woods. She leaped over streams, hurdled fallen trunks and limbs, and detoured around boulders and marshy pools. Ever mindful of her forest neighbors, she did her best not to disturb animal dens, nests on low branches, or intricate spiderwebs. But moving at such speed she crashed through many such obstacles and once stepped in a snake hole, twisting her ankle. Though her ankle began to throb, she kept on running.

Finally, the cloud of faeries reached their ancestral home, the Faery Glens. This network of mist-shrouded pools and bubbling cascades among towering, majestic trees exuded magic—both from the place itself and the faeries who had long lived there. To those with understanding, this was one of the most sacred places in the forest.

Atlanta had always loved visiting these pools, sitting quietly for hours to watch the faeries frolic and explore and tend their young. Their glowing wings zipped through the swirling mist, soared through waterfalls, and turned spins in the air. Faeries made magical flowers sprout from the surface of streams, crafted sculptures out of mud or honeycomb, danced on rapids, and dined on the nectar of wild roses, irises, and tulips. All the while, they sang ethereal harmonies that echoed around the glens.

Today, however, the faeries didn't sing or dance or do playful acrobatics. They merely slowed their flight upon entering the glens, then dived into hiding places under leaves or behind waterfalls. Whatever had frightened them so much was apparently so terrifying that they couldn't bear to lead Atlanta all the way there. By the time the faeries brought her halfway through the area, most of them had vanished from sight; when she reached the northernmost pools, all the faeries had hidden themselves away.

Except one. Quiggley continued to ride on her shoulder. Since he'd learned from the flock what had terrified them so badly, he knew where to go. And though he couldn't communicate to Atlanta in faery language (which was much too densely packed with meaning for her to comprehend), he could send her waves of encouragement to keep moving in certain directions.

Even so, Atlanta could tell that he was growing increasingly upset. He fluttered his wings nervously, sometimes even leaping into the air for a few seconds before forcing himself to return to his perch. His antennae quaked fearfully. And the shoes he'd made from hollowed-out berries clacked together nervously.

Suddenly, they reached a splashing stream whose banks looked severely trampled. By people! Fresh tracks from heavy boots marred the waterway, crushing patches of wild mint and strawberries, as well as destroying the den of a family of river otters.

Several trees had been toppled, felled for no apparent reason. One especially tall redwood had crashed down so hard that it had knocked down a dozen more trees. In addition, many branches had been intentionally broken off or marked with red flags, as if the whole area was being surveyed.

*Why?* asked Atlanta. *Why would someone ever do this?*

With Quiggley trembling on her shoulder, she pressed onward. The number of boot prints increased, as well as the amount of toppled trees. Then she saw, leaning on a boulder, a collection of axes, saws, and shovels. Beyond that stood an old willow whose dangling tresses hung like a leafy curtain.

Atlanta pushed through the curtain—and gasped. Quiggley squealed in horror.

Before them stretched a scene of unimaginable devastation. Vast open-pit mines exposed the rocks beneath, as if the very skin of the land had been ripped away and cast aside. Huge, lumbering vehicles drove inside the pits, scraping away more, while their engines shrieked and belched black smoke. Ditches and dams plowed across the landscape; only a few shrubs remained. Meanwhile, scores of men and women worked with shovels and wheelbarrows, hauling rocks, digging more ditches, and carting away unwanted soil and whatever plants had grown there.

Yet that wasn't the worst of what Atlanta and Quiggley saw. A toxic, yellow pool sat right in front of them, bubbling like a poisonous broth. From it rose fumes that stank of rot and death.

On one side of the pool sat enormous piles of rocks and mine tailings. Teams of workers poured buckets of liquid on the piles—liquid that sizzled like acid and washed more chemicals into the basin. Meanwhile, a stream of yellow liquid poured into the pool from a building whose chimneys belched thick black smoke.

Workers scurried everywhere. Some, with shovels, labored feverishly to expand the pool's size. Others hauled heavy loads on wheelbarrows between buildings. Still others, wearing uniforms of brown tunics and sea blue arm bands, bullied the workers constantly.

At least three of the workers staggered around, coughing and retching. Clearly sick from the toxic fumes, they looked too weak even to pick up their shovels. But uniformed supervisors continued to bark commands at them. When one of them collapsed on the mud, a supervisor kicked him until he rose to his feet again.

Suddenly they saw a new group of people moving toward the pool. Three supervisors were dragging someone, a red-haired girl, to the very edge! Despite all her struggles and shouts, she couldn't stop them. Nor could she keep them from tying heavy rocks to her limbs.

A wave of horror flowed through Atlanta. *They're going to drown her in the pool!*

Urgently, she looked around for some way to help. *I've got to do something! But what?*

On her shoulder, Quiggley shook uncontrollably. The entire scene struck his faery sensibilities with such violence that he reeled, almost losing his balance. His cotton hat slid off and fell to the ground.

Then, to Atlanta's surprise, the faery sent her a burst of regret—telling her how sorry he felt for what he was about to do. Still shaking, Quiggley flew off. He plunged back into the safety of the forest, leaving her entirely alone.

Turning back to the girl in peril at the toxic pool, Atlanta dashed into the fray. Ignoring her aching ankle, she ran full speed—and crashed right into two of the men, knocking them over backward. One of them fell so near the pool that he took a deep breath of the fumes and started coughing uncontrollably, while the other hit his head on a rock and lay motionless.

The third man raised his whip and struck at Atlanta. Instantly, she jumped aside. The whip barely missed her and slashed the mud instead. But she landed on her sore ankle and fell to the ground.

The supervisor roared angrily and raised his whip again. Atlanta knew that this time she couldn't escape, so she bravely locked gazes with her attacker.

Just then Shangri, who had managed to free herself from the rocks tied to her limbs, threw herself headlong into the supervisor. The force sent him sprawling. His whip flew into the pool, where it sizzled and then sank.

Atlanta sprang to her feet. Grabbing Shangri's arm, she pointed at the observation tower that overlooked the pool. Understanding, Shangri ran for it while Atlanta hobbled behind. Quickly, both of them jumped onto the rickety ladder that ran up one side and climbed to the top.

As soon as she reached the platform, Atlanta had an idea. A bold, desperate idea.

Looking over the toxic pool and all the workers at the mining complex, as well as the scarred lands beyond, she focused her thoughts. And then she shouted.

"Stop this, all of you! Can't you see what you're doing? You are killing the land—and also yourselves!"

Most of the nearest workers froze, as did their astonished supervisors. Several men and women dropped their shovels or set down their wheelbarrows. For a brief moment, all heads turned to the pair of young women on the tower—especially the one whose words rang out across the complex.

"This land was healthy and beautiful," Atlanta cried. "Now look at it! And look at yourselves—yes, do. Nobody can survive working here! You must stop!"

More workers dropped their tools. A few nodded their heads, while others looked nervously at their supervisors. One of the mining machines halted as the driver tried to understand what was happening. Then another voice rang out.

"Get back to your work, all of you!" ordered Karpathos. Tugging angrily at one end of his mustache, he glared at both of these intruders—the brazen young woman who had dared to slow his workers' productivity, and Shangri, who had somehow escaped the punishment he'd commanded. From the platform's railing, Shangri glared right back at him.

Raising his voice again, the foreman shouted, "Back to work, I say! Any laggards will be whipped and lose all their pay!"

Several of the workers grumbled, but picked up their tools. Supervisors stepped in, shoving and cursing anyone who dared to hesitate. One worker talked back and got slammed in the shoulder by a supervisor wielding a shovel.

Meanwhile, Karpathos commanded two of his uniformed men, "Get those girls down from there! They will be punished for what they've done today!"

Karpathos's men rushed the tower. Swiftly, they scaled the ladder.

Knowing her time was short, Atlanta called again to the workers. "Listen to me, please! This is wrong, all wrong. You must stop!"

"Back to your jobs!" bellowed Karpathos, purple with rage.

"You don't need to do what he says!" she urged.

Shangri chimed in: "All you need to do is stop!"

Atlanta shot her a grateful glance, even as Karpathos's men reached the top of the tower. "Remember," she shouted to the workers, "there are more of you than—"

A strong hand grabbed Atlanta by the arm and dragged her backward. At the same time, the other supervisor lunged at Shangri. She dodged him adeptly—and he tumbled over the railing. Immediately, Shangri pounced on the man who was trying to pin down Atlanta, and the three of them rolled to the edge of the platform.

Meanwhile, two more of Karpathos's men started scaling the tower. In just a few seconds, they would reach the top.

Looking over the edge, both young women had the same idea. With a wordless glance, they kicked free from the attacker and shoved him backward on the platform. Then, before he could recover, they rolled over the side and started climbing down the wooden structure of the tower. Near the ground, they jumped off.

Caught! Burly supervisors grabbed them both, wrenched their arms behind their backs, and hauled them over to Karpathos.

The foreman glared at them, his whole body twitching angrily. "Vermin! Both of you will drown in the pool for this! But first . . . I want you to feel some added pain."

He snapped his fingers. "A whip!"

Immediately, a supervisor handed him a whip. Karpathos directed his men, "Hold them tight."

Even as Atlanta and Shangri struggled to free themselves, the men twisted their arms harder. Atlanta groaned, feeling like her shoulders were about to break.

Glaring at Shangri, Karpathos said, "You first, wench. It's you who started all this trouble. Now you'll pay for it!"

Shangri stood tall and declared, "You're the one who will pay."

Seething, Karpathos raised the whip. Pausing just long enough to aim precisely at her face, he started to bring it down.

Suddenly someone shouted—loud enough to make him stop.

"Wait!" cried a big fellow who had been working to dig a ditch. "I know her, that red-haired girl! She's been bringin' pastries to my family fer years."

"An' look," shouted a woman who carried a shovel. "She's no older than my own daughter!" Throwing down her shovel, she yelled at the foreman, "Put down yer whip!"

Another worker shouted in support. More nodded their heads in agreement. Someone else bellowed, "The other one was right, too—what she said about this cursed job. It's killin' us!"

Shangri and Atlanta traded hopeful glances.

"Arrest thcm!" Karpathos shouted to his supervisors. "After I've punished these two intruders, I'll show everyone what happens to workers who dare to disobey!"

Two supervisors rushed at the woman who had thrown down her shovel, but the big fellow at the ditch ran over to help her. Together, they held their own. More workers ran over to join the scuffle, as did more uniformed men. A frenzied brawl broke out.

People punched and tackled one another, rolling in the mud. Some swung shovels or buckets, while others hurled rocks. One worker, struck in the head with a shovel, tumbled backward and fell into the toxic pool.

Though the workers greatly outnumbered the supervisors, many of them still held back, afraid to jeopardize their jobs. On top of that, the uniformed men were less tired from long days of labor, so they could muster more strength to fight. After a few minutes, the brief rebellion started to fade out. It seemed more and more certain that the men in uniforms would prevail.

At the same time, Karpathos glowered at the two young women who had started it all. He cursed them roundly, but they showed no fear. Though their bodies ached and they still couldn't budge, they just peered straight at their captor.

Wrathfully, Karpathos raised his whip. "No need to wait until the fighting's all settled," he told Shangri. "It's time to give your face those slashes I promised."

He lifted the whip higher. Just as he started to strike—

A vast swarm of faeries poured out of the forest. Led by Quiggley, they plunged into battle, diving at the men and pummeling their eyes and ears with tiny fists. As the horde of angry faeries descended, men scattered, dropped their tools, and ran. Even the workers driving the mining machines leaped out and ran for their lives.

Karpathos shrieked in fright and dropped his whip. Abandoned by his aides, he dived into a ditch and tried to shield himself from the onslaught under an overturned wheelbarrow. Yet dozens of faeries found gaps and kept bombarding him.

One of those faeries, after pounding his fists on the foreman's earlobe, flew back over to Atlanta. She sat on the ground, watching the faeries' rout with a broad grin. Instantly, she recognized the lone faery as he arrived.

"Quiggley!" she cried gratefully. "You came back for me!"

He landed on her thigh, placed his tiny hands on his hips, and waved his antennae at her. Even if she hadn't felt the wave of loyalty he was sending, she knew he was saying something like, *What else did you expect?*

She reached over so he could hop onto her wrist. Bringing him close to her face, she said with quiet appreciation, "Everyone needs a friend."

Meanwhile, Shangri stood just a few paces away, watching Atlanta and Quiggley with amazement. *I wonder,* thought the red-haired girl, *if that could be her.*

Continuing to talk to the faery, Atlanta said, "I certainly needed a friend today." With a glance over at Shangri, she added, "And so did she."

Then she looked out across the scene of devastation where all the work had ceased, at least for now. "And so did the land."

CHAPTER 33

# A Wave of Gratitude

hangri ambled over to Atlanta and sat down beside her—being very careful not to disturb the tiny faery resting on her wrist. Shangri had never been so close to a faery before, and was naturally amazed by the creature's luminous wings, delicate antennae, and translucent cloak. But what caught her attention most of all were his shoes made from hollowed-out red berries.

*Those are jest the cutest shoes I've ever seen,* she thought.

Quiggley, who had read her thoughts, promptly clicked his little shoes together. Then he bowed gallantly.

Atlanta chuckled, "Always a show-off, aren't

you?" Nodding at the faery on her wrist, she said to Shangri, "This is Quiggley."

Bowing her head of carrot-red hair, the young woman said, "Pleased to meet you, Quiggley. My name is Shangri."

Completing the introductions, Atlanta said, "And my name is—"

"Atlanta," finished Shangri. Looking into Atlanta's eyes, she added, "I know who you are."

Surprised, Atlanta asked, "How?"

Shangri brushed back some of her hair, and smiled bashfully. "From Promi."

That name struck Atlanta like a body blow. "Promi?" she asked, confused. "You know him?"

Before Shangri could answer, Atlanta felt a sharp pang of fear. Promi had replaced her with Shangri! That was why she hadn't seen or heard from him in so much time!

Atlanta stiffened, and her grin disappeared. Sensing her upset, Quiggley sent her a wave of compassion.

Shangri, too, sensed the change. Perceptive as ever, she suddenly realized what Atlanta must be thinking. Taking a deep breath, she explained.

"I knew him a long time ago, Atlanta. When I was jest a little tramp with braids! But I haven't seen him fer five whole years now."

Atlanta laughed with relief, a resounding laughter that rang like a bell. "I'm such a fool." She grinned at the red-haired young woman seated beside her. "So you were friends."

Shangri nodded. "I used to bring him pastries from Papa's bakery, 'specially cinnamon buns." She smiled at the memory. "What a thumpin' big sweet tooth he had!"

"That's Promi, for sure." Atlanta laughed again. "When I met him, he'd just stolen a pie."

"O' course," said Shangri quietly, "that's to be expected fer someone who is . . . immortal."

Atlanta caught her breath. "So you know about the Prophecy?"

Shangri nodded, loosening a clump of mud from her hair that fell in her lap. "A little. He told me about it on the last day we spoke—right after he'd had a terrible fight with someone."

Atlanta swallowed. "Who?"

Shangri took her hand. "Someone he loved a whole lot."

Clearing her throat, Atlanta asked, "He told you that?"

"With his words, his eyes, an' also . . . his whole way o' lookin' whenever he'd so much as *think* about ye."

"What else did he say?"

Shangri grinned, thinking back to that day on the cliffs above the sea. "He called you 'a true nature spirit.'"

At that, the faery on Atlanta's wrist fluttered his radiant wings.

Atlanta gazed at their surroundings—the vast open pit mines, the abandoned vehicles, the sooty buildings, and the putrid yellow pool. She sighed. "He was right about that."

"An' he also said," Shangri continued, "that you were the smartest an' bravest person he'd ever met. An' also . . . the most frustratin' person he'd ever met."

Smiling sadly, Atlanta said, "He was right about that, too."

Quiggley sent her a new burst of compassion. But this time it didn't help. Atlanta wasn't ready to be consoled.

For a long moment, they sat there on the muddy ground, immersed in their thoughts. Finally, Shangri squeezed Atlanta's hand and said, "Ye know what I remember best about what he told me?"

Atlanta peered at her, waiting.

"Yer name. Jest the way he said it . . . with so much feelin'."

A flicker of light returned to Atlanta's eyes—then abruptly

vanished. "Something must have happened to him in the spirit realm for him to stay away for so long. Something serious."

"It could be jest a few days fer him," Shangri reminded her. "Time up there is different."

Atlanta blew a long sigh. "*Too* different."

Hoping to change the subject, Shangri nudged her companion's shoulder. "By the way, thanks fer savin' my life today."

Atlanta grinned. "You did a good job saving mine, as well."

Shangri blushed. "Well . . . I'd have done better if we were in Papa's bakery. I'd jest fetch one o' our biggest pans an'—*slam!*—no more attackers."

"If I'm ever in trouble in a bakery," chuckled Atlanta, "I'll call for you."

"Good. An' if I'm ever in trouble in the forest, I'll do jest the same."

"Well," said Atlanta, "it's time I go back to the forest and soak this ankle in a cold stream." She glanced at the swollen joint, then at Shangri. "Someday, I'd love to show you where I live."

Quiggley fluttered up to Atlanta's shoulder, nodding in agreement.

"I'd love that," replied Shangri. "An' someday, let me show you where the best cinnamon buns around are made."

"That's a deal."

With Shangri's help, Atlanta stood. Though she couldn't put her full weight on the ankle, she found that she could still walk without much pain. The two young women hugged, then Atlanta turned and headed back into the forest.

Shangri watched her go, the radiant little faery riding on her shoulder. Just before Atlanta disappeared behind the tresses of the old willow tree, Shangri felt a sudden wave of gratitude pour over her. She knew, instinctively, that it was Quiggley's parting gift.

*Must be gettin' back to the bakery,* thought Shangri. *Before Papa and Lorno start to get worried.* She straightened her back with resolve. *But first . . . there's somethin' I need to do.*

She strode back down the rutted road, now free of vehicles, thinking about what she was planning. Crossing the bridge back into the City, she went straight to the market square and found an old monk selling prayer leaves. Since she had no money, she promised to come back the next day with payment in the form of his favorite pastries. Knowing he could trust her, he gladly agreed.

Speaking softly so no one would overhear, she dictated to the monk a personal prayer which he inscribed on the precious leaf. As she explained, it was an important message to a certain spirit in the immortal realm. Though the monk had never heard of a spirit by that name, he complied and addressed the prayer to Promi.

A few minutes later, Shangri stood at the edge of the rickety bridge that stretched halfway across the gorge—and, as Promi had described, all the way to the spirit realm. The Bridge to Nowhere, he had called it.

Far below in the chasm, the river thundered; mist billowed all around the bridge. From every post and railing, lines of prayer leaves fluttered in the vaporous wind.

"This is fer you, Promi," said Shangri quietly. She tossed the prayer leaf into the air, watching as it floated off into the mist, spinning and twirling until, at last, it disappeared.

In the distance, Shangri thought she heard the slightest sound—almost like the faraway roar of a lion. But there was no way to be sure.

CHAPTER 34

# One Faulty
# Gear

Reocoles, standing in the middle of
his room of machinery and inventions, glared at his foreman with
all the intensity of Zeus about to
hurl a thunderbolt. He swore in Greek and
slapped his metal leg brace angrily.

"You *what*?" he demanded.

Nervously, Karpathos clawed at his mustache. He swallowed meekly and said, "I hid in
a ditch, Master. Those cursed birds were so
deadly, they—"

"Birds?" fumed Reocoles. "You were
routed by a flock of *birds*?"

"But, Master, these were not ordinary
birds! They attacked without warning, pecking
out men's eyes and biting off their ears. Why,

they poured out of the forest like the winged gods in the old myths."

"Gods!" shouted Reocoles. "The gods favor *us,* you fool! Do you think Poseidon saved us for no reason? Do you think Hephaestus put his divine essence into my mortal body for no reason?"

Too nervous to speak, the thin foreman merely shook his head. But now he was convinced that he'd been right not to tell Reocoles about the troublesome red-haired girl, only the young woman dressed in forest garb. For if Reocoles knew that he'd bungled the red-haired girl's punishment . . . it would be Karpathos's turn to be punished. Most severely!

Reocoles took a wobbling step closer so that he stood face to face with Karpathos. For a long moment, he glowered at his aide, watching the man fidget. Then, in a voice frighteningly calm, he spoke again.

"Your incompetence has cost me valuable time. How long do you expect it will take to hire a new team of workers?"

"T-two weeks, M-m-master."

Reocoles slapped his brace again. "Why so long?"

"These local urchins," explained Karpathos, "are superstitious. They don't have our great Olympian gods to guide them."

"What does that have to do with anything?"

"They are troubled by the sudden attack of those deadly birds, Master. Cowards that they are, they're afraid the forest spirits are angry at them for digging up the land and cutting the trees."

The scowl on Reocoles's face looked as grim as King Agamemnon's would have looked if his army had lost the Trojan War. "Offer them double wages, then. We can get that money back in other ways later."

"Yes, Master." Karpathos tugged on his mustache. "And what do you want me to do about that rebellious girl? She's bound to cause more trouble."

"Ah yes, the one who wore what you called 'forest garb.'" The master machinist stroked his chin thoughtfully. "Young people can, unfortunately, act as if they have minds of their own."

Karpathos's expression darkened as he remembered that young woman with the striking blue-green eyes. She had incited the workers to rebellion, freed the redhead, and caused great delay in the work. All of which made her a dangerous troublemaker.

"Tell me about her," commanded Reocoles. "What was she like?"

"Arrogant," spat the foreman.

*So,* thought Reocoles, *she is passionate.*

"And insolent," added Karpathos. "More insolent than anyone I've ever known."

*That means,* Reocoles told himself, *she is brave. Very brave.*

"And also," added the foreman, "she is deceptively attractive."

*So she is also beautiful,* Reocoles concluded.

"All that," said the inventor firmly, "makes her very dangerous."

"Yes, Master."

Reocoles stroked his chin again, then beckoned. "Come with me, Karpathos. There is something I want to show you."

The master machinist limped across the room. Anxiously, Karpathos followed, pulling on his mustache the whole way. They passed the bellows, the furnace, and the experimental pesticides before finally stopping at the mass of gears that Reocoles called his astrolocator.

"Do you see this device?" asked the inventor with a wave of his hand.

"I do, Master."

"Eventually, I will perfect its mechanism so it can accurately predict the motions of the stars and even eclipses of the sun and moon."

Karpathos peered at the complex device. "Amazing."

"Yes," continued Reocoles. "It *is* rather amazing. But hear me out. If, after this machine is complete, even one small gear doesn't function properly—then *the entire machine is worthless.*

He moved closer to the contraption and tenderly stroked its gears. Then he turned back to his foreman and asked, "Do you follow my meaning?"

Karpathos shifted his stance nervously. "Er . . . well, no."

"All the gears must serve the larger purpose," explained Reocoles. "That is true for machinery, as well as society. If there is one faulty gear . . . it must be *eliminated*. Removed and destroyed."

Karpathos raised his eyebrows. "Now, Master, I understand."

"Good." Reocoles limped toward him. With a wicked gleam in his eyes, he declared, "That is why we need to engage the help of Zagatash."

Karpathos started. "Zagatash? But he's a criminal—a murderer, scheduled to be executed."

Calmly, Reocoles said, "He is all those things, yes. But he is also a great master of disguise . . . and an *expert* assassin."

Warming to the idea, Karpathos grinned. "You want me to offer to break him out of prison if he will do this new task?"

"That's right. If he fails, we will see that he is thrown back into prison. And if he succeeds—"

"That insolent young woman will never bother us again," finished Karpathos. "She will be dead and gone."

Reocoles nodded grimly. "A faulty gear eliminated."

# CHAPTER 35

# *Ulanoma*

*rowning! I'm drowning!* Promi's mind whirled as the waters of the roiling sea filled his lungs. Coughing, he swallowed even more. Despite his desperate flailing, he sank deeper and deeper.

Though he knew he was supposed to be immortal, right now he felt entirely mortal. As well as weak, vulnerable—and drowning. Pain exploded inside him, searing his lungs and chest. His mind reeled as it darkened swiftly. All he wanted to do was breathe!

Water poured into his lungs. What had his mother said about a spirit body perishing? *Any spirit can die from pain too intense or prolonged.* That had been the goal of Grukarr and his master before Bonlo had spoiled their plans.

*Bonlo.* A new kind of pain struck Promi as he realized he'd lost his hold on the old monk!

When they slammed into the sea, Bonlo's body had been ripped away. It was crucial to find Bonlo soon—before he drowned!

Promi flailed more wildly than ever, hoping at least to touch the friend he'd tried to save. And who had given his all to save Promi.

*Just like he did long ago in that dungeon,* Promi recalled with a stab of regret. *All for nothing.*

With his awareness quickly darkening, Promi remembered Bonlo's final words. As if the gentle elder were whispering right in his ear, those words echoed in his mind.

*I knew when I first met you, lad, there was something special about you. That you were destined for great deeds. And lad . . . you still are.*

Despair, more pervasive than water, overwhelmed Promi. He'd lost not only Bonlo, but everything else he might have done. His life, so full of promise, had been utterly wasted. The losses rolled like waves across his mind.

He'd never have a chance to save Jaladay.

Never take another ride on Theosor.

Never set things straight with his parents.

Never help the worlds he loved—worlds he himself had doomed by his own selfishness.

Shadows fell over his thoughts, a curtain woven from threads of sadness, shame, and regret. In his final spark of consciousness, his last thought was of one more loss:

He'd never see Atlanta again.

Promi's mind went completely dark. Like a ragged shred of kelp, he floated deep underwater, buffeted by the currents. For the first time since he'd hit the water, he was at rest . . . though that rest had claimed a terrible price.

Water moved around him, bending his neck and arms, pushing against his back. Water flowed over his slackened jaw and into his throat and lungs. And more water weighed down on his limp body, thrusting him down into the blackened depths.

Then . . . a new current stirred, brushing against his long hair. Rising from below, this current nudged him gently at first. Steadily, it grew stronger, supporting his form as it rose upward.

Higher and higher the current carried him—until, at last, it was replaced by something solid. Something rising from the bottom-most reaches of the sea. Something whose upward surge now lifted Promi rapidly to the surface.

All at once, Promi's body broke through the waves on the surface, carried by a gargantuan head covered with turquoise scales. Like a whole new island rising out of the sea, the head thrust higher. Rivers of water poured off the enormous brow, cascading over immense eyes and washing across scales that gleamed with their own inner light.

The turquoise dragon roared so loud she shook the sea itself. The wind from that roar sent huge waves racing away from the spot. A flock of seabirds gliding nearby screeched in panic and flew off; underwater, a group of giant sea turtles abruptly turned and fled.

Colorful starfish clung to the dragon's brow and the full length of her jaw, shining like undersea jewelry. And several huge conch shells, purple and pink and gold, were embedded between the scales of her chin. Her most striking jewel, though, dangled from her left ear.

Ocean glass. A huge chunk of radiant crystal, taller than a fully grown human, graced the dragon's ear, suspended by a silver net of mermaids' hair. *As rare as ocean glass* was a common phrase in the spirit realm. Indeed, the substance was so rare that even Sammelvar had only seen a single small fragment in his whole long lifetime. That piece he attached to an amulet, then gave it to Escholia at their wedding.

Many prized ocean glass for its lustrous, shimmering glow. Yet many others prized it for a quality even more unusual: this crystal changed colors depending on the fortunes of whoever held it. Right now, the dragon's ocean-glass earring glowed radiant blue, like ocean waves shot through with sunlight.

Still, nothing the dragon wore glowed nearly as bright as her eyes. Shaped like diamonds, they shone gold with flecks of turquoise. Beneath those colors burned the light of supreme intelligence.

With seawater still cascading down her head, the dragon arched her neck slightly. Promi's limp body slid off and plunged back toward the waves. But before he hit the water, she lifted the tip of one wing and caught him in the groove between two claws. There he lay, sprawled on the leathery webbing of her wing.

For a moment she gazed intently at the young man, as if searching inside him for any remaining spark of life. Suddenly her nostrils flared and she blew a long, steady breath on his motionless form— a magical wind that could, perhaps, kindle such a spark into flame.

The dragon's breath ruffled Promi's drenched sleeves and tousled his wet hair. Yet he showed no sign of life. He just lay there like an empty shell.

All at once, the turquoise dragon stopped blowing. Noticing something strange, she raised an eyebrow and peered at the young man's chest. For his tunic had started to ripple and bulge strangely. His chest seemed to be shifting shape.

Out of Promi's collar poked a small, furry head with wide blue eyes. Kermi! He shook his sodden head, crawled completely out from the tunic, and gazed at the dragon.

"So what are you staring at?" he grumbled. "Haven't you ever seen a blue kermuncle before?"

The turquoise dragon gave a rumbling laugh, a sound like distant thunder. Then in a rich, melodic voice that seemed as deep as the sea itself, she replied, "Neverrrrr one as wet as you arrrrre."

Kermi, who was using the bushy tip of his tail to swab out his wet ears, sighed. "Neither have I."

The dragon shook her head sadly, making the ocean-glass earring sway and clink against her scales. "I fearrrrr yourrrrr companion has been lost. He sufferrrrred too much and too long—morrrrre than most spirrrrrits could surrrrrvive."

Kermi scowled. "Don't underestimate his ability to suffer. He's unusually good at it."

The kermuncle shook himself, spraying water everywhere, then leaped on top of Promi's face. Using his tiny fists, he started pounding the young man's nose. This beating continued for several seconds, until—

Promi suddenly gasped for air. He belched seawater, spraying Kermi. Then he coughed vigorously, belched some more, and finally drew a few ragged breaths.

Focusing his gaze, he jumped when he saw the enormous face of the dragon staring down at him. "You!" he exclaimed. "How . . . what?"

"Articulate as ever," said Kermi crustily. "Show some manners, manfool. This dragon rescued us both."

Promi's jaw opened in astonishment, closed again, then opened again to say, "Well . . . thank you, great sea dragon."

"You arrrrre most welcome, young man." The enormous creature tilted her head thoughtfully, making her earring sway again. "I could tell, even frrrrrom fathoms below, therrrrre was something special about yourrrrr spirrrrrit. Something perrrrrhaps worrrrrth saving."

"Bah," snorted Kermi, sitting on Promi's chest. "The only thing special about him is the extent of his *idiocy*."

"Kermi!" A broad grin spread over Promi's face. "I do believe I'm actually glad to hear your sarcastic voice." After a pause, he added, "You do look a bit ragged, though."

"No thanks to you, manfool." Grabbing his tail, Kermi started to swab his ears again. "You don't look so presentable yourself."

Promi sat up on the dragon's wing, staying well away from her immense claws. "Believe me, I don't feel very good." Suddenly puzzled, he reached up and felt his swollen nose. "For some strange reason, my nose feels really sore."

Kermi shrugged and shot a wink at the dragon. "Who knows why?"

Again, the turquoise dragon laughed. Then, noticing something visible through a tear in Promi's tunic, she opened her massive, teeth-studded jaws in surprise. Closing her jaws with a resounding *snap*, she spoke again to the young man she'd saved.

"Now I know why yourrrrr spirrrrrit seemed so special. Just as I know yourrrrr name—Prrrrrometheus."

Catching his breath, Promi peered at her. Suddenly realizing what she must have discovered, he glanced down at his torn tunic and saw the mark of the Prophecy on his chest. As always, the mark resembled a bird in flight . . . but this time, it almost could have been a dragon.

"Yes," he replied. "That is my given name. But you can call me Promi."

"Hmmmpff," sneered Kermi. "I prefer *manfool*."

The turquoise dragon's powerful legs kicked in the water, lifting her body higher above the waves. "Having seen the marrrrrk on your chest, I know morrrrre than yourrrrr name. I also know yourrrrr destiny: to do grrrrreat deeds forrrrr the world."

Promi blanched. He'd never, in his whole life, felt deserving of the high expectations that came with the Prophecy. Especially now, after he'd failed so miserably to do the one deed he'd set out to do: to save his sister. *I'm sorry, Jaladay,* he thought. *Wherever you are right now . . . I'm sorry.*

At this moment, though, what made the dragon's words bite

extra-deep was how much they echoed what Bonlo had said. Just before the end.

Biting his lip, Promi turned to the kermuncle. "I lost Bonlo," he said morosely. "After everything he did for us . . . and I just couldn't hold on to him. He must have drowned."

Before Kermi could respond, the dragon spoke. "The destiny of the frrrrriend you lost is beyond yourrrrr rrrrreach, young voy-agerrrrr. Allow him to find his way, just as he helped you to find yourrrrrs."

"Is he," asked Promi, "gone forever? Totally destroyed?"

The dragon thought for a moment—and as she did, the crystal of ocean glass darkened to a deeper shade of blue, like the waters of a stormy sea. Finally, she said, "I cannot tell. His fate is utterrrrrly hidden."

She raised her enormous head higher. All up and down her long neck, turquoise scales sparkled as water ran down them, mak-ing her body seem more liquid than solid. "But yourrrrrs," she declared, "is not."

Her diamond-shaped eye peered down at the two bedraggled creatures resting on her wing. "My name is Ulanoma, eldest of all the sea drrrrragons," she said in her deep, melodic voice. "And ourrrrr fates are entwined, like rrrrropes of sea kelp."

As she spoke those words, the ocean-glass earring darkened even more. Shadows crept across it, until it looked more like a piece of black obsidian than the sparkling crystal it had been just moments before. Then Ulanoma said the last thing Promi ever expected to hear.

"Forrrrr I shall help you find the one you seek—the one named Jaladay."

## CHAPTER 36

# Swirling Shadows

Both Promi and Kermi jolted, as if they'd been hit by an electrical shock. And indeed they had, for the name *Jaladay* sent a current right through them.

Promi sat upright in the notch of the turquoise dragon's wing. "What—I mean, how? You *would*? You will?"

Kermi rolled his wide blue eyes. He shook the remaining water off his whiskers and said, "What my articulate friend here is trying to say is . . . er, well—you *would*? You will?"

"Thanks for clarifying," grumbled Promi.

"Indeed," declared Ulanoma, "I will try to help you find herrrrr. But I must warrrrrn you—that will not be easy."

Having regained his composure, Kermi hopped up to the base of one of the dragon's perilous claws. "How is it even possible? Have you ever met Jaladay? Do you know anything about her?"

The turquoise dragon raised her mighty head, making the ocean-glass earring clink against her scales. "We spoke only once, verrrrry brrrrriefly. Yet she made a clearrrrr and strrrrrong imprrrrression on me. She seemed highly awarrrrre of herrrrr surrrrroundings, in the way of a Seerrrrr, as she sat therrrrre on that purrrrrple cloudfield."

"Wait," said Promi. "How long ago was this?"

"Severrrrral days ago."

"And," Promi pressed, "was the cloudfield full of tiny flower worlds?"

Ulanoma lowered her head so that one huge golden eye was right beside him. "Yes, young voyagerrrrr. How did you everrrrr know?"

"Because that was the place where she disappeared! You might have been the very last being to have seen her."

The dragon's eyebrow lifted, knocking off a few starfish that had been clinging to the scales. As they splashed into the sea below, Ulanoma nodded her huge head. "Now I underrrrrstand."

"Underrrrrstand what?" asked both Promi and Kermi at once.

"Why herrrrr message came to me."

"What message?" Promi demanded.

The turquoise dragon lifted her other wing, gesturing toward the constantly shifting clouds of the spirit realm. "Everrrrry-wherrrrre, new worrrrrlds abound. The morrrrre I have explorrrrred this rrrrrealm, the morrrrre rrrrremains to be discoverrrrrred. And each of those worrrrrlds has its own individual rrrrrules."

Promi pushed the wet locks of hair off his brow. "What does that have to do with Jaladay?"

"Only this," rumbled Ulanoma. "One of the rrrrrules that

applies in any parrrrrt of the spirrrrrit rrrrrealm is that someone who is a Seerrrrr can telepath a message to the last being she saw! No matterrrrr how farrrrr away."

"I never knew that," said Promi.

"Like most things, manfool." Kermi jumped onto his shoulder and growled, "Let me handle this, will you?"

Turning his tiny face toward the dragon's immense one, the kermuncle said, "So she contacted you, did she? What did she say?"

Ulanoma sighed, making her great nostrils flare. "Verrrrry little. You see . . . the message was hurrrrried, incomplete. Not at all underrrrrstandable."

Promi shook his head in disappointment. So did Kermi, who grumbled, "Then we have no way to find her."

"Not trrrrrue," declared the dragon. She shook her head, flashing her luminous scales. "I was about to say, herrrrr message was not at all underrrrrstandable—*except* to anotherrrrr Seerrrrr."

As her two companions stared at her in surprise, Ulanoma explained, "My powerrrrrs as a Seerrrrr arrrrre bound up with my ocean-glass crrrrrystal. It magnifies whateverrrrr visions I have, painting images both in the crrrrrystal and in my mind."

Tilting her head so that the suspended ocean glass rested securely against her jaw, she declared, "And what I saw, only yesterrrrrday, was this."

Deep within the swirling shadows of the crystal, a small point of light appeared. It swelled like a distant explosion, growing more luminous by the second. Soon, misty light filled the whole crystal.

Suddenly, shapes started to emerge. Broken and half-formed, they flashed briefly, then vanished. A thin, pointed chin . . . an ominous shadow that trembled with black sparks . . . an empty stone cell . . . a jagged cloud that looked like a dark row of icicles . . . an eye, so fiery red it seemed to sizzle.

The shapes abruptly stopped—as if someone's scream had been stifled.

From deep in her throat, the dragon growled—a sound that terrified any fish or seabirds near enough to hear. "Mistwrrrrraiths," she said scornfully, "arrrrre therrrrre."

"As is Narkazan," added Promi, with equal scorn. "I'd know that eye anywhere!"

"Few have seen that eye," Ulanoma observed, "and surrrrrvived."

Kermi's tail thumped against Promi's shoulder. "He tried awfully hard *not* to survive . . . but alas, he did."

Ignoring the provocation, Promi said, "If only Jaladay can hang on long enough for us to find her."

"But how?" Kermi demanded. His tail twisted anxiously in the air. "We have absolutely nothing to go on—nothing to guide us."

Promi blew a long, discouraged breath. Peering up at the great golden eye of the dragon, he asked, "That's right, isn't it?"

For several heartbeats, Ulanoma said nothing. Her earring darkened swiftly, as if most of its light had been extinguished. Then, in her deepest rumble, she spoke.

"Once, in my trrrrravels long ago, I saw those icicle clouds. They may have moved farrrrr away. They may be impossible forrrrr us to find—orrrrr even surrrrrvive."

She clenched her massive jaw, grinding hundreds of sword-sharp teeth. "But if they still exist . . . we shall searrrrrch everrrrry bit of them."

"Yes," agreed Promi as he pressed his hand against the leathery webbing of her wing. "And rescue Jaladay."

"Therrrrre is anotherrrrr prrrrroblem." The dragon's earring went completely dark, as black as a starless night. "Mistwrrrrraiths."

Ulanoma paused, then growled again. This time, though, the sound was mixed with something almost like a sob. "I hate them morrrrre than anything in the entirrrrre rrrrrealm. Forrrrr they killed my mate, my one trrrrrue love. Even now, many yearrrrrs laterrrrr, I can hearrrrr his scrrrrreams of agony when they touched him."

Both Promi and Kermi kept silent. Nothing they might say could possibly help to heal the dragon's broken heart.

"Therrrrre is morrrrre you should know, Prrrrrometheus," she continued. "Not only do I hate mistwrrrrraiths . . . but I also fearrrrr them."

Promi shifted uneasily in the notch of her wing. "If this is too much to ask, Ulanoma, you don't have to help us."

Her great golden eye, sparkling with flecks of turquoise, peered down at him. "Yes, son of the Prrrrophecy, I do. Forrrrr yourrrrr sisterrrrr . . . and also forrrrr my mate." She nodded, making her earring bounce. "But it is good that my two childrrrrren arrrrre big enough now to fend forrrrr themselves. Forrrrr we may neverrrrr rrrrreturrrrrn."

Bending closer to Promi, she asked, "Do you have a plan, Prrrr-rometheus?"

Under his breath, Kermi muttered, "This should be entertaining."

Promi chewed his lip, then confessed, "Er . . . no. I don't."

"Then," the turquoise dragon announced, "I have a plan to offerrrrr."

"Tell us," said both Promi and Kermi at once.

"We shall searrrrrch the icicle clouds forrrrr the hidden forrrrrtrrrrress of Narrrrrkazan. If we find it, I shall face my worrrrrst enemy—the mistwrrrrraiths—and do my best to drrrrraw them away."

Bending her enormous head closer, she said gravely, "Then you shall face yourrrrr own worrrrrst enemy—Narrrrrkazan—and trrrrry to save Jaladay."

His expression grim, Promi nodded. "We have a plan. Let's hope that it works."

"And that," Ulanoma added, "when it is all overrrrr . . . we shall meet anotherrrrr day."

Suddenly, a deep roar echoed across the ocean waves. Though it came from far away, Promi recognized it immediately. And his face brightened.

"You know that rrrrroarrrrr," declared the dragon. "I sense it comes frrrrrom no strrrrrangerrrrr."

"Right." Promi stood up on the dragon's wing. "It comes from Theosor!"

Just then, the wind lion appeared out of the misty sky. Giving his thick mane a shake, he hovered over their heads, his invisible wings whirring.

"Greetings to you, great dragon," he declared, his voice booming across the water. "I am Theosor. And I see you have met my friends."

The dragon nodded, making her turquoise scales shimmer. "I am Ulanoma. Have you come to join us on ourrrrr quest?"

"To rescue Jaladay," added Promi. "We're just about to leave— searching for a place with jagged clouds like icicles." Hopefully, he asked, "Will you join us?"

"No, young cub." The wind lion's immense eyes peered at Promi. "I cannot, for I am very busy patrolling the perimeter of a certain afterglow."

Promi frowned. "My fault, I know." After a pause, he questioned, "So why are you here?"

Theosor flew lower, hovering close enough to Promi that the young man could feel the wind from his wings. "I am never too busy to bring a message to you, young cub."

"A message? From who?"

"From a mortal—someone named Shangri. She sent you a prayer leaf from the very same bridge where we first met."

"When I leaped," Promi recalled, "and you caught me."

"That I did," thundered the wind lion.

"Shangri," said Promi, feeling surprised, as well as pleased. "What did she say?"

"Just this, young cub." And Theosor recited:

*"Promi, it feels jest like yesterday we talked on those cliffs above the sea. But five years have passed for us here on this world."*

"Five years!" exclaimed Promi. "That can't be true."

"But it is, young cub. Now hear the rest.

*"Those years have not been good for Atlantis. We are in trouble, Promi—mainly from the people on that ship you rescued."*

At this, Kermi groaned loudly and Promi scowled. But Theosor went on.

*"We need yer help, Promi. Atlantis is in peril . . . an' what are we to do?"*

Promi shook his head. How could he have caused so many problems in both of his worlds?

*"There's one more somethin' you must know,"* recited the wind lion. *"An' it's the most important fact o' all: Atlanta still loves you. I jest met her an' she still holds a place in her heart fer you."*

The force of those words almost knocked Promi off the dragon's wing. He steadied himself, but his head spun with questions, doubts, and longings.

*"If ye really get this,"* concluded the message, *"please answer yer old friend Shangri. An' if ye ever do come back to us . . . cinnamon buns will be waitin', that's a promise."*

Theosor studied the young man below him. "Do you have any reply?"

Furrowing his brow, Promi answered, "Just this. Let Shangri know that I got her message. Tell her that I will never abandon Atlantis, if it's the last thing I ever do! Tell her not to lose hope. Trust me, hope has great power. And finally . . . tell her that I feel the same way about Atlanta—even if we can never be together."

Theosor nodded, shaking his great mane. "I shall deliver your message, young cub. The next time her thoughts turn to you, she will hear your voice on the wind."

Lifting himself higher, he said, "Now I must go. But first, I have two more things to say."

Turning to the turquoise dragon, he declared, "There is only one formation of icicle clouds anywhere that I know. It lies far from here, near the Caverns of Doom."

Ulanoma's golden eyes narrowed. "Those caverrrrrns arrrrre known to me. Forrrrr that is wherrrrre my mate was murrrrrderrrrred."

"Be careful, brave dragon," said Theosor.

"I shall trrrrry."

The wind lion faced Promi again. "If you are attacked by mist-wraiths, remember your father's advice. It sounds crazy, I must agree, but Sammelvar has great wisdom. Perhaps you should trust him."

"No!" retorted Promi. "I won't—can't—do that. His advice doesn't just sound crazy, it really *is* crazy. No one could love one of those evil beings!"

Theosor merely gazed at him with the deep brown pools of his eyes.

"I can't do it," repeated Promi.

"No one," growled Ulanoma, "could everrrrr love a mist-wrrrrraith! They arrrrre the most loathsome beings anywherrrrre."

"So be it," declared Theosor. "Good luck to you all."

There was a whir of invisible wings—and the wind lion vanished.

# CHAPTER 37

# War of Glory

Jaladay crawled slowly across the vapor-stone floor of her cell. She grimaced, realizing how much more effort that required than it did when Narkazan's mistwraiths had first captured her, however many days ago. Now even the simple motion of crawling made her feel dizzy and exhausted.

*All part of his plan*, she reminded herself. *He wants to weaken me—first my body. Then my resolve.*

Indeed, the crumbs Narkazan had allowed her to eat were just enough to keep her functioning. Barely. He knew that even an immortal's body needed some sustenance, but he wasn't going to give her more than the minimum. After all, she'd only use her added strength to try to escape.

*Or to try to send a message,* she thought grimly.

Weakly, shoulders trembling, she crawled toward the wall that held a door—a door that had opened only rarely since she'd arrived. Even in this utter darkness, with her second sight deadened, she knew exactly where to find that door. How? From the faint rays of light that filtered through the narrow food slot. And also from the hint of fresh air that wafted through that small opening.

Right now, it was the promise of better air that had motivated her to move herself across the cell. Her prison felt more stifling by the hour, so tightly enclosed that she had trouble breathing. Yet again—she knew that was part of the warlord's plan.

*Survive,* she told herself firmly. *Must survive! For as long as I can.*

But even as she made that vow, she wondered how much longer that could be. For as Narkazan knew, the worst kind of starvation came not from lack of food—but lack of hope. And here in this cell, with nothing to stir her senses or her second sight, with barely enough air to breathe, with no one to talk with, and no way to escape . . . hope could not last long.

*Why should I try so hard to stay alive? What's the point?* Discouraged, she ran a hand through her straggly hair. *Maybe it's best for everyone if I just . . . die.*

Panting, she reached the food slot. Lowering herself flat on the stone floor, she turned her head toward the thin opening. The faint wisp of air that flowed over her face struck her like a plunge into a cold lake.

She knew, of course, that a little bit of air really wasn't much of an improvement. But for the moment, at least, it revived her. Not enough to do anything remarkable, since she was still so weak she could hardly stand. Yet . . . enough, perhaps, to shift her thinking.

After all, she was still alive. Still herself. And still aware of Narkazan's plans for war—what he called *my war of glory.*

That war would begin very soon. Forces were getting ready. Battle plans were being finalized.

She'd heard, through this very slot, a few scattered clues about those plans. Nothing detailed, unfortunately. But she'd learned enough to know that the whole spirit realm was about to explode in chaos and wrath. The wrath of Narkazan.

Mistwraiths had gathered secretly in the Caverns of Doom.

A vast army had assembled somewhere behind a spell of concealment.

The warlord had offered a huge bounty on the lives of Sammelvar and Escholia. And a far greater one on her brother, Promi.

*I don't know what to do with all this,* she thought. *But maybe I can still do something that could help!*

Lying by the bolted doorway, she clenched her jaw. For she'd remembered exactly why she needed to stay alive.

Suddenly, she heard Narkazan shout angrily at someone. Then, as that person spoke, she caught her breath. For she recognized his voice—a man who had battled Promi and Atlanta fiercely on Earth, and who now served his master in the spirit realm.

Grukarr.

Pressing her ear as close as she could to the food slot, she strained to hear. She didn't want to miss a single word they said.

# CHAPTER 38

# The Gift

Imbecile!" shouted Narkazan, so loud it seemed to shake the walls of his chamber.

The scars on his face turned dark red, as if they were rivers of blood. "Let me understand this. You actually had him in your grasp? Right there inside the flying ship?"

"Y-yes, Master," answered Grukarr, shuffling his boots on the vaporstone floor.

"You are certain it was him? That miserable young meddler marked by the Prophecy? The one who stole my Starstone?"

"Y-yes, Master."

Narkazan leaned forward in his thronelike chair, thrusting out his narrow chin as if it were the point of a sword. As he peered at Grukarr, his fiery eyes burning, the pair of mistwraiths floating by his side released an angry crackling noise. Black sparks sprayed on the floor, almost scorching Grukarr's boots.

Speaking in a voice that was much quieter—and much more frightening—the warlord asked, "And you had him under control?"

"Completely," the former priest assured him.

Narkazan raised an eyebrow.

"Well . . . maybe not *completely*. But, Master, I promise you it seemed that way! I had him bound up in a net made of fibrous vaporstone, tightened securely all around his body. Why, I even had that furry blue beast of his bound up, too."

Narkazan bared his teeth and growled, recalling the moment when that very same beast had attacked him and nearly gouged out his eyes.

Grukarr scowled. "There was no way they should have escaped. No way!"

"Except they did." Narkazan's eyes seemed to sizzle. "Of all the idiots, fools, and half-wits ever to serve me, you are the *worst*."

Swallowing hard, Grukarr said meekly, "As you say, Master."

"No! This is exactly *not* as I say!" The warlord's shouts echoed inside the chamber—and, no doubt, in Grukarr's head. On the other side of her cell door, Jaladay heard those shouts clearly . . . with the first hint of a grin since she'd been captured.

"I commanded you to capture him," Narkazan ranted, "and bring him straight to me! Instead, you bungle everything and set him free again!"

The mistwraiths crackled ferociously. Black sparks flew into the air. One spark landed on Grukarr's pant leg, instantly burning a hole in the fabric. It very nearly burned his skin, as well, but he brushed it away just in time.

Glaring at his subject, Narkazan tapped one of his bloodred tusks. "Something tells me, imbecile, that you tried to inflict a bit of torture on your prisoners. Is that right?"

Shuffling nervously, Grukarr mumbled, "Well . . . I might have tried using a few blades on them."

"Is that all?"

"And . . . well, maybe giving them a bit of skinmelt potion."

Narkazan tapped his tusk. "And?"

"M-m-maybe also . . . hanging them outside the ship. But that never happened! I never actually did it."

"Because they escaped, you moron!" The warlord slammed his fist down on the arm of his chair. "Your desire for vengeance spoiled everything!"

He leaned forward even more, jutting his chin. "For that, you shall suffer dearly."

Grukarr's face went white. "B-but, Master . . ."

"*Unless,*" continued Narkazan, "you can successfully hunt down that young man and his troublesome pet. Can you do that simple, straightforward task?"

"Oh yes! I most certainly can, great and forgiving master."

"Good. Because if you fail me again . . . I shall make certain that you experience all the tortures you tried to inflict on your prisoners. That's right—*all of them.*"

Grukarr made a sound like someone choking. He took a step backward.

"And, Grukarr," concluded the warlord, "when I torture some-one . . . he *never* escapes."

For several seconds, Narkazan glared at his subject. Then, with a wave of his hand, he spat, "Go! Get out of my sight."

Hurriedly, Grukarr backed away, then fled down the darkened hallway that was the room's only entrance. As he departed, the mistwraiths crackled angrily, hovering beside their master.

"Yes, yes," he grumbled at them. "I did let him off far too eas-ily. But he might still prove useful to me."

Narkazan peered at the hovering mistwraiths. "I must leave

briefly to inspect my growing army. I must make certain all the preparations are in order before we attack."

The shadowy beings crackled with approval.

"My trip won't take long," the warlord continued. "Until I am back, you and your fellow warriors must guard my lair. Be always alert! If any intruders dare to come near, give them the most exquisitely painful deaths you can."

A fountain of black sparks sprayed from the mistwraiths.

"Good." Narkazan grinned malevolently. "When I return, I shall look in on our prisoner. And if she has not changed her mind and decided to cooperate, I shall commence her tortures."

On the other side of her cell door, Jaladay shuddered. Her imprisonment, she knew, would soon come to an end. A most horrible end.

Suddenly another mistwraith swept into the chamber, blowing out of the hallway like a dark, menacing cloud. Approaching Narkazan, the mistwraith crackled noisily, releasing a fountain of black sparks.

Listening closely, the warlord sat bolt upright. "Are you *certain*? A red glow in the mist of the borderlands?"

Excitedly, the mistwraith crackled. More sparks erupted, sizzling on the vaporstone floor.

A predatory smile creased Narkazan's face. "Well, well. The afterglow from mist fire!"

He sat back in his chair, tapping his tusk thoughtfully. "How very careless of you, Sammelvar! For now you have told me what you least wanted me to know—that the veil between the worlds is so weak you were worried enough to check it."

On the other side of her prison door, Jaladay gnashed her teeth. *The veil,* she thought miserably. *So weak it can no longer shield the mortal world from Narkazan. And what's worse . . . he now knows about it!*

Though she was already lying flat on the floor of her cell, she felt as if she'd slumped even lower. Her brief taste of hope had vanished. What remained in its place was the most bitter taste of all, a mixture of helplessness and despair.

In his chamber, however, Narkazan was feeling quite different. Almost giddy with this unexpected news, he chortled with delight. The mistwraiths, unsure what to make of this mood they'd never seen before in their master, huddled together anxiously.

Finally, Narkazan's chortling ceased. "At last," he said to himself with satisfaction, "I am getting some of the good fortune I so deserve." With a vengeful gleam in his eyes, he added, "And now . . . I have an idea of how to give that meddling son of Sammelvar the ill fortune *he* so deserves."

Leaning toward the mistwraiths, Narkazan declared, "The young man of the Prophecy seems unduly fond of the mortal world below. Have you noticed?"

In unison, the shadowy beings crackled angrily.

"A wasteful dalliance on his part," the warlord went on, "since the creatures of that world last just a few short breaths of our immortal lives. Besides, they exist only to serve our needs."

He stroked the length of one of his tusks, savoring his new idea. "Let us turn his fondness for mortals to our advantage! I have a gift for you to deliver to that place he so cherishes. Yes . . . a gift he will long remember."

As the mistwraiths trembled with excitement, Narkazan explained, "This will surely make him come out of hiding and speed back to the mortal realm. Then we can find him more easily! And this time, *he will not escape.*"

A chorus of ominous crackling greeted his words. "The poetic justice of this plan is simply beautiful," crowed Narkazan. "For when he goes to Earth for this gift, he will cause further damage to the veil, weakening it even more."

The mistwraith who had brought the news about the veil shook vigorously, snapping its dark folds.

"Yes," agreed the warlord. "By then, the veil might have collapsed completely." In a voice drenched with sarcasm, he added, "How very disappointing."

The mistwraiths started to rustle noisily. But the instant Narkazan thumped his fist on the arm of his chair, they halted. "Now," he commanded, "come closer together. All of you."

As the mistwraiths pressed together, he thrust his whole arm deep into the center of their shadowy forms. Keeping his hand inside the knot of darkness, he grimaced. Then, slowly, he pulled it out. In his open hand, he held a crackling mound of black sparks—so many that they pulsed with negative energy, like an explosive weapon.

Narkazan squeezed the sparks in his fist. Shaking with the strain, he condensed them smaller and smaller. At last, when he opened his hand again, the sparks formed a glittering black lump no bigger than a pebble. Yet that lump vibrated in his hand, sizzling with enough power to cause terrible destruction.

"There," announced Narkazan. "It is ready."

He chortled once more. "Now," he commanded the mistwraiths, "while I go to the army, you go to the place whose image I have just planted in your minds—and deliver this gift."

# CHAPTER 39

# The Dragon's Eye

s Ulanoma flew across the spirit realm, with Promi on top of her head and Kermi perched on the young man's shoulder, nobody spoke. Although Promi was near enough to the dragon's ears to be heard easily above the constant wind, there was really nothing to say. The plan had been hatched, the commitment made, the warning given. All that remained now was to try—and hope—to survive.

Misty air blew across Promi's face as they flew, sometimes offering glimpses of marvelous, endlessly varied worlds. He caught sight of one world in the shape of an upside-down tree sprouting from a deep blue cloud. Its fruit, hanging upward from every branch, glittered like newborn stars . . . and smelled, somehow, like the fresh passion fruit he'd tasted in the Great Forest. With a pang, he wished he could show this place to Atlanta.

Then he saw a bubbling cloud of mist that gave birth continuously to worlds in different geometric shapes—a flat triangle, a squat pyramid, a quirky polygon, a perfect sphere, and more. At the moment of each world's birth, the bubbling cloud released a different sound, like the chime of a bell, that ranged from deeper than the deepest roll of thunder to higher than the first peep of a newborn robin. As a result, the cloud literally bubbled with sounds—a celestial symphony that knew no beginning and no end.

Most of the time, however, Promi just watched Ulanoma's ocean-glass earring as it swayed and jostled with their journey. Though the magical crystal stayed dark, revealing nothing specific about their ominous future, sometimes Promi caught glimpses of what looked like tiny pieces of complete darkness, blacker than the rest of the crystal. Did they foretell the black sparks of mistwraiths? Or did they result from the dragon's own dark thoughts?

*Do not trrrrry to rrrrread the futurrrrre frrrrrom my earrrrring,* Ulanoma cautioned him telepathically. *It is harrrrrd enough forrrrr me to sense its many meanings, even afterrrrr all these yearrrrrs.*

Onward they flew, soaring on dragon wings across the limitless expanse of the spirit realm. Ulanoma's turquoise scales flashed and rippled with each wingbeat or turn of her massive head.

Finally they reached a massive gray cloud punctured with ominous, lightless pits. The air around them grew sharply colder; Promi could see the dragon's breath as she flew. He knew without asking that they were passing the Caverns of Doom. The dragon's earring, now utterly dark, made a sound like ice breaking. A web of tiny cracks spread across its surface.

Clenching her enormous jaw, Ulanoma flew even faster. She wanted to move past this place, as quickly as possible.

Not long after that, all the companions suddenly tensed. The dragon slowed her flight, gliding on the cold wind. For there, dead ahead, was a jagged cloud in the shape of icicles.

Suddenly Ulanoma banked to the right. For her golden eyes had spied, hidden in the crack between two icicles, a rectangular structure made of solid vaporstone. Compact and impregnable, the structure gleamed darkly.

Narkazan's fortress.

*It is time,* the turquoise dragon told Promi and Kermi telepathically. *Do not trrrrry to enterrrrr until I have drrrrrawn off all those miserrrrrable warrrrriorrrrrs.*

Promi placed his open hand on the scales of her immense brow. *May you succeed, my friend. And may you survive this day.*

Deep in her dragon's throat, she growled. *I wish you the same, Prrrrrometheus.*

Promi leaped off the dragon, carrying Kermi on his shoulder. They flew off to one side where a swath of gray mist provided cover. Just before they hid themselves, Promi caught one last glimpse of the dragon's eye. Within its diamond shape, he saw a mixture of rage, determination, and revenge.

Plus one more quality—something he recognized immediately. Something he'd never seen before in a creature as immense and powerful as a dragon.

Fear.

Then Ulanoma roared, loud enough to shake many distant worlds. Her roar echoed across the icicle clouds.

Instantly, a horde of shadowy beings poured out of the fortress. At least fifty mistwraiths flew in tight formation, swiftly pursuing the dragon who had dared to approach their hideaway.

With another powerful roar, Ulanoma beat her wings hard. She flew off into the mist, trailed closely by the deadly mass of shadows.

# CHAPTER 40

# The Deepest Fear

As soon as the dragon and the horde of mistwraiths vanished in the distance, Promi flew out from behind the swath of gray mist. With Kermi clinging to his shoulder, he plunged toward the small but secure fortress.

Would Narkazan be waiting there? Would Jaladay? And would his sister, after whatever tortures the warlord had inflicted on her, still be conscious? Sane? Alive?

*We'll find out,* Promi thought grimly.

*Indeed we will,* answered Kermi, looping his tail around the young man's neck for added stability. *Just try not to get us killed before we do.*

Apart from the pair of narrow windows in the roof of the fortress, there was only one entrance—an archway that opened into a long tunnel. It led straight into what looked to Promi like the main chamber. There, he felt sure, he'd find the answers to his questions.

He landed under the archway. Like the tunnel and the rest of the fortress, it had been built from solid vaporstone, strong enough to withstand any attack from the outside. Except for intruders so bold—or foolish—to try to walk right in.

Stepping as lightly as possible, Promi entered the dark tunnel. Silently, he moved farther inside, always alert for any movement or sounds.

Deeper and deeper he walked, trying his best to calm his racing heart, a skill he'd learned during his years living as a thief on the streets. But this time, for some reason, he couldn't slow his heartbeat down.

Nor could he stop the burning feeling on his chest. Starting at the mark of the Prophecy, the sensation spread across his skin, stinging his abdomen, shoulders, and upper arms. And with every step, that burning grew hotter.

Kermi's tail tightened around Promi's neck. Uncomfortable as that felt, the young man couldn't do anything about it. He knew that the furry blue kermuncle was every bit as tense as he was.

At the far end of the tunnel, a dim light gleamed. It seemed to emanate from the inner walls of the main chamber. What, Promi wondered, would await them there?

Silently, he kept walking. Each step brought the main chamber nearer and made the tunnel a tiny bit lighter. Dark shadows still clung to the tunnel walls . . . but the hint of light helped him feel a bit more confident. The burning sensation on his chest diminished slightly.

As Promi passed one of the shadows—it suddenly leaped at him! Black sparks exploded everywhere. The force flung him hard against the wall, smashing the shoulder where Kermi was riding. As Promi staggered to regain his balance, the kermuncle dropped to the floor, unconscious from the impact.

Flailing, Promi tried to escape from the mistwraith's shadowy folds. But in the narrow confines of the tunnel, he had nowhere to go. The mistwraith pressed closer, holding him against the wall.

*Trapped!* he thought desperately. *Completely trapped!*

Tentacles of darkness flowed around him, squeezing and suffocating. Worse yet, everywhere the mistwraith touched burned with agonizing intensity. Pain shot through his entire body—his head, his arms, his chest. That pain wasn't only on the surface; he felt a swelling agony deep in his bones.

The more he fought to break free of the being's death grip, the weaker he felt. For the mistwraith was feeding on his fear, as well as his pain, devouring his inner magic, sucking every drop of life out of his spirit body.

Curtains of darkness fell over Promi's mind. He could feel himself fading, losing his ability to think.

Or move.

Or live.

Then, from a distant corner of his mind, he heard his father's faint voice: *Somehow . . . give it your love.*

Even though the idea made Promi recoil with horror, he remembered the rest of his father's advice. *You must truly give it your all. And you must hold on long enough that you won't be destroyed.*

But how was that possible? With his awareness swiftly fading, Promi fought to comprehend. How could anyone feel compassion—let alone love—for one of these murderous beings?

Yet . . . he needed to try. Nothing else could possibly save him. And, more importantly, nothing else could allow him to save Jaladay.

*All right then,* he told himself, *I will do this. For her.*

While his body burned with pain down to the blood within his veins, he tried with all his remaining strength to move beyond his anguish. To abandon logic. To release fear.

Instead . . . he let himself feel the mistwraith. Comprehend it. Maybe even accept it for what it really was.

*I embrace you,* he thought weakly.

Seeming surprised, the mistwraith only squeezed harder. Black sparks erupted from every fold, scorching Promi mercilessly. Dark fire pierced him like flaming swords, devouring his energy.

Yet he still hung on. With the thin wisp of awareness he had left, he imagined the mistwraith's life of torment right from birth. Its constant torture from Narkazan, the cruelest master imaginable. Its fear of his wrath at every waking moment.

Its anger at beings who could somehow live in comfort, peace, and even joy.

Its resentment that the only pleasure it could feel was from the suffering of others.

Its separation from all other forms of life.

Its loneliness, complete and unending.

Again, the mistwraith tried to squeeze out of Promi whatever shreds of life remained. It blasted him with a new onslaught of black fire, burning the inside of his brain and the walls of his heart. Yet strangely . . . all that didn't produce more terror or pain. Instead, it spawned some other feeling, one the mistwraith had never experienced before.

In panic, the mistwraith squeezed even harder. It poured all its wrath, all its hatred, into this unusual prey, willing it to perish once and for all.

Weaker by the second, Promi continued to let his compassion flow deeper. Finally, with his last hint of awareness, he discovered the mistwraith's deepest fear.

*You fear that you must always be alone. That you could never truly love anyone.*

Even as his last bit of life drained away, he realized, *You are so much like me.*

*Which is why . . .*

*I love you.*

With that—the mistwraith suddenly dissolved. Nothing remained of its shadowy form, save a few black sparks that flickered darkly in the air, then vanished.

Promi collapsed to the stone floor. Weak and dazed though he was, still feeling the ripples of pain inside his body, there was one feeling that rose above all the rest.

Gratitude.

*Thank you,* he thought weakly, conjuring in his mind the care-worn face of his father.

Summoning his strength, Promi sat up. Facing the main chamber, he realized that the opposite wall showed the lines of a door and a heavy bolt.

A prison cell.

Frantically, he crawled across the chamber to the door. He stood, grasping the bolt with both hands, and slid it open. As the door swung aside, he saw a windowless cell—and a frail body lying on the floor.

"Jaladay!"

He ran over and kneeled by her side. She lay as limp as a rag, her eyes closed. Bending down, he put his ear to her mouth . . . and felt the barest hint of a breath.

"Jaladay," he cried, cradling her head. "You're alive!"

Slowly, her eyes opened. She drew a ragged breath, then another. To herself, she whispered, "I can see again."

Then, focusing on Promi, she said, "And I see *you*." A thin, trembling smile touched her lips. "You found me, at last."

"I did," he replied, hugging her head against his chest. "And I'm going to get you out of here. You're so weak . . . you're almost finished."

"That makes two of us," said a grumpy voice from the doorway. Kermi stood there, rubbing his sore head. "So glad I didn't miss anything."

"Nothing at all," said Promi dryly. "Now let's get her out of here!"

Kermi sniffed the foul air of the cell and frowned. "The sooner the better."

"Right," said Promi urgently. "Those mistwraiths could come back at any moment. Not to mention Narkazan himself."

He lifted Jaladay to her feet, slung her arm across his shoulder, and wrapped his own arm around her waist. Then he helped her to hobble out of the cell. Kermi padded along beside them.

As they passed through the main chamber, she whispered, "Battle plans. Over there."

Following the direction of her gaze, Promi saw several scrolls on the metal chest beside a cot. Gently setting down his sister, he raced over to the scrolls and stuffed them inside his tunic.

As he lifted her again, she said, "Narkazan won't be happy . . . to find those gone."

"Not to mention," Promi added, "his prisoner."

Jaladay almost grinned—then suddenly looked terrified. "And, Promi . . . he's sending something to the mortal world. A trap! For *you*."

"No time to worry about that now, Jaladay. You need healing! As well as food and water."

"That's right," agreed Kermi. "And most of all—a bath."

Amused by the kermuncle's familiar snide tone, she managed a grin. Turning her head to catch his gaze, she said, "I'll wait to hug you until after that."

"You've got that right," he said crustily . . . though it wasn't hard to hear the affection underneath.

Hurriedly, they made their way down the dark tunnel. At the archway, Kermi scampered up to Promi's shoulder—just before the young man leaped into the sky. As they flew away from the icicle clouds, he tightened his grip on Jaladay, determined to deliver her safely home.

Casting a glance back at the fast receding icicle clouds, he thought of Ulanoma. Without the turquoise dragon's exceptional bravery, they never could have succeeded. *I just hope she, too, can return home.*

Flying fast through the swirling mists of the spirit realm, he thought of the infinite variety of worlds that existed all around. Many of them he longed to explore. Yet of all the possibilities, there was only one world that aroused his deepest feelings.

For on that world was an island full of magic, surprise, and peril. And on that island lived the person he most wanted to see— Atlanta. He needed to speak with her right away . . . and recalling what his mother had said about dreams, he knew just how to do it.

It is possible, Escholia had explained, for a spirit to appear physically in the dream of someone mortal. *But only,* she'd added, *if they truly love that someone with deep devotion.*

And so, even as he flew through the mists of this faraway realm, Promi focused his thoughts on Atlanta.

# CHAPTER 41

# The Visit

A tlanta always loved to sleep at home. Despite Etheria's sometimes eccentric behavior, at bedtime she gave the whole house a feeling of serenity and peace. The oversized acorn, set among the trees, would literally glow with warmth. A crackling fire would magically appear in the woodstove, the scent of lilacs would waft through every room, and shutters would open and close themselves with a rhythmic creaking sound.

On this particular evening, Atlanta went to bed feeling especially grateful for such a comfortable home. Though the terrible experience at the mining complex had happened more than a week earlier, it still haunted her thoughts. During all the chores and meals of that day, she'd worried about the future of her beloved forest—and of Atlantis. And the conversation with Shan-gri had reminded her how much she still missed Promi. Not even Quiggley's waves of encouragement had made her feel better.

But now, as she climbed into bed, those cares faded away. She fluffed her pillow made from soft feathers (the gift of a family of geese she'd sheltered during a wild storm). By the time she stretched herself out on her simple mattress of meadow grass and pulled up her blanket woven from softreeds, she was half-asleep. It was all she could do to glance over at Quiggley's perch by the window, know-ing that he'd return after his evening explorations of the forest.

She closed her eyes and immediately drifted off. Soon she was immersed in deep, peaceful slumber.

She dreamed that she was walking slowly along a mossy path by the edge of a lake. Water birds chattered and fluttered their wings by the shore. A family of river otters playfully slid down the muddy bank where a stream poured in. And a pair of moths, yel-low as butter, hovered over the first marsh marigolds of spring.

"Well, well," said a voice. "You picked a good place to dream."

Startled, she looked up—and saw Promi, striding toward her on the path. She flashed a bright smile, genuinely happy to see him. But she coyly replied, "Normally, though, I dream up better company."

He came up to her, standing face to face. She noticed that, while he used to be a bit taller than herself, they were both now the same height. Other than his black hair being a bit longer than she remembered, he looked just the same.

Looking straight into her blue-green eyes, he said quietly, "Atlanta. This visit isn't a dream."

Seeing her look of puzzlement, he explained, "Sure, we're in your dream. But this is really me. I'm visiting you from the spirit realm. In a way that won't tear the veil."

Slowly, she nodded. "I feel it. I really do!" She cocked her head thoughtfully. "So . . . you forgive me for being such an idiot last time you were here?"

"Only if you forgive me! And *I* was the bigger idiot."

Toying with one of her curls, she said, "No disagreement there."

Taking both her hands, he said, "You were right, Atlanta. About putting the needs of others ahead of my own. About protecting our worlds. Basically . . . about everything."

"Well," she said mischievously, "I guess an apology five years later is better than none at all."

He winced at the reminder of how much time had passed in the mortal realm. "It's really been that long?"

She looked suddenly sad. "And, Promi . . . some horrible things have been happening. Caused by people, new people."

"I know," he said guiltily. "I brought them."

"What?" Atlanta pulled her hands away from his and scowled. "How could you?"

"Not on purpose," he protested. "Their ship was about to go down in a whirlpool! I just wanted to save all those innocent lives. So I, well . . . asked for some help. From the ocean goddess."

Softening, she gave a nod. "I see. But, Promi, I wish you hadn't helped them! Those people have been doing so much damage. It's terrible."

Frowning, he said, "Something tells me they've had some encouragement from the spirit realm."

"You don't mean—"

"Yes. Narkazan is back. He's preparing for another war of conquest. We just dealt him a blow . . . but he'll be back, angrier than ever, very soon."

• • •

While Atlanta was deep asleep, immersed in her dream, all was not well with her home. Etheria, alert for trouble like any reasonably sentient house, felt a disturbing new presence. Yes—from the spirit realm!

In some way Etheria couldn't fully understand, that spirit had violated the space of Atlanta's home—and had even intruded on her peaceful dreams. Well, Etheria wasn't about to sit idly by while that happened! There was only one solution to this outrage: to wake up Atlanta.

Doors slammed. All the shutters opened wide, then crashed closed. The floor under Atlanta's bed started shaking.

Still, Atlanta stayed sleeping. But if Etheria had her way, that wouldn't last long.

• • •

Glancing over at the water birds by the lake, Atlanta said, "Let's walk."

"Good idea. It's been too long."

Together, they started strolling on the mossy path. Beautiful as their surroundings were, neither of them were in much of a mood to notice. A dark cloud seemed to have settled over them.

"I'm so worried," said Atlanta as she stepped over a turtle on the path. "About everything. The forest. My world. Your world."

She stopped, peering at Promi. "And also . . . about you."

He swallowed. "And I'm worried about you."

"You know," she said, running her hand down the length of his arm, "that even if we can't . . . um, find a way to be together—"

"Don't say that. There still might be a way."

She nodded, but her expression was not hopeful. "Whatever happens . . . I just want you to know that *I bless your eternal qualities.*"

Hearing her say her favorite blessing, he almost smiled.

"And, Atlanta," he began, then cleared his throat.

• • •

Increasingly upset, Etheria slammed her doors with even more force. Shutters crashed, while floorboards creaked and groaned.

Then she started to shake violently. From top to bottom, the whole house rocked as if struck by an earthquake.

• • •

After clearing his throat, Promi took both her hands in his own. "There's something I've been wanting to say to you. Something . . . important."

Her eyes widened. "What is it?"

• • •

Frantic with concern, Etheria started shaking more violently than she'd ever done before. The whole house rocked side to side, sending Atlanta's bed sliding into the wall.

• • •

"It's, well," fumbled Promi. "It's . . . important."

Warmly, Atlanta watched him. "Go on."

He drew a deep breath. "You know, the way my life started out, I was—well, *alone* much of the time. So . . . there wasn't anybody around who I could trust. Or . . . come to love."

She blinked the mist from her eyes.

"Well, this thing I want to say to you—it's, um, something I haven't really said before. Haven't *wanted* to say before."

She gave him an encouraging nod.

He gazed at her for several seconds. Then, at last, he said, "Atlanta . . . I really do—"

• • •

Atlanta woke up—torn away from her dream, as well as the young man who visited her there.

# CHAPTER 42

# Utter Darkness

At Reocoles's mining operation, a strange quiet had descended. For the first time in years, the giant rock-scraping machines sat in silence. No black smoke belched from them; no grinding metal jaws tore away at the land. And no workers had yet returned, so nobody coughed or retched from the fumes rising out of the toxic waste pool.

Since no trees remained standing, the wind couldn't blow through branches to rustle any leaves. Nor did any songbirds share their lilting melodies. Dragonflies and bees didn't whir and buzz. Frogs didn't croak at twilight.

The only sound to permeate the silence came from the toxic pool. Not from anything on its shore, marked only by the carcass of the bear cub—but from the liquid of the pool itself. Bubbling and churning like a deadly brew, the yellowish liquid roiled incessantly as its chemicals mixed, repelled, and recombined. As fumes rose from the surface, so did the sulfuric stench.

During those days before any new workers could be found and the operations resumed, no eyes came near enough to view the mining operation. So no one saw what happened one day in the dim light of dusk.

High above the toxic pool, a dark cloud appeared. It wasn't caused by the rising fumes, and it wasn't produced by the atmosphere. Rather, this cloud had traveled all the way from the spirit realm.

Crackling with negative energy, the cloud of mistwraiths swelled until its shadow covered the whole waste pool. Mistwraiths, dozens of them, swarmed in the center of the cloud. Their dark, rippling tentacles reached outward, groping like limbs of night.

All at once, from the innermost center of the cloud, a bolt of black lightning exploded. It flashed darkly, sizzling, as it shot toward the toxic pool. At its leading edge, it carried the condensed lump of utter darkness fashioned by the vengeance and greed of Narkazan.

The black lightning struck, hurling Narkazan's weapon into the depths. As the lump splashed down, ripples raced across the surface. The mistwraiths crackled louder than ever, as if they couldn't contain their satisfaction.

Then, with surprising swiftness, the mistwraiths vanished. As their cloud disappeared, so did their ominous shadow.

The pool, meanwhile, fell still. No more liquid boiled and bubbled. No more chemicals churned. Even the fumes stopped rising from its surface.

Suddenly . . . something stirred. Deep inside the pool, a new creature struggled to be born, to take shape, to satisfy its overwhelming desires. And when it started to emerge, reaching part of its body made of utter darkness above the surface, it released a cry of unrelenting rage.

That cry shattered the air, echoing ominously.